THE PRAIRIE MARTIAN

JONATHAN EATON

Copyright © 2016 Jonathan Eaton

All rights reserved.

ISBN-13: 978-1535359900
ISBN-10: 1535359900

Cover Art by Tony Masero

Revision 1.1

> To Dani &
> Michael
> Sherman's
> god parents
> — [signature]

For Steve and Rosemary

Part 1

1 THE PRISONER

Sheriff Frank Westfall was a man who believed in adhering to a schedule, and as it was well past his bedtime, he put the CLOSED sign in the window, checked on the prisoner in the lockup, and went upstairs to bed. He rarely suffered from insomnia, but given the strange and difficult day he'd had—given the possibility that he had a Martian in the lockup—well, a man can close his eyes, but *sleep*—that was a thing that came and went of its own accord, like the flu or a cat. Why was that? When a man is thirsty, he can drink. When his bladder is full, he can take a piss. Why can't a man who is worn out simply will himself to sleep?

While Frank pondered that question, exhaustion quietly uprooted the thorny bramble of his concerns and sent it tumbling away across the silken prairies of Nod. Frank's long limbs relaxed. His bony feet, extending well beyond the jurisdiction of the covers, twitched once; twice; thrice—and were still. And just then, just at the instant of most delightful surrender to blissful oblivion, he was wrenched painfully back to awareness by the sound of kicking and pounding on the door downstairs. Only one person in all of New Halchita had the balls to beat on the door like that when the CLOSED sign was in the window. *Damn you to hell, Germaine*, Frank muttered. He took the pillow out from under his head and put it over his head.

"I know you're up there! Come down and let me in!" Frank's pillow softened the impact of Germaine's voice about as much as smoke would deflect the blow of a sledgehammer. He got out of bed, shoved the window open, and stuck his head out. Germaine, along with half the population of New Halchita, was down in the street below looking up at him. Frank figured the other half was out in Mr. Habushaki's bean field stomping the poor farmer's plants into the dirt in their eagerness to get a look at that giant cast-iron cockroach the Martian (if that's what it was) rode in on. Frank had posted deputies Orland and Soon out there with strict orders not to let anyone get close to the thing. He hoped no one would be stupid enough to try. He didn't want his deputies to have to shoot anyone. Though maybe there were one or two he wouldn't mind so much if they did.

"Read the sign!" Frank yelled, at the crowd in general and at Germaine in particular. "The sheriff's office is closed for the day! Go away! Go home! Come back tomorrow if you have *legitimate* business with the sheriff!"

The crowd quieted down, but no one went away. Naturally, they were keen to observe the outcome of this classic confrontation between Authority and Compassion. They did back off some, all except for Germaine, of course. Frank was in no mood to perform a balcony scene in his red flannel union suit for these gawkers. On the other hand, maybe it would do them good to see someone stand up to Germaine for once.

"You have to let me examine the prisoner," Germaine said. "You know the law."

Frank did know the law. As New Halchita's physician, Dr. Germaine Perry had every right to examine the prisoner. But she should have come during regular hours. At the very least, she should have knocked respectfully, instead of pounding and kicking on the door. The sheriff's office wasn't just his office, it was his home. She should show some respect for his authority, especially on his own turf. Law and Order didn't have to bow down before Kindness and Mercy, and despite what she might think, the rules applied to her, just like everyone else.

"The sheriff's office is closed," Frank said. "If you were so concerned about the prisoner's health, you should have come earlier."

"I would have," Germaine said, "but Mrs. Ramos' new baby girl had other ideas."

Another thing Frank hated about Germaine was how she always had a perfectly good reason for not following the rules everyone else had to follow.

One of the gawkers spoke up: "They doing okay, Doc?"

"Beautiful and healthy," Germaine said. "Both of them."

The good folks of New Halchita whooped and cheered. A few hours earlier, the whole town was going berserk over the arrival of the spaceship, and the sheriff and his deputies were summoned to protect the terrified citizens. But Dr. Germaine Perry delivers a baby that would have no doubt delivered itself given half a chance, and suddenly Martians are old news. She was the hero of the moment, and any resolve on his part to enforce perfectly reasonable business hours for the sheriff's office would be seen as pettifoggery. He knew it, Germaine knew it, and he was pretty sure she'd worked it all out beforehand.

"Now come down and let me in," Germaine said. "Don't make me call an emergency session of the council."

Frank cursed, closed the window, put on his sheriff clothes (slowly and deliberately), and went downstairs. He unlocked the door and opened it just enough to let Germaine and her enormous black bag squeeze through. The citizens outside craned their necks in an attempt to get a look at the Martian monster—which they couldn't possibly do because it was in the lockup down the hall. They tried though. Frank shut and locked the door behind Germaine.

Germaine looked Frank up and down—but mostly up.

"Have you grown again?"

"Oh, lay off with that already, Germaine. Are you here to examine me or . . ." Frank motioned with his head towards the lockup, ". . . or that?"

"You need to come to the clinic," Germaine said.

"Like I need a hole in the head."

"Don't tempt me." Germaine started towards the lockup but Frank grabbed her arm to stop her, wrapping his long fingers all the way around her muscular arm—and then some.

"What?" Germaine said.

Frank let go of her arm. "Let me see what's in the bag."

Germaine set the bag on the floor and opened it. Shiny metal tools, rubber tubing, glass syringes—all of which Frank could easily see from the perspective of any desperate, psychotic, or extraterrestrial prisoner with a little imagination: a tempting smorgasbord of murder weapons.

"Wait," Frank said. He unlocked the gun cabinet and,

perusing options that seemed especially inadequate to this particular situation, eventually selected a sawed-off shotgun. "Alright," he said, "let's go."

"You're kidding," Germaine said.

"I'm not," Frank said, "and if you don't like it, feel free to take it up with the council."

The thing—the Martian—the woman—whatever it was—stood up and smiled as Frank let Germaine into the lockup.

"Hey, Sweetie," Germaine said, "what's your name?"

"Nancy. What's yours?"

"Dr. Perry."

"Dockerperry?" Nancy said.

"She's not so good with titles," Frank said. "I guess everyone's on a first-name basis on Mars."

"That's okay," Germaine said, "you can call me Germaine. How have you been treated here?"

"Frank has been most kind. Germaine."

"I'll bet he has. Sit back down for a minute, Nancy. How old are you?"

"Twelve. That's cold."

"Sorry, I should have warned you. Breathe in. Good. Breathe out. Good. But Sweetie, you are *not* twelve years old."

"I assure you I *am* twelve—oh! I'm sorry. I would be about . . . twenty-two in Earth years."

"That sounds more like it. How long were you in space?"

"About six months. Earth months, I mean."

"Do you feel weak? Dizzy? Nauseous? Any difficulty standing up or walking?"

"No."

"That's good. Go ahead and stand up. You'll need to take your shirt off."

When Nancy started unbuttoning her shirt, Frank, leaning against the wall outside the lockup with his shotgun at the ready, looked away. He couldn't help himself—he'd been raised a gentleman—sometimes that upbringing wasn't a good fit for a lawman. Nor could he help it when his eyes meandered back to the prisoner just for a second. He was a man, after all.

Germaine was prodding around in Nancy's armpits and Nancy, hands up like she was being robbed at gunpoint, was looking straight at him, unequivocally catching him indulging a weakness. Weakness? Maybe—but he had every right—what if she had been strangling Germaine with her own stethoscope? Frank looked up at the ceiling. Whatever it was in his lockup, it did a fine job of impersonating a healthy woman of twenty-two Earth years.

After the examination, Frank put the shotgun back in the gun cabinet, shut the cabinet door and locked it.

"Well?" he said.

"Well what?"

"Is she from Mars?"

"How would I know?"

"There must be something . . . after six months in space?"

"I can't discuss my patient's medical conditions with you, Frank."

"I see. You can tell half the citizens of New Halchita what just popped out from between Mrs. Ramos' legs, but you can't tell me whether or not the woman in my lockup is from Mars. That's all I'm asking, Germaine. Do you think she's been in space for the last six months? Is she really from Mars?"

"Honestly, Frank, I can't say one way or the other. I

might have expected some indication of recent bone and muscle loss, and I didn't find any. But I don't have a baseline for her, and I don't have a clue as to what kind of medicine or technology they might have to prevent that kind of thing. So . . . I don't know."

"You're a big help."

"Wherever she's from, I can tell you she's a human being and she has rights. You should release her."

"And I can tell you she's staying right here in my lockup for now. Anyway, where would she go? Back to Mars?"

"Have you charged her with something?"

"I've been over this with Mr. Delgado already and I'll tell you what I told him: the law says I can hold a suspect for 48 hours without formal charges."

"Suspect? Suspected of what?"

"Aiding and abetting Scabs."

"She's no Scavenger spy, Frank, you know that. Twenty-two years old and no scars, no tumors, all her fingers, all her teeth? And that thing out there in the bean field—does that look like a Scavenger ride to you?"

"Maybe it's a Trojan horse," Frank said. "Maybe they want us to bring it inside the gates. Maybe it's crammed full of Scabs."

"You don't believe that."

"I don't know what she is," Frank said. "I can tell you I took a good look at that . . . thing in Mr. Habushaki's bean field, and it doesn't look like any scrapride I've ever seen, Scab *or* Civvy. So maybe she's from Mars like she says. But if she's from Mars, something's not right. Did you notice how she's dressed?"

"So her outfit is a bit . . . showy."

"Showy? Do you think that's what Martians wear when it's two-hundred degrees below zero and they're mining for water crystals or whatever they do on that rust ball? It's not 'showy,' it's a strategic diversion meant to confuse and distract us."

"She's not on Mars, and the outfit she's wearing is not a crime."

"Just barely not a crime. In any case, it's suspicious behavior."

"Only you would consider a young woman dressed up to attract attention 'suspicious behavior,'" Germaine said. "When you release her, she can stay with me."

Sometime during the night, he lets himself into the lockup with the Martian. "Stand up," he says, and she does so. "Take off your clothes," he says. He means to explain to her that he has to make sure she isn't concealing any weapons. But she doesn't ask why, she just steps out of her clothes, and to his dismay, he sees she is not human after all. Not from the neck down, anyway.

"Be kind," she says as she scuttles towards him. He tries to get away, but he's managed to lock himself in the cell with her and he's got nowhere to go. There's a strange noise coming from inside . . . what would you call it? her thorax? . . . like a baby crying or something even less human than she is that wants out.

Frank woke, heart pounding. The horrible noise in his dream resolved itself into the bleating of goats someone was herding down Main Street. At 5:30 a.m. Again. Oh, the things he would arrest people for if only he could. No sense trying to get back to sleep. Might as well get up—see if the Martian wants any breakfast.

While putting on his sheriff clothes, Frank counted this single blessing: for once, the woman of his dreams wasn't Germaine.

2 THE INQUIRY

*Minutes of the Proceedings of an Inquiry into
the "Visitor from Mars,"
by the Honorable Council of New Halchita,
in the Main Council Room, upon this 26th day of September,
2473.*

PRESENT.

His Honor, NOÉ LOPEZ, Mayor.
MEMBERS of the council:
Mr. ISAAC GOODHUE
Mrs. DORENE CRANE
Mr. W.H. DOWNES
The "VISITOR FROM MARS," also known as NANCY
Attorney PABLO S. DELGADO, ESQ., Advocate for the Visitor
Sheriff FRANK B. WESTFALL, Acting Bailiff

His Honor the Mayor Noé Lopez appeared in the main council room, and all persons noted above were admitted and seated. The order of Mayor Lopez to the council to question the Visitor was read. The several members of the council were sworn, and the Visitor was also sworn. The Visitor and her advocate, being asked by the Mayor, declared they had no objection to opening the proceedings to the public. By the order of Mayor Lopez, the public was then admitted and seated. The Visitor, being asked by Councilman Goodhue if she understood that she was participating in these proceedings of her own free will, and not under threat of harm or force of law, replied in the affirmative.

Question (by the Council). Please state your full name, age, and current address.

Answer (by the Visitor). My full name is Nancy. That's all the name I've ever had. I'm twelve Mars-years old, or about twenty-two in Earth years. I'm currently residing in the lockup at the Sheriff's office.

Question. Are you a Martian?

Answer. Yes, I came here from Mars.

Question. When did you come to Earth, and why?

Answer. I achieved Earth orbit fifty-two days ago. After observing the planet for most of that time, I released my ship from the orbiter and landed it in the field outside your settlement. I came to Earth to—"

Question. You have another ship in orbit?

Answer. Yes.

Question. Are there others from Mars on that ship?

Answer. No, I came alone.

Question. And why did you come here? I mean, to Earth?

Answer. Almost 300 years ago, my ancestors, the men and women of Mars Experimental Colony #3, lost contact with Earth. The colonists tried to re-establish communications, but their transmissions went unanswered. That the people of Earth had met with some unexpected and horrific catastrophe seemed the only possible explanation. The colonists had little hope of survival without resupply from Earth. Most of them died in the first year after what we call "The Disconnect." But a few did survive, and the descendants of those survivors flourished. About a decade ago, we had achieved the technology and infrastructure necessary to build a spaceship, so we did. When the ship was completed, I was sent to find out what happened to Earth, and to re-establish contact if there were survivors.

Question. And why did you come to New Halchita? Wouldn't it have made more sense to contact, say, the government in Washington, D.C.?

Answer. After observing Earth for almost two months, New Halchita was selected as the most favorable place to make our initial contact: populous, orderly, and peaceful.

Question. So you chose to come to New Halchita because you saw us as docile?

Answer. I didn't say docile, I said peaceful.

Question. So your decision to come to New Halchita was based on your impression that New Halchita would submit peacefully to an invasion by a force armed with superior weapons and technology?

Answer. No . . . that's not it at all . . . I . . .

Answer (by Mr. Delgado, Esq.) Your Honor, and esteemed members of the council, Nancy has clearly stated that her purpose in coming here was to discover why Mars Experimental Colony #3 was so cruelly abandoned, and to re-establish contact with Earth if there were any survivors of what they correctly assumed was a planet-wide disaster. If she is to be questioned as though she is a scout or a spy for an invading army, I will advise her to invoke her fifth amendment rights under the U.S. Constitution.

Question. Ma'am, would you agree with your counsel? Would you characterize the purpose of your mission—the *sole* purpose of your mission—as an attempt to determine why communications with Earth ceased 300 years ago, and to re-establish relations with Earth?

Answer (by the Martian). Yes.

Question. You said you have a ship in orbit?

Answer. Yes.

Question. And no one is currently aboard that ship. You are, as you said, 'alone' here?

Answer. Yes.

Question. But surely, from your ship, you can communicate with the other descendants of the Mars colony? So in that sense, at least, it's not accurate to say you are "alone."

Answer. Yes, that's true.

Question. When was your last communication with Mars, and what was the nature of that communication?

Answer. I said that I had landed my ship at the selected location—

Question. You communicated this from the ship you landed outside New Halchita?

Answer. Yes, I can communicate with Mars from the orbiter or from my ship.

Question. Okay, please continue.

Answer. I said that I had landed my ship at the selected location, and that a delegation from the community was approaching, and that it looked to me like the delegation was armed. As I recall, my very last communication was, simply, "Wish me luck."

Question. And that was your last communication with Mars?

Answer. As I haven't had access to my ship since then, I haven't been able to contact anyone on Mars. It's likely they believe I'm dead.

Question. Are you seeking citizenship or asylum in New Halchita?

Answer. (by Mr. Delgado, Esq.) Not at this time.

At the request of His Honor the Mayor, a fifteen minute recess was called, and the mayor and council retired to chambers. When the mayor and council returned from chambers, the following statement was read: The mayor and council members have determined that the Martian, hereafter known as Nancy, is to have no further communications with Mars, nor is she to be given access to her ship, until further notice from the council.

The council further stated that if Nancy agrees to abide by the rule of the council, and not attempt further communications with Mars until and unless such communications have been approved by the council, she may be released into the custody of Dr. Germaine Perry.

After a brief consultation with Mr. Delgado, Nancy agreed to abide by the rule of the council.

Mayor Lopez then asked if the librarian, Mrs. Barlow, was seated with the public in the council room. Mrs. Barlow stood and replied in the affirmative. Mayor Lopez asked Mrs. Barlow if she would be so kind as to check the old books and see if there was a record of the existence of a "Mars Experimental Colony #3" around the time of the GIW. Mrs. Barlow replied that she would do so.

By the order of the Honorable Mayor Noé Lopez, the inquiry was then adjourned.

3 LAGAMACHIES

What do you do with a visitor from Mars? Germaine didn't have a clue. There hadn't been a stranger in New Halchita since they caught those Scavenger kids breaking into a dry goods store—and that was many years ago now, when she was a kid herself. But surely a walk around the town was obligatory. It would occupy all of an hour.

Or maybe it would take longer. The Martian proceeded as slowly and carefully as if she were traversing a rope bridge suspended over a canyon. Crossing Main Street caused her particular difficulty—she didn't seem to trust the dirt under her feet. When they had attained the other side, Nancy stopped and leaned against an awning post in front of Otis' dry goods store.

"You look a little pale," Germaine said. "Are you feeling all right?"

"No," Nancy said, "I'm not feeling all right. I'm feeling . . . I don't even know how to describe it. On Mars, I live in a hole in the ground. In fact, I live in a machine that lives in a hole in the ground. This—standing outside in the sun. Buildings rising up into the air. Trees. Wind. And so much . . . so much *room*, everywhere. It's terrifying and wonderful."

New Halchita was so familiar to Germaine that she hadn't really taken in the view, such as it was, in a very long time—maybe never. She tried her best to see her world through the eyes of a visitor from another. Main Street was a wide dirt road with a ditch running along either side. The buildings that lined the street were of stone and mortar or wood planks, and stood wall to wall, as though they needed to hold each other up. Once, long ago, the buildings might have been white or some other color with a name. In front of each building, a board or two served as a bridge across the ditch into the street. Looking north, there wasn't much to see other than the North Gate. Looking south, she could see the council building with its little dome and a few trees out front, and beyond that, the reserve silos and the South Gate. *Terrifying and wonderful* was not how Germaine would have described it.

"The sheriff's office is just a couple of blocks down the street," Germaine said. "I'm sure Sheriff Westfall would be more than happy to throw you back in the lockup."

"Do you think he would?" Nancy said. "I found the lockup quite comfortable."

"I was kidding," Germaine said. The two started walking again, continuing west on Lancaster Street. Nancy seemed to be getting her Earth feet, and they picked up the pace, but where Lancaster turned to the south, Nancy stopped, a look of deep concern, if not exactly terror, on her face.

"What's that noise?" she said.

Germaine laughed. "Children. We're coming up to the school. There, to your right. Mr. Elson's third graders must be on recess."

"They run around like . . ."

"Like what?"

"Like the sun won't burn them into dust. Like there's air to breathe."

"It's nice to see New Halchita through the eyes of someone who finds it so exotic," Germaine said. "I guess you had no idea what you would find here."

"We didn't know if we'd find anything," Nancy said. "—anything living, anyway. We always assumed an asteroid strike—a planet killer—but it wasn't, was it?"

"There was a war—or what we call a war because we don't have a better word for it," Germaine said, "but there were no speeches, no declarations, no soldiers, no invasions, no battles—just death, in the billions."

"Over what?"

"Over nothing, as far as we know. A mistake, maybe. Someone screwed up. Someone went crazy. We don't have much in the way of records about what happened, because there wasn't much in the way of survivors. They called it the GIW—the Great *Something* War. We don't know for sure what the 'I' stood for. Inadvertent. Idiotic. Inevitable. All we know for certain is that one day, around three hundred years ago, it started raining nuclear warheads. And then it was over—that's what the survivors thought—until they tried to rebuild. Then came the lagamachies.

"Lagamachies?"

"The lagamachies are nuclear warheads designed to stay in orbit for centuries, looking for radio signals, indications of power generation—we don't know the criteria exactly—that's the problem—but if a lagamachy decides a settlement is using inappropriate technology, down it comes."

"Why?"

"We don't know. Maybe someone decided there's not much point in bombing your enemies back to the stone age if they're just going to rebuild their civilization in a few generations."

As they walked past the clinic, Germaine kept her eyes straight ahead, resisting the tremendous urge to *just run in for a minute and check on things*. Nurse Jim could handle it for a few hours. He was young, but he could handle it. He could.

"So when I communicated with my ship in orbit—" Nancy said.

"We're still here—that's a good sign. But you can understand why that would make people nervous."

"I think I talked to them," Nancy said.

"What do you mean you talked to them?"

"When I was approaching Earth, I detected a lot of satellites in orbit, all of the same design. I signaled them to let them know I was coming, so we wouldn't run into each other. They made the necessary adjustments, but there was something decidedly unfriendly about them. They must have been lagamachies."

"Unfriendly?" Germaine said, "I'm surprised they let you live. The library's right around the corner. We can stop in for a few minutes if you want to get out of the outside for a while. There are plenty of cramped little nooks and crannies in the library."

The library was a square stone building, rather small, but with a muscular look about it, and it stood proudly in its own small courtyard. There were wide stone steps and columns in front, and to one side, an enormous oak tree. In the shade of this oak, Deputy Orland and the assistant librarian, Miss Melody St. Clair, were standing very close together engaged in a conversation so gripping that even the approach of a visitor from Mars in the company of the town's physician merited little more than a quick glance.

What do you do with a visitor from Mars? Germaine didn't have a clue—but some things were older than the GIW and must extend at least to the orbit of the red planet.

"Do you have a man back on Mars?" Germaine asked.

"No," Nancy said.

"In that case," Germaine said, "I'll introduce you to Nurse Jim. You could do worse."

4 THE LURE OF THE MARTIAN

Mayor Lopez held up a hefty binder for the other council members to see. "As always," he said, "Mrs. Barlow has been quite thorough. Her report confirms the existence of Mars Experimental Colony #3, established around six months prior to the GIW. The colony consisted of one-hundred and twenty-five scientists and engineers. And I have received some new information from Dr. Perry as well. She measured Nancy's levels of ionizing radiation, and found those levels astonishingly low. Dr. Perry said Nancy cannot have been on Earth a year, much less twenty-two. In short, what evidence we have been able to gather so far supports Nancy's claim of being from Mars in every particular."

"I don't need an old book or a Geiger counter to tell me that woman is not from around here," Mr. Downes said. "I was working in the fields when that thing came in for a landing—a fireball coming straight for New Halchita. I thought a lagamachy had finally sniffed us out. I thought, *well, that's the end of New Halchita—three hundred years—and poof!* Then the fire went out and it sprouted wings and fluttered right down into Mr. Habushaki's bean field. If you dropped your handkerchief on the ground it wouldn't land any softer. Just before Sheriff Westfall and his deputies showed up, this . . . I don't know what . . . like a great heap of boiled spinach fell out of the belly of the thing. Something—that woman—Nancy—she wriggles her way out of the spinach, and stands up, and there she is, pretty as you please. She's not the girl from next door, Mr. Mayor. She's at least from Mars. What's the one after Mars? Saturn? Maybe she's from there."

"It's Jupiter after Mars," Mrs. Crane said, "and if you'd paid attention in my eighth-grade science class, you'd know that, Mr. Downes. But otherwise, I completely agree with you. She's other-worldly, to say the least."

"I propose the following resolution," the mayor said, "that the council of New Halchita hereby states and affirms that the woman known as Nancy is a human from Mars, a descendant of a colony established on that planet prior to the GIW known as Mars Experimental Colony #3."

"Seconded," Mr. Downes said, firmly.

"All in favor?" The mayor said.

Four hands went up.

"I suppose it's stating the obvious," the mayor said, "that circumstances warrant a letter to the president of the United States in Washington D.C."

"He won't believe it," Mr. Downes said. "Would you?"

"We have good evidence," Mayor Lopez said. "Mr. Downes, your own eyewitness account of the landing; Dr. Perry's measurements of her remarkably low levels of ionizing radiation; Mrs. Barlow's report on the history of Mars Experimental Colony #3, supporting Nancy's story—"

"And when the president gets the letter, it's all just ink

on paper," Mr. Downes said. "At best, he'll think we've gone mad. At worst, he'll think we're trying to be funny."

"Why not let Nancy take the letter herself?" Mr. Goodhue said. "Presumably she could fly her ship to Washington if we would let her."

"We've already voted on that, Mr. Goodhue," Mrs. Crane said, "and you lost, so don't think you can sneak your way around the will of the majority. The decision was we don't let her near that machine—not until we are certain of her true intentions."

"I'm curious, Mrs. Crane," Mr. Goodhue said, "how exactly do you plan to determine her 'true' intentions? And why do you assume she means us harm?"

"Why do you assume she doesn't?" Mrs. Crane said. "Six months in space, eighty million kilometers—she didn't just drop by to say howdy." Mrs. Crane took off her glasses and crossed her arms, allowing Mr. Goodhue to see both the resolve in her eye and the pointiness of her elbow. "There's something she's not telling us," Mrs. Crane said.

"And you think holding her hostage here will—"

"No one's holding anyone *hostage* Isaac. She's a guest at Dr. Perry's house, for Christ's sake. Are you saying *Dr. Perry* is holding her hostage? Why do you always have to exaggerate—"

The gavel that Mayor Lopez lifted had a head and handle carved from a single block of yellow bois d'arc, the head inlaid in a floral pattern with teardrops of polished steel and colored glass. Both the gavel and the table the council was sitting at had been made to the specifications of one of New Halchita's early mayors by a talented young woman as her masterwork for acceptance into the woodworker's guild. The genius of the design was in how the two parts worked together, like clapper and bell, though the notes produced were not at all agreeable to the ear. Mayor Lopez banged the gavel and didn't stop until the other council members gave up trying to argue over the noise. He let the silence sink in for a moment for dramatic effect (and to catch his breath, as it was, per necessity, a very heavy gavel), and then he spoke, softly and calmly.

"There is a point here that I think the council is missing," the mayor said. "Apparently, we have a Martian. By the grace of God, if you will, or by luck or fate, if you'd prefer, but however it happened, we have a Martian, and if we send the Martian to Washington, we have nothing.

"Every member of this council is aware of how desperate our situation is. Ten years ago, we had enough grain in our reserve silos to get us through two—maybe three—years of crop failure. Today we'd be lucky to sweep up enough beans and corn to last three months. Every year the spring rains end sooner and the fall rains start later. The old books say this whole area was a desert. Our weatherman says the GIW changed the weather patterns across the entire planet, but now it's going back to the way it used to be. In a few years, if we don't move, we'll starve. But move where? And how? How do we get every man, woman, and child in New Halchita from here to there, wherever *there* is, through a wilderness controlled by the Scavenger hordes and infested with bloodthirsty ticks? And once we're there, how do we feed ourselves until first harvest?"

Mayor Lopez looked at each of the other council members in turn, and, as none of them had an answer, he continued: "Every year we send Postmaster Skint to Washington D.C. with a letter to the president. We tell him we need help. We tell him we don't know how much longer we can make it on our own. Every year Postmaster Skint returns with the same reply, 'As soon as resources permit.' And we never get any help. But now we have a Martian. And if we can get the president to come to New Halchita to see the Martian, we'll shake his hand, we'll introduce him to Mrs. Ramos' baby girl, we'll take him to the school and have the children sing for him, and we'll hope he's not the kind of man who, after all of that, can look a desperate mayor in the eye and say *I can't help your people*. So the question before us is, how do we get the president to believe we have a visitor from Mars, without actually sending him the Martian?"

After a long silence, the Mayor suggested that the meeting be adjourned for the day, and the council members think about the problem, and return the next day with some ideas. Mr. Downes cleared his throat once, and then again.

"Mr. Downes," the mayor said, "do you have a suggestion?"

"Well," Mr. Downes said. He looked down at the table and seemed unwilling to continue.

"Go ahead, Mr. Downes," Mayor Lopez said.

"When my beloved Helen passed away a year ago," Mr. Downes said, very softly, "Mr. Lyons took a lovely photograph of her . . . and he also took . . . you know, one of those stereoscopic pictures . . . the kind you look at through a viewer. And I . . . I looked at it once and tore it to shreds immediately . . . it seemed unnatural, like she was right there, and I was afraid I had taken her away from heaven. And then I was sorry I'd done it—I mean, I was sorry I tore up the picture. I thought she might be looking down on me and not understand."

Mr. Downes buried his face in his hands and wept. Mrs. Crane patted him gently on the back. "We all miss your sweet Helen," Mrs. Crane said. "And I know she knows you loved her very much and she knows why you tore up that picture. She knows it just hurt you too much to look at it. But Mr. Downes, it *is* a marvelous suggestion. I've seen some of Mr. Lyons' stereoscopic photographs, and they are *quite* convincing."

"All right," the mayor said, "I move that the council engage the services of Mr. Lyons for the production of a stereoscopic photograph of the Martian and her ship, to be included with the letter we will send to the president of the United States in Washington D.C."

"Seconded," Mr. Downes sobbed.

"All in favor," the mayor said.

Three hands went up immediately. Mr. Downes, keeping one hand over his face, slowly raised the fourth.

5 DINNER WITH THE DOCTOR

Postmaster Skint was considerably shorter than Sheriff Westfall, and somewhat taller than Mr. Delgado. He was not as pale as Nurse Jim and not nearly as dark as Germaine. His hair was brown, his eyes, green, his nose, long, thin, and a little crooked. His rather average appearance was something of a relief to Nancy, who found the wide variation in human form in New Halchita unsettling—an unnecessary complication on top of an already difficult condition. What puzzled Nancy was that it was clear from the moment that Spencer Skint walked in the door that Germaine found him *exceedingly* remarkable. The way Germaine looked at Postmaster Skint, you'd think he was the sun, two moons, and all the stars in the sky, rolled into one single luminous celestial phenomenon.

Germaine served Nancy a thumb-sized piece of cornbread and about two tablespoons of chicken stew. Spencer Skint, on the other hand, got about as much as his plate would hold. Germaine served herself considerably more than the former and considerably less than the latter. The instant the three of them were seated (or perhaps an instant before) Skint dug in. Nancy lifted a pea-sized crumb of cornbread up to her lips on her fork, and then, rather than putting the crumb into her mouth, she tasted it by touching it with her extended tongue. Even Skint, whom little could distract from his victuals, stopped eating to watch.

"I take it you don't care for cornbread," he said.

"I find most Earth food problematic," Nancy said.

"So what *do* you like?"

"Blackberry spritz."

"Oh, right," Skint said, "I heard about that—Nurse Jim and the Martian at Mr. Fitz's apothecary—one cup, two straws. It's the talk of the town. So you liked the spritz—the question is, did you like the nurse?"

"He's very informative."

"The boy does love to talk," Skint said. Skint buttered his cornbread thoroughly, then turned to Germaine. "Speaking of people who love to talk, guess what brilliant plan the council has come up with for dealing with our Martian friend here?"

"I heard already," Germaine said. "They're going to send a letter to the president of the United States in Washington D.C."

Skint, his mouth full of well-buttered cornbread, snorted. "Yep. That's their answer to pretty much everything, isn't it? If it were up to me, I wouldn't send a letter to the president in Washington D.C.—I'd send a letter back to Mars with this young lady right here."

"What would the letter say, Spencer?" Nancy asked.

"It'd say: 'Come back with about a thousand of your friends and help us wipe out the Scabs, and we'll split this country with you fifty-fifty.'"

Nancy looked at Germaine.

"I don't think the council would have much

enthusiasm for a plan that includes stirring up the Scavengers," Germaine said.

"Of course not," Skint replied. "Here we are in New Halchita, America. We survived the GIW and kept the torch of civilization burning through hell and high water for the last three hundred years. But hey, let's not guarantee our survival if it means stirring up the Scabs. Let's not worry about our children's future—let's worry about the *Scabs'* future."

"It's easy to say that when you're not on the council, and what you say doesn't end up getting people killed," Germaine said.

"It's easy to say 'send a letter to the president' when you're not the one carrying the letter," Skint said.

"You don't have to go," Germaine said. "You've been once already this year. They can find someone else."

"No they can't," Skint said. He turned back to Nancy, as he had already explained to Germaine on several previous occasions what it took to get a letter to the president. He held up three whole fingers and a stump, felling each in turn as he iterated over the requirements: "You have to be smart, you have to be quick, you have to know how to deal with Scabs, and you have to be able to smell a tick nest a mile away."

"What does a tick nest smell like?" Nancy said.

"I'd say like strawberries. You might think a man would have to be crazy to walk straight into a nest of ticks, and you'd be right. But when they hatch, ten thousand all at the same time, they make a fume—a miasma—that spreads out for miles around the nest, and when you breathe it in it plays with your head."

"That's what we call a tall tale," Germaine said to Nancy.

"No, sir," Skint said. "I know from personal

experience. I was a tick-juicer before I was a postmaster, so I know a thing or two about ticks. You get one good whiff of that stuff and you start thinking about who's waiting for you at home, or what you're going to have for dinner, or a funny joke you heard. You take a wrong turn, and you forget to look where you're going. Next thing you know, you're standing in the middle of a tick nest, along with ten thousand juveniles looking for their first feed."

Skint stood up, turned around, and pulled off his shirt. He had a semi-circular scar on his back, just below his left shoulder. The cicatrix resembled a lip, raised and red, with many fine creases along its length. It was dotted on either side with the pinpoint tracks of sutures. "Does that look like a tall tale?" Skint said.

"Maybe you weren't paying attention," Germaine said.

Skint put his shirt back on and sat down. "Think whatever you want," he said, "I can tell you this: My predecessor, Postmaster Larkin, made four trips. The fifth time he set out he never came back. Me? Nine times already I've gotten a letter to the president in Washington D.C. and brought back his reply. You think eighty million kilometers in a brand-new spaceship is something? It's a walk in the park. Try driving down three thousand kilometers of busted pre-GIW road in a scrapride made from three-hundred-year-old truck parts with Scabs trying to put a bullet in you and ticks trying to suck you dry and radiation hotspots trying to boil your brains and God knows what else. Now *that's* something."

Spencer Skint waited for a suitably complimentary reply from Nancy, but none was forthcoming.

"I always worry about Spencer when he's on the road," Germaine said, breaking the uncomfortable silence. "Who's at home worrying about you, Nancy?"

"No one," Nancy said.

"That can't be true," Germaine said. "You must have family . . . or friends?"

"It's not like that on Mars," Nancy said. "There were one-hundred and twenty-five original colonists, and not all of them survived The Disconnect. There are thousands of us now, but as you can imagine, we're all very much alike. No one on Mars is going to worry over the fate of this one Nancy. There are plenty more where I came from."

"There are some boys in this town if they heard you say that, they'd set right to work building themselves a spaceship," Skint said.

"The ones who stare at me, you mean?" Nancy said.

"Them," Skint said, "and the ones who don't. Maybe especially the ones who don't. What's for dessert, Germaine? And if the Martian finds dessert *problematic*, I'll take her share."

Previously, Germaine and Nancy had shared Germaine's bed, but on this particular night, Germaine made a pallet on the kitchen floor, and suggested politely (but firmly) that Nancy might sleep quite comfortably there.

For a little while Nancy listened to the low voices of Spencer and Germaine coming from the bedroom, and for a little while after that she listened to their moans and sighs and grunts. A strange image came into Nancy's head—Germaine's dark hands on Skint's pale back, the doctor's fingertips just touching that raised, lip-like scar. For a moment, Nancy thought she herself could feel it. She dismissed the thought and directed her attention to her ship's video feed. There wasn't much to see on that channel: a cloudy night in a field of beans in the yellow light of a single lantern. It was late enough that early would be along shortly. Only Deputy Orland and a young woman, the one Nancy had seen talking to the deputy near the library, were out there now.

Deputy Orland was leaning back against one of the ship's legs, like he and the ship were old chums. The young woman stood several feet away, clearly unwilling to get close to the ship. She told Deputy Orland it looked like a giant bug. He said she should come closer and touch it—it was smoother and warmer than you would think. She said she didn't dare. He said he wouldn't tell anyone. She said he was very brave. It started to rain.

"Come on," Deputy Orland said. He took her hand and pulled her under the ship. The woman squealed in obviously feigned horror. Nancy could hear them, but no longer see them. "We'll stay perfectly safe and dry here," Deputy Orland said. "there's nothing to be afraid of, it's just a big hunk of metal—a wheelbarrow from Mars."

Very slowly, Nancy extended an eye-segment on its cable, curving it down and under the side of the ship until she could again observe Orland and the woman. They were standing very close, their faces mashed together. Orland had one arm around the woman's back in order to press her firmly against him, and the other down lower, so he could get a good grip on her buttocks.

A noise in the house brought Nancy back to the sensations of her organic self. A rise and fall of murmuring and rustling from the bedroom was soon followed by the sound of Spencer Skint coming down the hall in that footwear of his that seemed especially designed to underscore his arrivals and departures. The thunk of his heel-irons on the wooden floor stopped at the entrance to the kitchen, and Nancy knew that if she opened her eyes, she would see Spencer in the hallway watching her. A few seconds passed, and then Spencer thunked on—out the front door and onto the porch. The thunk became a thud when he stepped onto the hard-packed dirt of Lancaster Street. Spencer Skint coughed, spat, and thudded off into the night.

Nancy turned her attention back to the ship. The woman's shirt was now undone and the Deputy's hand that was not on the woman's buttocks was clutching one of her breasts. While the buttocks-hand remained stationary, the breast-hand turned this way and that, giving the breast a squeeze after each repositioning, as though Deputy Orland was searching for, and not finding, a favorable grip upon the woman's mammary protuberance.

If her ship hadn't been able to see considerably more of the electromagnetic spectrum than the human eye, Nancy might not have noticed a shriveled little man in an oversized gray fur coat hunkered down in the beans, not fifteen yards away from where the deputy and his girl were grappling with each other. The shriveled gentleman's bulging yellow eyes were fixated on the ship—he seemed to have little interest in the deputy and the assistant librarian. Nancy wasn't sure how long he'd been there. She wasn't certain he hadn't observed the extension of the eye segment. It concerned her, but there wasn't anything she could do about it now.

Sensing the orbiter coming over the horizon, Nancy prepared a short transmission: *This morning, Germaine took me to see a new-born female they call Pilar Ramos. The infant appears to be of the finest quality and in every respect suitable for conversion. Please advise.*

6 HOW TO EMBELLISH A MARTIAN

"First," Mr. Lyons said, "I would like to say that I am honored by the council's request for my services in this matter. Second, I would like to thank the council for calling a special session in order to allow me to voice my concerns."

"The council thanks you for being here," the mayor said.

"I hope the council will not think it rude of me to speak plainly," Mr. Lyons said. "As a man who has spent his entire life practicing the photographic arts, I most humbly suggest to the council that stereoscopic images alone are not adequate for a historical event of this magnitude. By necessity, the photographic prints that make up a stereoscopic image are rather small, as they must fit into a viewer. Allow me to demonstrate. I have brought with me a viewer, and here is a typical print. The print fits into the viewer thusly . . . and now . . . Mr. Mayor, why don't you take a look . . ."

The mayor brought the viewer up to his eyes, and was immediately greeted by the image of a tick big enough to swallow a small dog whole, its scissor-like chelicerae parted, and the long, serrated scoop of its hypostome fully extended. The tick appeared to be soaring through the air, as though caught in the act of leaping for its victim's throat. The mayor gasped and dropped the viewer.

Mr. Lyons chuckled. "I'm sorry, Mr. Mayor, I couldn't resist. I am quite proud of that particular effort, both for the quality of the photograph and for the excellent manner in which I was able to preserve the life-like qualities of that specimen of Ixodes Giganticus—but the point is, though the image is convincing, it is also quite small."

Mr. Lyons picked the viewer up off the table and removed the print, the print being somewhat smaller than a playing card. He handed the print to the Mayor. Without the viewer, the side-by-side images of the tick were about as large and frightening as a couple of almonds.

The mayor, after a few attempts, was able to place the print back into the viewer in its proper orientation. He handed the viewer over to Mrs. Crane, who, having witnessed the Mayor's reaction to the scene contained therein, brought the viewer very slowly and cautiously to her eyes, and then, scowling, quickly passed it on to Mr. Goodhue.

"I believe I will not be contradicted," Mr. Lyons said, "when I say it is the wise intention of this council to convince the president of the United States in Washington D.C., that the arrival in New Halchita of the Martian in her most remarkable spaceship is the kind of historical event that would be greatly enhanced by his presence, and greatly diminished without it."

"You have captured the purpose of our request for your professional services most eloquently," the mayor said, "please proceed with your recommendations."

"If we are to convince the president of the importance of what has happened here in New Halchita," Mr. Lyons said, "we must believe it ourselves, and act accordingly. Great historical events are not recorded solely on a few two-inch by four-inch stereoscopic prints. You have asked for my recommendation, Mr. Mayor. I most respectfully ask that the mayor and the council look around."

The portraits that adorned the walls of the chambers were so familiar to the council that they were, for all intents and purposes, completely invisible to them. But Mr. Lyons' words, like a mystical incantation, caused them to gradually reappear. There, for example, above and to the left of a squat bookshelf containing many handsomely bound volumes of ancient (and for the most part long-forgotten) statutes and acts of the council, was Mr. Downes' great aunt, Henrietta Downes Wasserman, who had stood at the door of the schoolhouse with a hammer in one hand and a frying pan in the other, using them first to beat out an alarm and then to single-handedly defend the children within from Scavenger raiders until help arrived. Though she was a much older woman when the photograph was taken, the essence of her courage on that day was palpable in her fierce demeanor. And there, over by the coat rack, was Dr. Germaine Perry's maternal grandfather, Dr. William Lancaster Navarro, who had nursed the sick during the great blood-flu outbreak of aught-seven. The photograph, so the story went, was taken when it was thought the danger had finally passed—and shortly before Dr. Navarro himself succumbed to the ravages of the disease. The love Dr. Navarro held for his fellow man, and perhaps an intimation of his own impending demise, could be seen in his sorrowful eyes. Between the door and the window hung a photograph of young Posey Sebastian, credited with leading the charge that broke the siege of New Halchita during the last Scab War. In the photograph, he is seated in a chair with a rifle across his lap and his eyes open—but there is no life in those eyes—the photograph was taken post-mortem.

Mr. Goodhue squirmed in his chair uncomfortably as he looked into the dead eyes of Posey Sebastian and recalled how that tragedy had played out. Posey's mother started drinking heavily after the death of her boy. One night she got in a row with her husband and shot him dead. She was brought before the council to answer for her crime. The inquiry and judgment was expected to go badly for her, as her late husband's brother was on the council. The first question he asked her she answered by shooting him dead as well. How she had gotten her rather enormous six-shooter into the council chambers undetected, and what her beef was with her brother-in-law, was a mystery that had never been solved—some said she must have had help. In any case, an election was held to replace the murdered councilman, and that was how it happened that Mr. Goodhue was now sitting in the same chair where Councilman Sebastian had breathed his last.

"Imagine," Mr. Lyons said, after a suitable time for reflection had passed, "what images might adorn these walls in a hundred years. Those are the photographs we must take today—the chance will not come again."

Mr. Lyons' passionate plea did not fall on deaf ears. He fully convinced the council of the necessity of recording the historical events unfolding in New Halchita both thoroughly and reverently. But whether from a lack of imagination or a lack of experience (and what experience is ever truly preparatory for the next great lurch of history?), in the end, there were only two things the council could think of for Mr. Lyons to photograph: the Martian's ship, and the Martian.

The council was easily persuaded to allow Mr. Lyons to photograph the ship from a variety of angles, and from each angle, to take photographs both with and without attendant persons. An unobstructed view of the ship was wanted for some purposes, Mr. Lyons explained, but a photograph with persons in it generally created the most interesting and desirable aesthetic effect, and as a historical and scientific record, having persons shown alongside the spaceship would give the viewer an immediate sense of its size. Furthermore, if the persons happened to be known to history, the historical era of the photograph would thereby be firmly established for future generations. In Mr. Lyons' view, no persons would serve better to that end than the Mayor and his council.

Deliberations turned to photographing the Martian. As that discussion proceeded, the Mayor had less and less to say, until he was saying nothing at all, and a troubled look came over him.

"Mr. Mayor," Mr. Lyons said, "if you have concerns, please don't hesitate to voice them."

"I suppose I have no objection to the Martian standing for a photograph or two," Mayor Lopez said, "but I do wonder if we should send photographs of the Martian to the president. We must keep in mind that the purpose here is to convince the president to come to New Halchita. And I'm afraid that a photograph of an attractive, but in the end rather ordinary, woman claiming to be from Mars, won't be nearly as compelling as the female Martian of his imagination."

The mayor's point was well-taken, and the council and Mr. Lyons were stumped. It was necessary to convince the president of the veracity of their claims, but if the photographs satisfied the president's curiosity in every respect, why would he bother to come to New Halchita?

"All right," Mr. Downes said at length. "So we won't include a photograph of Nancy among those we send to the president."

"But the president will surely be suspicious of such a strange and obvious omission," Mrs. Crane said. "He may conclude we don't have a Martian at all."

"Under the circumstances," Mr. Lyons said, "perhaps a little harmless subterfuge is in order. I could, for example, quite easily place a third eye on the Martian's forehead when I make the print—a manipulation that I can assure you will be quite undetectable. In my experience, a detail of that sort invariably increases, rather than diminishes, the viewer's interest in the subject."

"He'll be unhappy when he meets the real Nancy," Mr. Goodhue said, "and if we gain the president, only to immediately lose his favorable opinion of us . . . ?

"Why would he be sore with us?" Mr. Lyons said. "Surely he knows that the Martian's distinctive third eye is a reaction to the harsh and unforgiving environment on that planet, like a sunburn or a callus, and once the human returns to Mother Earth's warm and nourishing embrace, the wound soon heals over. Of course, if he isn't aware of that well-known fact, we'll educate him.

7 DEATH OF A BETTER ANGEL

"I believe the key to this case," Pastor Craddock said, "is to determine the motivation of the perpetrator. What if whoever took the communion tray didn't take it for its monetary value? What if they took it because they were angry at God—though possibly on a subconscious level? Perhaps you could shed some light on that kind of thinking, Frank. I myself cannot understand it."

Sheriff Westfall looked down at the report on his desk as though studying it intently for clues. Surely this was Pastor Craddock's way of punishing him for never going to church: to show up every few days and quiz him over his progress on the seven-month-old "case"—the theft of a silver communion tray—and at the same time bully him over his spiritual ambivalence.

"Not a crime of greed, but a crime of passion?" Sheriff Westfall said.

"Exactly," Pastor Craddock said.

"Well, now," Sheriff Westfall said, "that's a possibility that had not occurred to me. In fact, you've given me an idea. I think I'm going to take a walk—talk to some folks."

"I'll go with you," Pastor Craddock said.

"I appreciate the offer," Sheriff Westfall said, "but if a suspect were to see you with me, they'd know why I wanted to talk to them. They'd be on their guard, and I'd lose the element of surprise. Thank you for your offer of assistance, Pastor, but I'll take it from here."

Sheriff Westfall incarcerated the offending paperwork in a desk drawer, stood up, and strapped his gun around his waist. He opened the door of the sheriff's office, exposing a brilliant rectangle of fall afternoon. "After you, Pastor," he said.

Pastor Craddock left, knowing full well Sheriff Westfall had no intention of talking to any suspects. He hoped Frank would at least feel guilty about the lie.

Walking by the scrap yard on Main Street, Frank saw that all three techs were hard at work on the postal delivery truck Postmaster Skint would use to deliver the council's letter to the president, their legs sticking out from under the hood and chassis of the scrapride as if they were worms gorging their way to the core of a giant mechanical apple.

He tipped his hat to Mrs. Otis, standing in the open door of her dry goods store. He walked past the school. There were children on recess running around screaming their heads off, and older kids grunting in unison as they responded to the shouted commands of their hand-to-hand combat instructor. In other words, things were exactly as they should be. Lancaster Street then bent around to the south, leading Frank past the gun and tool works on one side of the street, and the clinic on the other. The smoke and the smell of the furnace, and the rhythmical tock-chocking of the trip hammer, indicated business-as-usual at the works. Frank waved at one of the apprentice machinists who had brought her work outdoors to enjoy the pleasant weather, or perhaps for the better lighting. The apprentice was hard at work building a tiny desk and chair out of cut, welded, and polished pre-GIW scrap metal.

Frank turned east on Wasserman, crossed Main Street and strolled by the twin reserve silos. The silos were by far the tallest structures in New Halchita, gray except for the dark green band that ran around the top of each silo, upon which was painted, in enormous white letters, *NEW* on one and *HALCHITA* on the other. Frank figured that was in case there were any Scabs around who didn't know the name of the town.

New Halchita's post office, located at the corner of Wasserman and Navarro Road, was closed—no surprise there. The post office was open when Postmaster Skint wanted it to be open, which was rarely if ever. Folks who wanted to send a letter delivered it themselves. Oddly enough, they generally felt honor-bound to put a stamp on it anyway. To that end, Skint had turned the sale of stamps over to Mrs. Otis at her dry goods store. Spencer Skint put his life on the line once a year taking a letter to the president in Washington D.C., and the council had determined that was asking enough of any man. Any other services Skint performed for New Halchita as Postmaster were icing on the cake. And that was one naked cake.

It was an exceedingly pleasant and entirely uneventful walk right up until Frank got to the corner of Navarro and Possum Race Road. A plump young woman was coming down Navarro towards Frank at a good clip. It took Frank a moment to place her—the Tyler girl—and not a girl any more, either, a full citizen. He remembered that he'd put a ribbon around her neck when she finished her coursework—what for, he couldn't recall—it must have been two years ago already. Miss Caroline Tyler. Miss Tyler worked at her family's bakery a couple of blocks up the street. The Tylers were at work at some awful hour of the morning and closed up shop around two in the afternoon. So Miss Tyler might have been walking home, only the Tylers lived on Chester Loop, and Chester Loop was in the other direction.

The way Miss Tyler looked straight ahead and not at all at Frank and picked up the tempo of her already quick step convinced Frank she did not want to stop and talk to him. She seemed to think that a show of determination and an abundance of momentum would be enough to convince Frank to step aside.

"Hold up there, Miss Tyler," Frank said, when she came even with him.

She stopped, but she didn't look up. Even so, Frank could see the fire in her cheeks—exertion perhaps—or the heat of a lie as yet untold.

"It's a beautiful afternoon isn't it?" Frank said.

"Yes sir," she said, without enthusiasm.

"How are your folks? I haven't talked to them in a while."

"They're doing fine, Sheriff."

"Where are you headed in such a hurry?"

"It's such a hot day," Miss Tyler said, briefly fanning her face with her hand, "that I just had a terrible thirst for one of Mr. Fitz's spritzes."

"Well, don't let me keep you from your spritz," Frank said. "Say 'hi' to your folks for me." He tipped his hat and walked on.

Miss Tyler was not a very good liar, and Frank was a pretty good sheriff. He continued slowly up Navarro in the direction of the sheriff's office just long enough to give Miss Tyler time to turn the corner at Possum Race Road and look over her shoulder to make sure she hadn't been followed. When those few seconds had passed, Frank turned around and walked back to the corner, where a thick pomegranate hedge provided him with cover as he peered cautiously after the rapidly receding Miss Tyler.

She walked past Fitz's Apothecary without even slowing down, and Frank had a feeling he knew where she was going—because that was life's favorite joke, right?—to hand you the head of your better angel on a silver communion tray. Sure enough, Miss Tyler went straight to the last house on Possum Race Road—the house where Spencer Skint did whatever (and apparently whomever) it was he did when he wasn't delivering a letter to the president of the United States. When she got there, she flew up the steps and raised her fist to knock—a useless gesture—the door opened for her before she landed the first blow.

8 MINDING THE LIGHT

Mr. Lyons' admonition to the council to treat the arrival of the Martian with the historical reverence it deserved had an unintended, though predictable, consequence: word had gotten out, and as the photography session involved a combination of the Martian's ship and the town's notables, it certainly qualified as a diversion, and could conceivably rise to the level of an amusement. In short, practically every citizen of New Halchita was planning to be there. When it became clear there would be a crowd, Sheriff Westfall assigned Deputies Orland and Rhome to attend in an official capacity to keep an eye on things. For his part, the sheriff had been expecting, and had finally received, a formal request from the council to make "exploratory expeditions" (as the council liked to call them) into the Scablands, in preparation for Postmaster Skint's trip to Washington D.C., and the schedule Sheriff Westfall planned for those excursions precluded his participation in the festivities.

Having given his deputies the job of keeping the peace, and having complete faith in their abilities, Frank had dismissed the whole event from his mind, and on the afternoon that he left the sheriff's office headed for the Scablands, he was so wrapped up in his own thoughts that he was taken completely by surprise when he found himself joined by a regular swarm of citizens, all leaving New Halchita through the South Gate. It wasn't until he saw the crowd gathering in Mr. Habushaki's bean field, and Mr. Lyons carefully adjusting the legs of the tripod that supported his box camera, that Frank recalled the grand historical event he would be missing.

The council didn't require absolute secrecy regarding Frank's expeditions—absolute secrecy of anything was a near impossibility in New Halchita—but they did prefer for Frank's forays into the Scablands to proceed quietly and without fanfare. Sometimes he would pass farmers returning from their fields, but in general, only Gatekeeper Abernathy was around to see Frank when he left in the afternoon and returned at that hour of the morning that has a reputation for being the darkest. The last thing the council would want would be for a bunch of citizens to buttonhole Frank on his way out of town and ask him where he was going and what he would do when he got there. But Frank's concern that he might be questioned by curious citizens was soon put to rest. At Mr. Habushaki's bean field, all eyes were on the Martian's ship and the photographer, Mr. Lyons, preparing his equipment.

Frank decided there wouldn't be any harm in lingering for a moment to watch the proceedings, and confronted with the Martian's ship for the first time at his leisure, he was at once struck by how careless his previous observations had been. It was not the pebbly cast-iron black he thought it was, more of a smooth aluminum gray. Frank wondered if the difference was the late afternoon light, or a faulty memory, or if, contrary to the old saying, the leopard had indeed changed its spots. When he "arrested" the Martian, he had noticed the ship's overlapping scales, like those of an armadillo or a woodlouse, but only now did it occur to him that those scales might allow the ship to bend along its horizontal axis, if not entirely roll itself into a ball. Nor had he reflected on the fact that the eight legs the ship stood on were each jointed in three places. The ship could almost certainly be lowered until its underside touched the ground, or raised eight to ten feet into the air. And there were two more legs towards the front of the ship (or what Frank imagined to be the front, because of fish-eye-like bulges at that end) that Frank had not noticed all. The legs were considerably smaller than the "major" legs, and were folded up against the body of the ship, after the manner of a praying mantis.

At Mr. Lyons' urging, the mayor and the other members of the council now lined up in front of the ship. They were smartly dressed and stood shoulder to shoulder, and, Frank was surprised to see, were flanked by Deputies Orland and Rhome. Frank's deputies were in their dress uniforms, including the rather ridiculous tall blue hats they had previously only ever worn (and reluctantly at that) when marching in the Harvest Day parade.

Mr. Lyons draped a black cloth over the camera and stuck his head under it to make final adjustments to the focus. After a few moments he came out from under the cloth, placed a leather lens cap on the lens, and inserted the shielded plate.

"Quiet everyone, please," Mr. Lyons said. "Mr. Mayor, esteemed members of the council, deputies—I must ask you to stand as still as possible. Try not to blink. It will only be for a moment." Mr. Lyons was reaching for the lens cap when the mayor started waving his arms. "Mr. Mayor!" Mr. Lyons said, exasperated, "you *must* remain still."

"One moment, please, Mr. Lyons," the mayor said, "a word."

"If you must, Mr. Mayor. But quickly. We must be mindful of the light!"

The mayor approached Mr. Lyons and conversed with him quietly and at some length. This conversation, Frank noticed with alarm, was interspersed with regular, quick glances by both parties in his direction. Mr. Lyons shook his head—and again—and then, rolling his eyes, nodded in apparent submission to some request of the mayor's he was not overly keen on.

"Sheriff!" the mayor said, "Frank—please! A word. Quickly, quickly—we must be mindful of the light!"

Frank walked up to the mayor, and the mayor motioned for Frank to lean down, so the mayor could speak in his ear.

"Sheriff," the mayor said, "we really had not planned for your deputies to be in the photograph—"

"I'm sorry," Frank said. "I assure you I didn't suggest to them that they would be. It was their idea, not mine. I'll tell them to stand off to the side."

"No, no, no," The mayor said, "that's not what I mean. We hadn't planned for your deputies to be in the photograph, but when they showed up in their dress uniforms, they looked so sharp and all, Mr. Lyons thought it would be wonderful to have them 'framing the council' as he said, and I agreed. In the excitement of the moment, I confess it didn't occur to me . . . but I know how this must look to you and I completely agree that it was . . . simply unconscionable of me, simply *unconscionable*, to include your deputies and not include you, Sheriff—simply unconscionable and I'm sorry—it has all been so very exciting I suppose I lost my head. Please, come stand with us for this historic photograph, Sheriff Westfall."

"Mayor, it's kind of you to consider my feelings, but I don't—"

"No time, Sheriff, no time! We must be mindful of the light! Mr. Lyons said you should set your pack down and stand between Councilman Goodhue and Deputy Orland."

Once Frank had been inserted into the lineup between Goodhue and Orland, Mr. Lyons removed the shielded plate and the leather lens cap, threw the black cloth back over the camera and his balding head, fiddled around under there for a moment, then emerged from beneath the cloth and walked quickly up to Frank.

"Sheriff," Mr. Lyons said, "why don't you try standing at the other end, next to Deputy Rhome. Quickly, quickly, please."

After this adjustment was made, Mr. Lyons hurried back to the camera, dove under the cloth and just as quickly resurfaced, ran up to Frank, and this time, taking him by the elbow, he led him away from Martian's ship.

"Sheriff Westfall," Mr. Lyons said, out of breath from his exertions, "as I'm sure you are aware, you are, well, you are a rather tall gentleman."

"I'm aware of that," Frank said.

"And standing with the others you are, um, you are the tallest by a wide, or perhaps I should say a high, margin."

"That's true," Frank said.

"How tall *are* you, if I might ask?"

"You might not."

"No, of course not, of course not. Ahem. Aha. What I mean to say is, with all due respect, when you stand with the council, they all look rather like . . . comparatively speaking, of course . . . like dreadfully unattractive children playing dress-up, ha ha, if you see what I mean. But it occurs to me, that if you were to stand *behind* Mayor Westfall, only not *stand* exactly, but rather crouch or kneel down—"

Frank wrested his elbow from Mr. Lyons' grip. He shouldered his pack and walked away from the bean fields of New Halchita and into everything else, also known as the Scablands, without looking back. It was getting late already, and Sheriff Frank Westfall was always, always, mindful of the light.

9 IN THE WORDS OF A SUNSET

Frank was about halfway between New Halchita and his destination, an enormous sandstone extrusion known as the Ram's Horn, when the sun plunged into the earth, leaving behind a sky thickly splattered with blood-red clouds. Frank had seen some remarkable sunsets out in the Scablands before, but this one, a perfect storm of violence and beauty, spoke to him directly, and though he was too small and too far away to make out the exact words, the message was clear: *I am your everything—you are my nothing.*

He took off his pack and set it down in front of him. He took the gun out of his holster, sat down, and set the gun down in the grass beside him. From his pack he removed a green glass jar stoppered with a cork, and a wedge-shaped gray paper package. He set the bottle down next to the gun and he set the paper package in his lap, unwrapping it carefully, such that when he was done, the paper served as a plate for his dinner: a thick slice of yellow cornbread.

He alternated between bites of cornbread and sips of water to wash it down. When there was nothing left of the cornbread but crumbs, and nothing left of the sunset but a hoary fringe on the western hem of the night, Frank lifted the edges of the paper and channeled the crumbs into his open palm, and got that little hill of crumbs into his mouth the best he could. He took one last sip of water, then stoppered the jar and folded the paper into a small flat square, and put the paper and the jar back in his pack. He took a lantern out of his pack and also a match, and striking the match on a stone, he lit the lantern. He picked up his gun and holstered it as he stood. He brushed off the seat of his pants, put on his pack, and with the lantern held out to illuminate the remains of the old road before him, he continued, stiffly for the first few strides, towards the Ram's Horn. The sandstone formation, which to Frank had always looked more like a roosting chicken than a ram's horn, was now visible only in the sense that it was a certain place and shape in the night sky lacking in stars.

A few hours later Frank was sitting in the light of his lantern with his back against the wall of the extrusion, the stone still warm from the heat of the day. He waited, and he kept an eye out for ticks. Having nothing better to do, he thought about the hanky-panky going on between Spencer Skint and Miss Caroline Tyler, and what he should do about it. *Nothing* was almost certainly the wisest course of action. But then he had an idea—a real rotten egg of an idea—and for the remainder of the night, he couldn't stop himself from brooding on it.

10 THE MEASURE OF A MAN

Nurse Jim, having heard the tinkling of the bells when Frank opened the door, came into the waiting room and told Frank that Dr. Perry would be with him shortly.

"Tom Abernathy," Nurse Jim said, by way of an unasked-for explanation. "He and his buddy Billy McKay decided to skip school this morning and have some fun. They climbed over the fence and got into the scrap yard. Tom tripped and fell and cut his hand wide open on a piece of rusty sheet metal. Doc's sewing him up now."

"Will he be all right?"

"Doc says if he doesn't get the tetanus, he'll be fine."

Gatekeeper Abernathy and her boy Tom came out some fifteen minutes later, the boy with his hand wrapped up in a cotton bandage. They were headed for the door, but when Mrs. Abernathy saw Frank, she made a detour in his direction.

"You need to do something about Billy McKay," the gatekeeper said. "That boy is a menace—a bad influence. I know he lost his father, and I'm sorry about that, but if that boy doesn't get some discipline he's headed for exile for sure, and my idiot son will be right there with him."

Tom Abernathy, who had been quiet, let out a whimper, though whether the cause was a throb of pain in his injured hand or his mother's insult, Frank couldn't discern. Frank could see the boy was in considerable pain, but he was, what? fifteen or sixteen now—past the age of crying—at least in front of the sheriff.

Gatekeeper Abernathy had more to say. Frank figured she was going to tell him to have a word with Billy McKay, maybe even suggest Frank throw him in the lockup to teach him a lesson—but before she got the chance, Nurse Jim stuck his head out into the waiting room and called out *Frank Westfall*.

"Excuse me ma'am," Frank said.

"So . . . ?" Germaine said.

"You wanted to measure me," Frank said. "Here I am."

"That's why you're here?"

"No."

"Okay, take your boots off, put your back up against the wall there and stand up straight. I'll take some measurements, then you can tell me what's on your mind."

Frank stood up straight and tall, an unusual posture for him. His head very nearly touched the ceiling of the examination room. Germaine pulled a chair up next to him and stood on it to make a mark on the wall at the height of his head. She searched around in a drawer and found a tape measure.

"Stand over there for a minute," she said.

"How's the Martian doing?" Frank said, as Germaine, standing on the chair, dropped the tongue of the tape measure from the mark on the wall to the floor.

"Seems to be fine," she said. She stepped down from

the chair and made a note of her measurement. "She doesn't eat much. That worries me some. Hold your arm out."

"Is she upset about us keeping her from her ship?"

"If she is, she's not letting on. She says she's not in any hurry. She says it'll be eight months before Mars comes back around and she can head home. All right, the other one now."

"Eight months? What the hell is she going to do in New Halchita for eight months? I'd go mad if I had to live here for eight *days* and didn't have a job to do."

"She has a job. Put your weight on your left foot. She's helping Miss Carmen with the kindergartners."

"Wow. She's a trouper."

"We'll see how long it lasts. Now your right foot." Germaine stood up and made a few more notes. "Well, I guess that about does it."

"And . . . ?"

"You've grown three inches since I last saw you here . . . seventeen months ago. You have any pain in your joints? Headaches? You think you sweat more?"

Frank shook his head.

"I've checked all the old books," Germaine said, "and I can't find anything that fits. A man your age doesn't grow—not like you do—not like you're just a kid who hasn't finished growing yet. Closest thing I could find is a pituitary tumor. But the old books say a man your age wouldn't get taller—your head and your hands and feet would get bigger, but you wouldn't get taller. I can't help you and I can't even say if you'll stop. I'm sorry, Frank. I wish there was something I could do."

Frank shrugged. "If you can't, you can't."

"You said you had something on your mind?"

"A question."

"Let's hear it."

"Will you marry me?"

"You don't want to ask me that, Frank."

"Yes, I do."

"You know what I'm going to say."

"I want to hear you say it."

"Frank Westfall, I won't marry you."

"Okay," Frank said, "I'm sorry if I made you uncomfortable. I just didn't want to spend the rest of my life thinking about maybe if I'd asked—"

"You're a good man, Frank, but I'm in love with Spencer Skint. And you know that."

"Spencer Skint is just going to hurt you, Germaine."

"Forgive me if I don't think your opinion of Spencer is exactly objective."

"Has he asked you to marry him?"

"We've talked about it. I told him I've got all of New Halchita to take care of right now. I don't have time for a family. Until I can get Jim properly trained—"

"So he hasn't."

"It really isn't any of your business," Germaine said.

"You're right. It isn't. I won't bother you about it anymore. But would you do me a favor, Germaine? Would you not tell Postmaster Skint about . . . what I asked you just now?"

"I can't promise you that, Frank. We don't keep secrets from each other."

"That's all right," Frank said. "I understand."

11 THE INQUIRY (2)

Miss Carmen instructed the children to push their desks to the wall and set out their mats in preparation for naptime. Once they had their mats out, Miss Carmen told the children to lie down, be quiet, and close their eyes, and they did so. She then asked Nancy to keep an eye on them for a minute while she went down the hall. The children, so quiet and still under Miss Carmen's command, began to twitch and stir the moment she left the room. They had questions.

Little Broome, speaking with his eyes closed as if he were only talking in his sleep, asked Nancy if she was really from Mars. Nancy replied that she was. Little Habushaki had the nearly instantaneous follow-up—she wanted to know where Mars was.

"It's very far away," Nancy said.

"Is it in the Scablands?" Little Wasserman said.

"It's *in* the *sky*," Little Broome said, rolling his still firmly-shut eyes.

Little Habushaki sat up, crossed her arms, and tilted her head in a manner suggesting great skepticism. "Is it *really* in the sky?" she said.

"In a manner of speaking," Nancy said. "If you look up at the sky at night, you can see it sometimes."

Little Wasserman now sat up, and inquired sternly as to whether or not Nancy's mommy and daddy knew where she was.

"My mother and father died a long time ago," Nancy said.

"Oh," Little Wasserman said, her voice soft and sympathetic.

Little Rhome sat up and stated that his dad was killed by germs in the air. He wanted to know if Nancy's parents had met a similar fate.

"My parents died in a war," Nancy said.

All the children were sitting up now—the conversation was getting interesting. Little Wasserman wanted to know if Nancy had come to New Halchita because she was lonely.

"No," Nancy said, "I have lots of sisters on Mars. I wasn't lonely."

"Did you leave Mars 'cause you hate your sisters?" Little Broome asked.

"I don't hate my sisters," Nancy said, "but I wanted to make new friends. So I left my home and my sisters on Mars and came all the way here to New Halchita."

"I'll be your friend," Little Wasserman said.

"That's very kind of you," Nancy said. "I hope all of you will be my friends."

"Is Nurse Jim your friend?" Little Rhome asked.

"Yes, I think so," Nancy said.

"Are you going to marry him?" Little Wasserman asked.

"I won't be here long enough to get married," Nancy said. "I have to go back to Mars in a little while."

"Will you be here when we wake up?" Little

Wasserman asked.

"Only if you go to sleep," Nancy said.

"Can we go to Mars with you when you go?" Little Broome asked.

"Lie down and close your eyes now," Nancy said. "Miss Carmen will be cross with me if she comes back and you aren't taking your naps."

12 CONVERSATION WITH THE POSTMASTER

. . . and then there were goats. With an enormous effort of will, Frank, who had gotten back from the Scablands and into his bed less than an hour ago, got himself out of bed and to the window. He opened it and looked down. There wasn't much light yet, and a mist had settled in the streets. He counted seven goats, and a boy herding them. In the dim light and the mist and with eyes not ready to see, Frank couldn't make out the boy's face, but he could see that the boy had a stick in one hand, and the other was bound up in a cotton bandage. He closed the window and went back to bed.

Late in the afternoon he got up, dressed, ate, and finished up some paperwork, and then it was time to head out into the Scablands again—he hoped for the last time—for a while, anyway. He packed the necessities and walked out of the sheriff's office, heading down Main Street towards the South Gate. He heard the thud of Spencer Skint's boots coming up from behind him before the postmaster fell into step beside him.

"Can I have a word with you, Sheriff?" Skint said.

"Sure," Frank said.

"Would you slow down a little? I don't have those great long legs of yours. I guess you know what I want to talk to you about."

"Most likely," Frank said, without slowing down.

"Germaine said you asked her to marry you."

"That's right," Frank said. "You upset with me? Should I be in fear for my life?"

"No, no, nothing like that. But there's something I thought I should tell you."

"All right," Frank said.

"You might remember when I got back to New Halchita from D.C. in '70. I rolled into town with a tick on my back. He got in the truck somehow and was hiding under the seat, and latched on when I stopped to get some shut-eye—thought I was perfectly safe in the truck—but you're never safe, are you? Lucky for me he was just a pup, no bigger than a cabbage, and I managed to make it back to New Halchita. Germaine cut him off my back and hung that bastard bug up on an I.V. pole, and stuck one end of a tube down its throat and the other end in a vein in my arm to get my blood back into me."

"She's a good doctor," Frank said.

"You don't have to tell me that," Skint said, "I was three weeks in the clinic recovering, so I had plenty of time to get to know her—and we had plenty of time to talk—and one of the things we talked about was you. You were courting Germaine something fierce back then. And when the council made you sheriff, Germaine told me she was afraid the title would give you the courage to propose. And I asked her why *afraid*? And she burst into tears, and she didn't want to say it, so I said it for her. I said no reason to be upset with yourself, it's human nature to abhor a freak, and—"

"Wait a minute," Frank said, "Dr. Germaine Perry burst into tears?"

"Well, maybe she didn't burst into tears exactly, but she was moved. She was relieved to hear someone say what she was thinking—someone who wasn't afraid to speak the truth."

Frank and Skint stopped, having reached the South Gate. The gate was open to admit farmers coming in from the fields, and the gatekeeper, Mrs. Abernathy, was greeting each one by name as they passed by her.

"I've gotta go," Frank said, "so if you've got a point you were getting to . . ."

"The point is," Skint said, "Germaine Perry could never love a freak like you. When you and me and Pete worked together out in the Scablands, we looked out for each other. I'd even go so far as to say we were friends. I know it's harsh, but you need to hear it—I'm telling you this as a friend. Your best move is to step aside—show some grace—and quit making yourself miserable over what you can't change. I can't stand to see a man—an old friend—make a fool of himself."

"I appreciate your concern," Frank said, "But there's no need to feel sorry for me. It's true that it hurt considerably when Germaine said she wouldn't marry me—but I got some good news from the doctor as well."

"What's that?" Skint said.

Frank put his long-fingered hand on Skint's shoulder and gave it a gentle squeeze. "Germaine told me according to the old books, instead of being so tall, I should have been a smaller man with a great big head," Frank said, "and I can't imagine a fate worse than that."

Gatekeeper Abernathy scowled at the departing figure of Postmaster Skint. "I don't care for that man one bit," she said. "I don't know what Dr. Perry sees in him."

"You know what they say," Frank said, "'love is an obdurate sot.'"

"Do you believe we get what we deserve?" Abernathy said.

"I believe the universe shows us little in the way of mercy—I don't know if that amounts to fairness or not. Mrs. Abernathy, can I ask you something about your boy Tom?"

"What is it, Sheriff?"

"Is he the one that sometimes herds goats down Main Street—right past the sheriff's office—real early in the morning?"

"I hope it doesn't bother you," Abernathy said. "They're not our goats, Sheriff. They belong to Mr. Crane—Councilwoman Crane's husband. Mr. Crane asked Tom if he wouldn't mind taking them from the pens out into the grasslands in the morning. Tom's supposed to go around, but when he's running late for school, sometimes he takes 'em straight through town. If it bothers you, I'll tell him—"

"Naw," Frank said, "it's all right. And good for Tom for taking the job—kids his age need to know what a great deal of work goes into making just a little bit of money."

"He doesn't get paid for it," Abernathy said. "He's doing it as a favor because Mr. Crane doesn't get around like he used to, and Mrs. Crane's got all that work she has to do for the council."

Frank understood what the gatekeeper was telling him. Mr. Crane was a retired tech who got it into his head to make some extra money selling goat's milk and cheese. Turned out that was more work than he cared for, and he'd been trying to sell the goats for some time, but couldn't get the price he had paid, not to mention the price he wanted, for his "top-notch hornless milkers." And as for Mrs. Crane's council work, part of that was selecting occupations for young men and women soon to become full citizens of New Halchita. It used to be you could pretty much pick the job you wanted—even try another if the first didn't suit you. Now there were more citizens and fewer jobs and it wasn't so easy anymore. Tom might want to be a technician, teacher or doctor. A contrary word from Mrs. Crane and he'd wind up collecting night soil for the motohol plant, or with a career in law enforcement.

The walk to the Ram's Horn kept Frank plenty warm, but after sitting and waiting for an hour, the heat abandoned him and he shivered. The cold would immobilize any ticks in the area—nothing wrong with a cold night—except how cold it was. He shivered again and his teeth chattered. He stood up and did some jumping-jacks, his lamp casting an enormous, gangly, and flapping shadow against the sandstone wall behind him. Out of breath but not much warmer, he sat back down and held his cold hands over the feeble heat of the lamp.

Frank had his gun in his hand before the reason why was in his head. The shriveled little man in an oversized gray fur coat put his hands up, a look of mock-terror on his round face.

"Damn you, Kuzzer Wayd," Frank said, holstering his gun, "you scared the crap out of me. For sneaking up on people, you're worse than a goddamn tick. Can't you whistle a tune or something?"

"It's nice to see you, too, Sheriff Westfall," the kuzzer said, sitting down next to Frank. "When I was told you were waiting to see me—for the second time this year—I could hardly believe my good fortune. To what do I owe the pleasure of this visit?"

"It's a long story," Frank said, "but the end of it is, there have been developments recently in New Halchita that the council feels the president in Washington, D.C. must be made aware of."

"Don't tell me you've come to negotiate safe passage for Mr. Skint—*again*."

"I'm afraid so."

"I should have known. The only reason you ever come to visit me is to negotiate safe passage for Mr. Skint."

"My duties as sheriff keep me very busy, Kuzzer."

"Well, I should be happy I get to see you at all, then. What does the council have in mind?"

"The council was hoping that since we paid for safe passage once already this year—"

"Tisk, tisk, tisk," the kuzzer said, shaking his head. "That payment was for one safe passage only, not a *year's* worth of safe passages."

"The council thought that might be your position," Frank said, "in which case, the council was hoping you might agree to a discount based on economies of scale."

"I don't know what you mean by *economies of scale*, Sheriff, but I'm willing, as always, to hear the council's offer."

"One hundred pounds each of corn, peanuts, and beans, and thirty pounds of dried chili peppers. The council wanted me to tell you that the peppers are of a particularly excellent quality this year."

"I have to say I don't much care for economies of scale," the Kuzzer said, "they seem to tip the scales in your favor. Two hundred and fifty pounds each of corn, peanuts, and beans, and as the chili peppers are of such excellent quality, fifty pounds."

"Kuzzer Wayd," Frank said, "the truth is, the council is concerned about the harvest this year, and there are those on the council who find *any* negotiation with Scavengers distasteful. They consider paying Scavengers for safe passage nothing more than extortion, and twice in one year—"

"Extortion? Sheriff Westfall, you can tell your council we are under no obligation to allow anyone passage through our territories at any price. If your council thinks a few sacks of beans and peppers—"

"Kuzzer, please—let me finish," Frank said. "If I bring back an agreement they find odious, those on the council who dislike dealing peacefully with Scavengers are likely to sway the others to an alternate solution—to forgo negotiations completely, and instead, send an armed escort to protect Postmaster Skint."

"We would kill them," the kuzzer said.

Frank wondered if the council ever told Spencer Skint what actually went on at these "excursions" he made into the Scablands—if Skint had any idea how easy it would be for Frank to get rid of him. The problem, of course, was the collateral damage.

"And our peoples would be at war again," Frank said. "Nobody wants that. A hundred and fifty pounds each of corn, peanuts, and beans. The fifty pounds of dried chili peppers is acceptable. And that's the best I can do."

The kuzzer reached into his fur coat and pulled out a bulbous leather pouch. He removed a stopper from one end and took a drink, then passed the pouch to Frank. One quick sniff told Frank it was *sweeka*, a Scab drink. God only knew what was in it. But though the taste was abysmal, the liquor was not without its charms—two of them, to be exact. First, it was agreeably strong, and last, if you drank too much, it didn't taste any worse coming up than it did going down. Frank took a quick but substantial swallow, and passed the pouch back to the kuzzer.

"Unfortunately," the kuzzer said, "I have a similar problem. There is a young man of fiery disposition who would very much like to replace me, and if my people think I'm going easy on Civvies, I'll accidentally cut off my own head or jump into a panther's mouth, and he'll be there to step into my shoes. His political philosophy, one that becomes increasingly popular as the memory of the last war fades, is that a Civvy hole like New Halchita is no better than a nest of ticks—and you don't negotiate with a nest of ticks, you burn them out. Two hundred pounds, etc., etc,. And that's the best *I* can do."

"Then I'm afraid we're at an impasse," Frank said.

The kuzzer took a drink and passed the pouch back to Frank. Frank took as close a look at the kuzzer as the light of the lamp would allow. The collar of his gray fur coat came up to the ears on his small, round head. His hair resembled a porcupine's quills—thick, gray, and stiff. His amber eyes bulged out, he had a generous and unevenly distributed dollop of a nose, and exactly four white whiskers stuck out of his chin—three long and one short. Nothing Frank saw was any help—Kuzzer Wayd was ugly as sin, but he had an excellent poker face.

"These *developments*," the kuzzer said, "that necessitate sending Mr. Skint to Washington, D.C. for a second time this year—I assume it has something to do with that mechanical chiggy pig that has made a home for itself in one of your bean fields."

"I'd say that's a reasonable assumption," Frank said.

"Where did it come from?" the kuzzer asked.

"I'm not sure the council would want me to say too much about it," Frank said.

"Well, let's just say, hypothetically," the kuzzer said, "it came from . . ."

The kuzzer looked up at the night sky and pointed at one particular light, a bright and slightly reddish one, among the uncountable multitudes.

". . . that one," the kuzzer said.

In lieu of a reply, Frank took a swig from the pouch.

"Look at how small it is," the kuzzer said. "Wouldn't it be a shame if we allowed a little thing like that to bring thirteen years of peace between our people to an end?"

"Yes, it would," Frank said.

"Then we'll sit here until we think of something," Kuzzer Wayd said. "Pass me that sweeka."

13 THREE IN FAVOR, ONE OPPOSED

"First," Mayor Lopez said, "the council would like to thank you for your service in this matter. We know the risk you take going out into the Scablands alone."

"I'm happy to do what I can for the council and the people of New Halchita," Frank said.

"Did you meet with the Scavenger representative, and were you able to reach an equitable agreement?"

"Yes sir," Frank said. "Kuzzer Wayd agreed to provide safe passage through the Scablands for Postmaster Skint, in exchange for one-hundred fifty pounds each of corn, peanuts, and beans, and fifty pounds of dried chili peppers. I was sure those terms would be acceptable to the council, but there was one other thing the kuzzer asked for—"

"I don't find those terms acceptable at all," Mrs. Crane said. "I don't know why we give them anything. It's a free country. At least, it used to be."

"Please, Councilwoman," the mayor said, "let the sheriff finish. What was the kuzzer's other request?"

"I'm afraid it was something I was entirely unprepared for, Mr. Mayor, but the kuzzer insisted."

"I know you did your best," the mayor said, "what was it the kuzzer wanted?"

"Seven goats," Frank said.

"Seven goats?" Mrs. Crane said. "That's ridiculous. You didn't—"

"I'm afraid I did, Mrs. Crane," Frank said. "The kuzzer would not give one inch on the matter. He made it perfectly clear to me that the alternative was a renewal of hostilities. And I'm sorry to say, Mrs. Crane, he specifically asked for your husband's goats."

"Sheriff Westfall," Mrs. Crane said, "you have greatly exceeded your authority in these negotiations. You had no right to give away Mr. Crane's goats to that Scab. And how did Kuzzer Wayd even know about my husband's goats?"

"I don't know, Mrs. Crane," Frank said, "But he was very clear. He wanted Mr. Crane's goats and no others would do. He said he was only interested in 'top-notch hornless milkers.' I don't know where he got his information, but you yourself have said that there are Scab spies in New Halchita, and Mr. Crane made no secret of the great value he placed on his goats, and the high price he was certain he could get for them. If it is the will of the council, I'll go back and try to renegotiate the deal. But Scabs expect a man to keep his word—not come back later and try to change it. They'll probably kill me. Or they'll kill Postmaster Skint as soon as he's out of sight of New Halchita."

"We can't allow it," Mrs. Crane said. "We have to draw the line somewhere. We can't let them have something just because they want it. There'll be no end to it. Next, they'll be asking for our first born children."

"I don't believe we have a choice," Mr. Goodhue said. "We have always entrusted Sheriff Westfall with these negotiations. I see no reason to question his methods now. I'm sure he obtained the best deal he could under the circumstances. And I'm certain we all agree that it is vital for Postmaster Skint to reach Washington D.C. swiftly and safely. We can't afford to put this delivery at risk for a few goats. I'm sorry, Mrs. Crane, but we all have to make sacrifices."

"They're not your goats, Mr. Goodhue," Mrs. Crane said, "so I don't think you have any right to talk about sacrifices. Mr. Mayor, I must object—"

"Your objection is noted." Mayor Lopez said. "I move we accept the terms of the agreement with the Scavengers for the safe passage of Postmaster Skint through the Scablands as negotiated by Sheriff Frank Westfall."

"Seconded," Mr. Downes said.

"All in favor," the mayor said.

14 SINCERELY

Dear Mr. President,

I write to inform you that a woman has recently arrived at our settlement who claims to be from Mars. If I had not witnessed the landing of her remarkable spaceship myself, I'm sure I would be as skeptical as you must be regarding her astonishing story—but if you will examine carefully the enclosed photographs, especially the stereoscopic images we have prepared for you (Postmaster Skint will instruct you in the proper use of the viewer), and open-mindedly consider the evidence I present to you in this letter, I believe you will conclude, as I have, that her claim to be a Martian, as preposterous as that may sound, is nothing more nor less than the simple truth.

The visitor from Mars states that she is a descendant of a Mars colony that lost touch with Earth at the outset of the GIW. Our librarian has checked the old books and records, and has indisputably verified that such a colony did indeed exist at that time. The colony consisted of a mere one-hundred-twenty-five souls and was never intended to survive without regular re-supply from Earth.

However, according to Nancy (as the Martian calls herself), though they met with great difficulty and hardship, survive they did, and eventually, they prospered. I would go so far as to say, Mr. President, that though we have been long separated, we have much in common with these "Martians," having ourselves overcome similar adversities.

In order to further substantiate Nancy's claims, our esteemed physician, Dr. Germaine Perry, examined her, and Dr. Perry assures me that the physical evidence supports Nancy's claim to being a descendant of the above-described Martian colony in every detail.

Nancy has told us that the colony tried for years to contact Earth, but without success. However, they never gave up on us, and now, after almost 300 years, the descendants of the original colonists have sent this young woman, courageous beyond her twenty-two years, back to Earth, the sole purpose of her unprecedented and death-defying voyage being to discover our fate, and, if possible, to establish diplomatic relations between the descendants of the original Mars colonists and the people of their beloved home planet.

You may wonder why we do not simply send her to you, along with this letter. Unfortunately, it is a long and perilous journey for which we are ill-equipped to provide even the most rudimentary security. On many occasions in the performance of his duties, Postmaster Skint has had encounters with murderous Scavengers and nests of blood-thirsty ticks, narrowly escaping with his life. Though he is a brave and resourceful man, we dare not burden him with the protection of any life other than his own. I'm sure you would agree that it would be a tragedy of inestimable proportions if the ambassador from Mars were to accompany Postmaster Skint and come to harm along the way.

Mr. President, because the purpose of the Martian's visit is diplomatic, it is, without a doubt, a matter for the federal government. She has asked me to inform you in this letter that she is most anxious to make your acquaintance, and eagerly awaits the opportunity to discuss with you the establishment of diplomatic relations with Mars.

As eagerly awaiting your visit myself, I am, most sincerely yours,

> The Honorable Noé Lopez, Mayor, New Halchita
> "A Civilized Society"

With safe passage negotiated, photographs taken, and the letter written, it wouldn't be long before Postmaster Skint would be on his way to Washington D.C. to deliver the council's letter to the president. Sheriff Frank Westfall knew if he didn't do the stupid thing soon, he never would.

15 FRANK DOES A STUPID THING

"Nurse Jim!" Frank said, gasping for air, "I need Dr. Perry!"

"She's with a patient, Sheriff—"

"Unless that patient is dying, you better get her out here! And quick!"

Nurse Jim disappeared into the examination room and came out a moment later with Dr. Perry.

"It's Spencer Skint," Frank said, "I was walking by his house and he called out to me—said he was awful sick. I went inside and he looked like he was dying. He said he couldn't catch his breath—"

Frank had more symptoms to share but didn't need them—Germaine had grabbed her big black medical bag and was out the door.

16 A POMPOUS RIDE

Tom Abernathy herded seven bleating top-notch hornless milkers through the South Gate and into the fields, Frank following in a scrapride van loaded with the agreed-upon quantities of beans, corn, peanuts, and chili peppers. In the distance, the Martian's ship, its legs hidden in the morning mist, appeared to float in mid-air. Frank had told Deputy Orland he could leave the ship unattended for the morning to join with the rest of New Halchita in giving Postmaster Skint the traditional push-start from the North Gate—the fewer people who saw Frank paying off the Scavengers, the happier the council would be. If asked, Frank was supposed to say that Scavengers had contacted the council through back channels for help—that their hunters and gatherers had been coming home empty-handed and Scavenger children were starving. In all the years Frank had been handling the transaction, no one had asked. For one thing, the council always made sure the payoff took place at the South Gate at the same time Postmaster Skint was leaving from the North, so hardly anyone would be around to see it, and for another, most folks had a comforting picture in their heads of

New Halchita's place in the world, and a strong desire to leave that vision unpestered.

The South Gate had hardly shut behind Frank and Tom when two scraprides came bumping down the Old South Road in their direction. The scraprides were "mules," the small, high-riding flatbed design favored by Scavengers for hauling their few belongings from one camp to another. The leading mule had a severe case of polka-dots, and the one following behind had a chrome beak welded to the front, and shiny metallic wings on the sides that served to hold a large cage in place atop the bed. The elaborate decoration of their mules was a point of pride among Scavengers.

Kuzzer Wayd's chosen emissaries were a young man of a coppery hue, and a young woman of a lighter, rusty red. The gentleman's black hair was well-oiled and combed back stiff and straight, producing a quill-like effect, perhaps in imitation of his kuzzer. The lady's wiry red tresses were bound up in a thumb's-length of braided pony tail, chopped-off straight at the end and whipped like a rope with tarred twine. Both had silver hoops in their ears (more than a dozen between them) and their clothing, light in color and with goose feathers worked into the weave of the cloth, fit so loosely as to be suggestive of hand-me-downs from older siblings. They wore no shoes. The young lady's toenails, on her left foot only, were painted: blue-white-blue-white-blue. Frank wondered what the Scavengers must think of him and Tom, in their close-fitting jackets, shirts and trousers, and their feet encased in stiff brown leather, like seeds in old, dried-up pods.

While helping Frank and Tom load the sacks onto the polka-dot mule and maneuver the increasingly anxious goats up a ramp and into the cage carried by the hawk mule, the Scavengers were both polite and chatty. After the goods were secured, the young woman asked Frank if they could take a look at the "mechanical chiggy pig." Frank said it would be all right, but he would accompany them and they must stay close.

The two Civvies and two Scavengers stopped twenty meters from the Martian's ship, as close as Frank wanted to get, partly because he felt responsible for the safety of Tom and the Scavengers (and there was something about the ship that made him uneasy), and partly because he didn't think the council would approve of associates of the kuzzer getting too close a look at the thing.

"Shameful!" the young woman exclaimed.

"Pompous!" cried the young man.

The actual meaning of the words notwithstanding, the admiring tone in which they were spoken convinced Frank that the Scavengers were expressing an exceedingly favorable opinion of the Martian's ship.

"Is it alive?" the young woman asked.

"It's a machine," Tom said, "it's not alive."

She nodded, but did not appear convinced.

When the bleating of seven top-notch hornless milkers could no longer be heard, Tom asked Frank why they had given all that stuff to the Scavengers. Frank considered the truth he wasn't supposed to tell, and the lie he didn't want to tell, and came up with a different answer altogether, one his father had often used when questioned by a young Frank Westfall.

"Why do you think?" Frank said.

Apparently, Germaine had decided not to attend the sending-off-the-postmaster festivities. She was standing in front of the sheriff's office waiting for Frank when he returned from his business dealings with the Scavengers. Frank wasn't nearly as prepared for the confrontation as he should have been, knowing full well it was coming. But what was there to worry about? She'd ask him why he'd done it. He'd been asking himself that same question for days, and hadn't come up with an answer. He'd tell her he didn't know, and she'd have to be satisfied with that. Only that's not what she asked him. In fact, she didn't ask him anything—instead, she punched him in the gut with all her considerable strength. Frank could have stayed on his feet if he really wanted to, but it was easier to lie down on the ground curled up in a ball wondering when, if ever, the wind she had knocked out of him might find its way back home.

"There's two things I have to say to you," she said.

Frank, not yet able to speak, nodded his willingness to listen.

"Your timing was perfect," Germaine said. "I burst into Spencer Skint's house on Possum Race Road just in time to catch him and Miss Caroline Tyler in the final throes of what was clearly a glorious fuck. They didn't even stop when they saw me—I don't think they could. But I want you to think about this: what if someone had come to the clinic with a serious medical condition while I was halfway across town watching Miss Tyler and Spencer Skint playing horsey?"

Frank nodded his agreement that that was a possibility that hadn't occurred to him, but should have.

"And one other thing I want to say to you. That little stunt you pulled, asking me to marry you when you knew I'd say no. I guess that was to freshen up the hurt I caused you when I chose Spencer over you, to give you the nerve to hurt me back, now that you had the means. So with all the thought and effort you put into it, you'll be happy to know I'm hurting . . ."

Germaine's lips trembled, and the finger she was pointing at him started to shake. Frank thought Germaine was going to lose her composure, but even as he watched, she wrestled it down and pinned it under the knee of her will.

". . . I'm hurting worse than I ever thought I could," Germaine said. "And I hope you wanted me to hate you, because I do. I hate you as much as I hate Spencer Skint. Maybe more."

Germaine stepped over Frank, leaving him alone on the ground to consider her point of view. He took in a little air, and then some more, and then got to his feet. Slowly and carefully, he stood up to his full height. He rubbed his sore belly. As a doctor, Germaine would have punched him where it hurt most but did the least actual harm—he hoped. He had no intention of chasing after her to argue any points. It wasn't necessary—he was pretty much in agreement with everything she had said. In fact, she had cleared up some things about his puzzling behavior that he hadn't been able to figure out for himself.

17 THE DELIVERY

After three days of driving the truck, eating and sleeping in the truck, and only getting out of the truck to answer the call of nature, Spencer Skint arrived at the Colorado River, where he stopped, because there wasn't a bridge, and because Kuzzer Wayd and a half-dozen Scab Warriors were there waiting for him. Skint killed the engine and set the handbrake. He opened the door and slid out from behind the wheel onto the hard-packed grit that had inherited the name "Road" and little else from a cement ribbon nature had chewed to crumbs centuries ago. Skint stuck out his elbows and twisted his torso, bent and straightened his knees, and windmilled one arm around slowly and then the other. He looked around. The river ran gray-green through the shadows of the canyon, and reflected the bright blue sky and white clouds where it looped out into the sunshine. He inhaled deeply through his nose. He could smell the fish in the water. It was a beautiful day in a beautiful country.

Skint turned and reached under the driver's seat to retrieve the packet addressed to The President of the United States in Washington D.C. He handed the packet to Kuzzer Wayd, who broke the wax seal and removed the council's letter and photographs. The kuzzer read the letter quickly and then spent some time examining the photographs.

"This is the Martian?" the kuzzer said.

"That's her," Skint said. "She's a looker, isn't she? And she says there's plenty more where she came from. Oh—wait'll you see this." Skint walked around to the back of the truck, raised the gate and climbed in. After a few minutes of rustling around, he emerged, sweating, carrying a small wooden box decorated with floral inlays sculpted of bits of glass and steel. He opened the box to reveal the stereoscopic viewer resting on a red velvet pillow, and in a separate compartment in the box, the stereoscopic prints.

Skint inserted one of the prints into the viewer. "You look at it like this," Skint said, demonstrating the proper technique to Kuzzer Wayd. Skint handed the viewer to the kuzzer, and the kuzzer looked at the image through the viewer, then turned the viewer around to see if there was something behind the print. He handed the viewer to one of his warriors, who repeated the actions of his kuzzer before passing it on.

The kuzzer went through the photographs of the Martian and her ship again, taking a long look at one in particular.

"Are you thinking about a wife number seven?" Skint asked. "Or would she be number eight? I'm afraid I've lost track."

"Does she really have a third eye?" the kuzzer said.

Skint snorted.

Kuzzer Wayd scowled and stuffed the photographs and the letter back into the packet. "You Civvies are masters of the art of deception," he said.

Skint let out a long and hearty guffaw—stopping when he saw the look on the kuzzer's face darken threateningly.

"I'm sorry, Kuzzer," Skint said, wiping a tear from his cheek, "but under the circumstances—well, you have to admit—that's a pretty funny way of looking at things."

The kuzzer handed Skint the packet. "Useless," he said. "There's nothing in here I didn't already know. And for this I have to feed you for the next six weeks."

"I've got my own food in the truck," Skint said.

"You'll eat twice that much," the kuzzer said.

"My appetite never bothered you before," Skint said.

"It bothers me now," the kuzzer said.

Skint was puzzled. The Scab leader was generally delighted with the swag Skint brought him. It wasn't just the letters to the president, revealing the council's innermost thoughts and plans—Skint left New Halchita with enough fuel and ammunition for a two-month trek through the Scablands battling every enemy imaginable, and a dash more for the unimaginable ones. The Scabs would get all of his supplies except for what Skint needed to get to the Colorado River and back. Sure, Scabs could get a few bullets here and there trading with tick-juicers, and they could make a few liters of motohol in their rickety little converters, but moving around the way they did, they couldn't compete with a Civvy hole when it came to mass production. Constancy had its advantages.

And then there were the little things. Ever since Skint had taken the job of postmaster, he'd been plying the kuzzer with treats from New Halchita, taking careful note of his reaction, and over the years, Skint had gotten a pretty good idea of what the kuzzer had a taste for that only the postmaster could bring him. The Scab leader surely knew by now that along with the council's letter to the president, the sacks of bullets, and the tanks of motohol, there'd be a tin of Mrs. Otis' peanut brittle, three or four library books, and assorted other delicacies.

Skint snorted inwardly at the kuzzer's peculiar weaknesses. The Scab's obsession with Mrs. Otis' peanut brittle was something Skint could understand—keeping his hands off of it for the three-day drive from New Halchita to the Colorado River was a torment—but the library books—that was another matter. Here was a man who commanded (as much as any Scab commanded another) hundreds of warriors, had his pick of wives, and had all the thousands of square kilometers of Scablands for his hunting grounds, and yet, he loved nothing better than to sit in the sun on a warm rock, reading *Pride and Prejudice* for the umpteenth time.

So the kuzzer should be happy, but clearly, the kuzzer wasn't happy, and the kuzzer's emotional state would have a direct impact on Spencer Skint's well-being. A happy kuzzer was a generous kuzzer—a kind kuzzer—a kuzzer who would share his venison stew or roasted rabbit, his sweeka, and maybe one or two of his wives. An unhappy kuzzer would cut off two of your fingers, slap a tick on your back, and tell you it was necessary in order to convince your Civvy friends you'd been roughing it out alone in the Scablands. Skint needed to know what was bothering the kuzzer. He figured the best way to find out was to ask.

"Oh, stop your bitching," Skint said, "You're not mad at me, I just got here. Why don't you tell me what the problem *really* is—you'll feel better."

Kuzzer Wayd seriously considered killing Skint, or rather, signaling to his warriors to do it for him. The man was useful, but his mouth—it never closed. If it wasn't sucking in food and drink, it was spewing out disrespectful comments and unsolicited opinions. Kuzzer

Wayd reflected on the good and the bad of Skint, and fortunately for Skint, the scales tipped in the postmaster's favor, if only by the weight of a tin of peanut brittle.

"I liked things the way they were," the kuzzer said.

Skint didn't need any further explanation—he got it. Scabs and Civvies had been getting along for the past thirteen years because all the horror, death, and misery of the last war had accomplished only one thing of any value: it had convinced both sides that neither would ever vanquish the other. But now, a monstrous technological advantage had landed smack-dab in the middle of Mr. Habushaki's bean field, and the Martian who put it there was getting cozy with the Civvies. No wonder the kuzzer was in a bad mood.

Postmaster Skint didn't think he could soothe Kuzzer Wayd's fears, but he could stoke them, and in his long career as a purveyor of information, Skint had found that bad news was often as well-received as good, as long as it confirmed the recipient's darkest suspicions concerning his fellow human beings. Skint whipped up a tale fit for the occasion—something he'd always had a talent for.

"We've worked this deal for what—nine, ten years now?" Skint said. "I've always done my part, and you've always done yours—but you've done more than you had to, Kuzzer. You always treated me well, and to show you I'm grateful for your kindness and generosity, I'm going to tell you something that's not in that letter. You're not going to like it—you'll probably decide to chop off the messenger's head—but I'm going to tell you anyway, because you need to know. The council has asked Nancy to send a message to her people on Mars. They told her to tell her friends back home that if the Martians will come to Earth and help the Civvies wipe out the Scabs, the Civvies will split the country with 'em fifty-fifty."

"How do you know this?" the kuzzer said.

"Mayor Lopez told me—so I can tell the president. The council wants Washington D.C. in on it."

"Why isn't it in the letter?"

"Don't be dim," Skint said. "The council's not going to put something like that in a letter Scabs could get hold of."

"Isn't he worried Scabs could get hold of *you*?"

Skint drew his revolver—and instantly found himself covered by a half-dozen Scavenger rifles. Slowly, carefully, and keeping the muzzle of the revolver pointed down, Skint pushed out the cylinder, holding it where Kuzzer Wayd could see the cartridges. "Looky here," Skint said. "I leave the chamber under the hammer empty, so I don't shoot myself in the foot. That leaves five rounds. These four rounds are for Scabs, panthers, lobos—what have you. The fifth one, that one is for me."

"And the mayor believes you would put a bullet in your own head before you would let yourself get captured by Scavengers?" Kuzzer Wayd said.

"Absolutely," Skint said, "I told him so myself."

Skint pushed the cylinder back into place and holstered his gun. He put his hands on his hips and tilted left and right. He leaned back as far as he could without tipping over, then bent forward, reaching for his toes. He stood up straight and looked at the sky, squinting. "When the opportunity presents itself," he said, "I'll kill the Martian—as a favor to you, Kuzzer."

"You'd kill her for me?" the kuzzer said.

"Well, not *just* for you," Skint admitted. "The Martian said she reconnoitered Earth from orbit for almost two months before landing in New Halchita. She must know there's nothing in Washington D.C. but a lot of radioactive granite. That's a problem for both of us."

"But she hasn't told the council?" the kuzzer said.

"If she had," Skint said, "I'd already be swinging from the old oak outside the library. The funny thing is, the council asked her directly why she hadn't contacted the President in Washington D.C. instead of coming to New Halchita. I was right there in the council room with everyone else when they asked her. I thought I was a dead man—but she didn't say Washington D.C. would boil your brains—she just said she liked New Halchita better. The council ate it up and moved on. I wish I knew what the hell it is she's up to."

"I appreciate your willingness to share this information with me," the kuzzer said. The conciliatory statement was growled out from under the kuzzer's breath, but it sounded to Skint like a sincere growl.

Skint licked his lips. "Say, Kuzzer," he said, "you wouldn't happen to have any of that sweeka on you, would you? I've had nothing to wet my whistle but water for the last three days, and I need something to clear out the rust."

Part 2

1 MATTERS OF WHEN

The citizens of New Halchita could agree on the following: That Postmaster Skint had been gone one week, and that it would be two more weeks (at least) before he arrived in Washington D.C. with the council's letter to the president and the photographs of the Martian and her ship. What would happen after that was anyone's guess, and anyone and everyone did, endlessly. Some said Postmaster Skint would return on the North Road leading a kilometers-long convoy of scraprides carrying the president and his entourage. Others (followers of the librarian, Mrs. Barlow, who had researched the matter thoroughly) were confident that once Postmaster Skint reached the president with news of the Martian visitor, the president and Postmaster Skint would return to New Halchita aboard *Air Force One*, a magnificent airship bristling with weapons. No one suggested that the president might choose not to come to see the Martian, as no one was interested in discussing that possibility.

Estimates of when Postmaster Skint and the president would arrive in New Halchita, whether by land or air, varied widely. Most of the citizens of New Halchita were hoping it would be soon, because they feared they'd die if they had to wait much longer. Mr. Ellinger, the music teacher, was a notable exception. He had been called on by the council to write, score, direct, and, upon the arrival of the president, premier an elementary school production of "A Musical History of New Halchita." Mr. Ellinger prayed nightly that Spencer Skint and the president would arrive by scrapride, and that the road they travelled would present a variety of obstacles that, while not entirely insurmountable, would prove quite challenging. "If you think about it," he would say, just before getting up off his knees, "it's only fair. Amen."

Under the circumstances, the disappearance of Billy McKay came as something of a relief—a distraction that the townspeople hadn't even realized they desperately needed. Mrs. McKay reported to Sheriff Westfall that Billy had not come home from school, and Sheriff Westfall soon determined that Billy had not attended his afternoon classes. When the sheriff questioned Billy's friend Tom Abernathy, Tom confessed that Billy had, that very morning, mentioned the alluring ripeness of the blackberries growing along the banks of the San Juan. Hardly an hour after Mrs. McKay reported her son missing, a search party of some thirty citizens, organized and led by Sheriff Frank Westfall, marched out of the North Gate with every expectation of finding Billy McKay quickly and bringing him home safely.

The searchers soon found a stand of blackberry bushes where it was clear that someone, quite recently, had pulled down the cane to reach the ripest fruit. At this discovery, the mood of the search party became almost jovial—the weather was fine, the late-afternoon light on the rock face carved out by the river was beautiful, and the general consensus was that Billy had gone in search of more fruit, and would soon be located, publicly chastised, and then publicly smothered by his mother until he was sorry as hell for his thoughtless behavior.

Sheriff Westfall divided the searchers into three groups. One party he sent upriver and one party he sent down, each calling out for Billy as they went. The third party, which included Mrs. McKay, made camp near the blackberry stand to serve as a center of operations, and in case Billy somehow managed to elude the searchers and return to that location.

A few hours later, the up-river search party came back to camp empty handed, as did the down-river searchers. Every effort was made to appear optimistic for Mrs. McKay's sake, but it was impossible not to consider the many dangers of foraging along the banks of the San Juan alone: cliffs, currents, Scavengers, panthers, lobos, and ticks to name only the most obvious—all perils that would increase exponentially once the sun went down.

Most of the searchers decided to head back to New Halchita while there was light enough to do so safely, vowing to return to the river at dawn with reinforcements and supplies. Sheriff Westfall and a few others chose to remain at the camp with Mrs. McKay, making what dinner they could out of blackberries, since no one had been so pessimistic as to prepare for an overnight stay. A fire was made when night closed in, and the fire, the worry, and the lack of a proper dinner reminded some of the older citizens of their soldiering days. Naturally, talk turned to the last Scab war. One of the veterans, a man by the name of John Broome, said that Frank had been a scout during the last Scab war, and though quite young, had shown a remarkable talent for the job.

"He knew this whole area like nobody's business," Broome said. "We'd send him out at night and he'd come back at dawn and tell us where the Scabs were camped, how many there were, how well they were armed and supplied, and what they planned to have for breakfast."

"Give us a story of the war, Sheriff," one of the younger men said.

"What I recall from my days as a scout," Frank said, "is that I did considerable crawling around on my belly, and that I was cold, hungry, and scared, in that order or some other, depending on circumstances. I don't know if that's a story, but if it is, you're welcome to it."

Songs were sung both to keep up spirits and in the hopes that the noise might help a young man gone astray find his way to the camp. By midnight, there was nothing left to sing or to say, and the camp fell quiet. For a while, every creak or rustle in the brush was met with an enthusiastic "I'll bet that's him!" followed by a chorus of shouts of "Over here, Billy!" and "Follow our voices, Billy!"—but the look on poor Mrs. McKay's face as her hopes were repeatedly raised and dashed soon put an end to that practice. Silence then prevailed, except for the occasional deep sigh, as each of the searchers, though alone with his or her thoughts, came to the same conclusion: that the boy would not be found alive.

In the midst of this silence, the light of a lamp was seen approaching the encampment from upriver. The steady approach and occasional gentle swaying of the light indicated that the lamp was attached to the bow of a small boat, and soon, the sound of oars dipping into the water could be heard. There was considerable speculation at the camp over what news the rowboat would bring. When someone suggested that Billy McKay might have made his way back to town, and the rowboat had been dispatched to bring the campers the good news, only Sheriff Westfall's quick thinking and long arms prevented

Mrs. McKay from diving headlong into the river in an attempt to gain the boat and the news more quickly.

Dr. Germaine Perry, the boat's single passenger and motive force, turned the boat and buried a few feet of the forward keel into the riverbank near the encampment. She did not bring the hoped-for good news, but did bring welcome supplies, including food and blankets, to the campers. When Sheriff Westfall came up to the boat to do his part in unloading, Germaine said, softly, "I need your help."

"What?" Frank said.

"I need your help," Germaine said.

"Help with what?"

"Take this," Germaine said, handing Frank a bundle of blankets. "Hello, Mr. Broome. Mrs. Broome made this—she said it was your favorite—but she said to tell you that she expects you to share."

After the supplies were unloaded, Germaine said she was going to take the boat downstream a ways, in case Billy had decided to camp out somewhere near the river.

"It's no use," Broome said. "We've already searched downstream all the way to where the river runs into the canyon. He couldn't have gone any further unless he jumped in, and even Billy McKay's got more sense than that."

"I'm going anyway," Germaine said, "just in case. And I could use some *help*."

"Um . . . Mr. Broome's right," Frank said, "but if you're determined to go, I'll go along."

Once out of sight of the camp, Germaine showed Frank a piece a paper with a single undulating black line running from one side to the other. It didn't take Frank more than a moment to recognize the line as a simple but accurate map of that section of the San Juan that he and Germaine were now floating on. Apart from the line, there was only one other notation on the paper: a dot had been scribbled inside one of many tear-drop shaped bulges that indicated a gooseneck in the meanderings of the river.

"Okay," Frank said, "it's the river." He pointed at the map. "We're about here."

Germaine pointed at the dot. "How far?"

"About four-and-a-half—five kilometers."

"That's where we'll find Billy McKay," Germaine said. "The problem is, I don't know where I am on this river—not in the dark."

"I'll know where we are," Frank said. "But what makes you think that's where we'll find Billy McKay?"

"We'll talk later," Germaine said, pulling hard on the oars, "right now, I need to save my breath for rowing."

Some forty-five minutes later, Frank told Germaine they had reached the location indicated on the map, and Germaine turned the boat into the bank on the north side of the river. She jumped out and took the lantern, and Frank pulled the boat up onto the narrow spit of reddish-brown sand. There wasn't much to search—about two hundred feet of wet sand between where the river ran right up against the cliffs to the east and west. They found Billy McKay face down at the water's edge. Germaine turned him over and checked his pulse. "He's alive," she said.

To his rescuers' surprise, the boy opened his eyes, looked around, and sat up slowly. "Howdy Sheriff . . . hey Dr. Perry," he said, "have you met my friend here?" Billy McKay pulled off his wet shirt and revealed a tick—a big one. Billy patted the tick on its slick, rust-colored dorsal shield. The way the bug had thrown its sticky palps around the boy's bony chest was suggestive of an affectionate embrace, but the mouth-parts buried deep in Billy's flesh near his armpit told a different story. The boy was not at all frightened—in fact, he had a kind of goofy, inebriated look on his face. A tick had something in its saliva to keep victims from feeling anything when it punctured the flesh—a powerful anesthetic known as "ticktox." A common side effect of getting ticked was a kind of euphoria. Frank had heard that getting sucked dry by a tick was a pleasant way to go. He didn't believe it.

"I've got a couple of blankets in the boat," Germaine said. "You just stay right there."

"I'll stay right here, Dr. Perry," the boy said.

"How'd you get out here?" Frank said.

"Ate so many blackberries I had to take a nap," Billy said. "Fell asleep, woke up with this little piglet nursing on me. I thought maybe I could drown him, so I jumped in the river and floated along with him underwater. Don't know how long. Is he dead?"

The tick, as if in reply, slowly adjusted each of its eight legs in turn.

Germaine returned with the blankets.

"Will you get him off me now?" Billy said, "I'm getting tired of lugging him around."

"We've got to get you back to the clinic first," Germaine said. "I promise I'll get him off of you. Actually, it's a 'her.' In any case, you'll have a nice scar to show off."

"I'm sorry for the trouble I've caused you, Dr. Perry," Billy said, turning suddenly maudlin. A tear coursed down his cheek. "Please don't tell my ma."

"We've got to get him warmed up," Germaine said.

"Well now wait a second," Frank said. "Billy said he jumped into the river to try and drown it. He didn't drown it, but maybe the cold water slowed it down."

Germaine thought Frank might be right. It was a miracle the tick hadn't drained the boy dry already. If the tick got to work, the boy would be dead well before they got him to the clinic. Germaine knelt down next to Billy McKay and put her hands on his face, then on his chest. Cold. She looked up at Frank and shook her head. No good choices.

"I've got two blankets," Germaine said. She threw one to Frank. "Go soak this one in the river. We'll wrap a dry one around Billy and a wet one around the tick."

Frank took the oars for the return trip. Billy and his tick, all wrapped up in blankets, leaned against Germaine in the stern of the boat. The boy was drifting in and out of consciousness. For a while, the only sound was the oars dipping in the water. Then the boy woke up in terror, as if from a nightmare, only to discover the nightmare was real.

"Get it off me!" he cried. He started pulling at the tick, and Germaine had to pin his arms to his sides. In the unlikely event he was able to break the sticky grip of the tick's palps and pull the serrated hypostome out of his flesh, he would bleed to death soon after. Blood around a tick bite wouldn't clot. Not for hours. At the clinic, Germaine could cut the tick off at the mouth parts, plug up the hypostome and leave it for a day or two until the blood could clot normally again. Then she could remove the hypostome surgically. All of this predicated on getting the boy to the clinic alive.

"Why won't you get it off me?" the boy blubbered.

"We have to get you to the clinic first," Germaine said. Billy McKay let out a wail.

"Have you ever seen that reciprocating saw she uses?"

Frank said. "It's really something else."

"Saw?" Billy said.

"Yeah, she had it built special." Frank said. "It'll cut through a tick like nobody's business."

"Quiet, Frank," Germaine said. "You're going to scare the poor boy to death."

"I'm not afraid, Dr. Perry," Billy said. "You're going to saw it off me?"

"That's right," Germaine said, "once we get you to the clinic."

"Will it hurt?"

"Take a look at that tick," Frank said. "Take a look at her shell. Go ahead—just a peek."

Billy, whimpering, lifted the wet blanket up enough see the edge of the tick's carapace.

"See how red her shell is? Ticks use the iron in blood to make their shells really strong. I heard they figured out how to do that after the GIW. You can hardly even shoot a tick dead—not from any distance. But Germaine had the techs and the smiths at The Works build a special saw for her. Hardest steel they could find. I'd bet anything your mom had a hand in it. Pneumatic—that means air powered—what a racket that thing makes! And wait till you see the sparks fly—it's really something. I'll work the pumps when we get to the clinic. If you ever wanted to see your sheriff sweat buckets, you'll get your chance. Did you know Germaine cut a tick off Postmaster Skint a few years ago? Not anywhere near as big as this one, though—I think you broke the record. Skint'll be jealous."

The boy, having drifted off again, didn't answer. Germaine unwrapped the tick, wrung the blanket out, and soaked it again in the cold water of the river. When she wrapped the wet blanket around the tick, she had to fight with it—it kept trying to push the blanket away with its legs.

"She's warming up," Germaine said, "getting active—but I think we're going to make it."

"The boy's lucky you knew where to find him," Frank said, "and how *did* you know where to find him?"

"I was thinking about the currents," Germaine said, "and I thought, if for some reason he jumped in near—"

Frank lifted the oars out of the water and set the blades down inside the boat.

"What are you doing?" Germaine said.

"I asked you how you knew where to find Billy McKay, and I want an answer—a *real* answer."

Germaine didn't immediately reply. Lacking the guidance of the oars, the boat surrendered to the influence of the current, and the bow began to turn.

"I had a hunch," Germaine said.

"You didn't have a hunch," Frank said, "you had a map. We're drifting Germaine."

"You won't let the boy die," Germaine said.

"Neither will you," Frank said. "When you talk, I'll row. Who drew the map?"

"Nancy drew the map," Germaine said, "Now please, Frank, row. We don't have a lot of time."

Frank lifted the oars. "Start from the beginning," he said. "As long as you're talking, I'll be rowing."

"We got the news that the search party hadn't found Billy McKay," Germaine said. "Nancy told me she could help. She said she had a chip in her head that would let her communicate with her orbiter, and from the orbiter she might be able to locate Billy McKay by his body heat."

Frank put one oar in the water, and pulled, in order to point the bow upstream again. "Communicate?" he said, "you mean with radio waves?"

"Yes," Germaine said.

"Jesus Christ, Germaine," Frank said, pulling hard on the oars, "she could have brought a lagamachy down on us. For all you know, there's one on its way right now."

"She told me it would be safe," Germaine said. "She said the lagamachies talk to each other, and that she communicates with the orbiter using the same frequency and protocol."

"What does that mean?" Frank said.

"It means she speaks their language," Germaine said, "and she's convinced them—"

"Convinced them of what?" Frank said, "that she's just one of the boys? What have you done, Germaine? Why didn't you tell her to leave it alone—let us deal with it our way?"

"Because I couldn't let Billy McKay die out here," Germaine said.

"For one life, you risked killing us all," Frank said. "The council is going to have a fit."

"You can't tell the council," Germaine said.

"Why not?" Frank said.

"What do you think they're going to do, when you tell them that the only way they can keep Nancy from communicating with the orbiter, or with her friends on Mars, is to split her head open and take the chip out?"

Frank rowed and didn't answer. He damned Germaine Perry to hell for always having a perfectly splendid reason for tying everything up in knots. The council wouldn't exile Germaine because New Halchita needed her. Germaine would get a slap on the wrist. But the Martian—the council would never allow a woman who spewed radio waves out of her head to live in New Halchita. They'd want her out—probably tell her she had to go back to Mars—unless they got worried about what would happen if she decided to shack up with the Scavengers after getting kicked out of New Halchita. To be able to see people from space would be a huge advantage if there was another Scab war—and there was always another Scab war. And who knew what other powers the Martian had at her command? Nancy's abilities were unfathomable, her trustworthiness doubtful, and her intentions suspect. The council would have to choose between killing her and keeping her—they could never take a chance on letting the Scavengers get hold of her. And if they decided the safest thing to do was to kill her, it would have to be quick and quiet, so she wouldn't have a chance to tell her friends on Mars what the "peaceful" citizens of New Halchita were capable of. Frank cursed under his breath. He knew who they'd pick to do the job.

2 SCAVENGER ATTACK!

The Martian made dinner. The cornbread was gummy, the collards cooked to mush, and the chicken dry, but Germaine was happy the Martian wanted to help out, and the good doctor had an effective remedy for a bad case of anemic provender. She got a jar down from a shelf in the kitchen, and along with it, two small, egg-shaped, red-tinted glasses. As Germaine turned the lid of the jar, it made a sound like the granite top of an old sarcophagus being pushed aside, and a sprinkling of rust sifted down to float on the oily and shimmering surface of the liquor. Small as the glasses were, Germaine only filled them halfway. She set one in front of herself and one in front of Nancy. Nancy took a sip and made a face.

Germaine laughed and was about to say something, but her thoughts and words were swept away by the hard, dull clang of the North Gate bell.

"What is it?" Nancy said.

Germaine stood up. "Scavengers at the North Gate," she said, "I've got to go to the clinic. You might as well come with me. Maybe you can help."

Germaine and Nancy ran down Lancaster, and

crossing Main Street, dodged men and women in various states of dress running in all directions armed with everything from rifles and revolvers to axes and knives. Nurse Jim was already at the clinic when they got there. He had lit the lamps and was engaged in setting up cots in the waiting area. Germaine propped the door to the clinic open, and heard a sound she hadn't heard in a long while and hadn't missed in the least: the *pop pop pop* of gunfire.

Frank, crouched down on the raised walk near the North Gate, peered over the wall and counted a dozen Scavenger rides—more than he'd ever seen in one place at one time. The Scavengers had taken cover behind their rides and were keeping up a steady fire, Civvies returning that fire, bullet for bullet. The noise was terrific, but, Frank noted, the battle was like the proverbial "tale told by an idiot," full of sound and fury, but entirely ineffective, on both sides. The Scavengers had set up their skirmish line about a hundred meters north of the gate, just outside the effective range of either side's rifles. Now that the Civvies were at the wall, the Scabs wouldn't be able to advance without getting cut to pieces by the fire from above. At the same time, the doughty defenders of New Halchita had little chance of inflicting serious damage on their attackers as long as they remained at that distance and fired from behind their mobile steel breastworks.

If the Scavengers had hoped to breach the North Gate, their attack had failed, and failed so utterly that Frank had to wonder if that was ever their plan. Perhaps the attack was a test of the town's preparedness and resolve, or the lodging of a complaint. Maybe Mr. Crane's hornless milkers weren't as top-notch, or the dried chili peppers as excellent, as Frank had led the kuzzer to believe. Or the attack at the North Gate was a diversion.

Frank pulled a dozen citizens from the firing line, intending to divide them into two squads, one led by Deputy Rhome, to check the western perimeter of the town's defenses, and the other led by himself, to check the eastern, leaving deputies Orland and Soon in command of the forces at the North gate.

Orland and Soon were easily located, but Rhome was nowhere to be found. Frank was preparing to be quite cross with the deputy *in absentia*, until Orland reminded Frank that Deputy Rhome was on "roach watch" that night—"roach watch" being what the deputies had taken to calling the job of standing out in Mr. Habushaki's bean field all night long keeping an eye on the Martian's ship. Rhome would have no doubt heard the ringing of the North Gate bell, but having a significantly greater distance to cover, she might yet be on her way. It was even possible, Orland remarked, that as no clear instruction had been given—but completing that thought proved unnecessary, when Rhome, entirely out of breath, made her appearance.

Frank divided the dozen citizens selected for the mission between himself and Deputy Rhome, then gave his instructions: "Keep out of sight and under cover as much as is practicable. Make sure that sentries are at their posts along the wall, and keep an eye out for any sign of infiltration of our fortifications by tunnel or other subtle means. It is not at all necessary for the sentries to see you, or for you to make your presence known to them. Make your inspections quickly, quietly, and move on. If you do find any section of the wall that you feel is not sufficiently defended, don't make a big fuss about it—you don't know who might be on the other side listening. Continue on and report it to me when we meet at the South Gate.

If you do encounter the enemy inside the city, find the best cover you can before engaging them. If we hear gunfire, we'll come running, and you will do the same for us. Otherwise, we'll see you at the South Gate."

After a 10cc injection of a 5% solution of ticktox into the leg just above the knee, Mr. Ward relaxed considerably.

"What happened?" Doctor Perry said.

"When I heard the North Gate alarm," Mr. Ward said, "well, it's been so long since I had the need for it that I couldn't hardly find my rifle. I finally found it in a crate with a bunch of junk piled on top of it. I saw the barrel sticking out and I was in such a great hurry I grabbed it by the barrel to pull it out. The trigger caught on something." Mr. Ward shook his head as if he found the whole incident completely mystifying and inexplicable. "I'm sure I wouldn't have stowed it away loaded."

"It was loaded," Doctor Perry said.

"Frank's gonna give me hell," Mr. Ward said.

"We could tell him you got shot by the Scavengers."

"He'd ask was I standing on my head. Best I tell him the truth."

"Maybe he won't ask."

"Maybe if a hundred others were wounded he wouldn't think to ask. But this place is empty. You even got anyone else in here?—anyone stupid as me?"

"Irwin Otis, if it makes you feel any better," Dr. Perry said. "Ran into a shovel and cut his head open. Or the shovel ran into him, to hear him tell it. Nurse Jim is sewing him up. He'll be fine."

"We're a worse enemy to us than the Scabs."

"So far," Dr. Perry said. "I hope it stays that way."

"I'm going to miss the fight, aren't I?"

"I'm afraid so."

"You gonna take it off?"

"Take it off? You mean amputate your leg?"

Mr. Ward nodded. "Look at that hole. You could stick your hand through there."

"I know it looks bad," Dr. Perry said, "but let's not give up on the leg quite yet. The kneecap is shattered and can't be repaired, but otherwise it's mostly a nasty flesh wound. If we get it cleaned up, you'd be surprised, even in pieces your kneecap will work okay. You're going to be awful sore."

Nurse Jim stuck his head in the door. "Dr. Perry, um . . ."

"What is it?"

"I was suturing and Nancy was cutting with the scissors. I told her to cut with the tips of the scissors and not the middle and she said why? and I said so you don't accidentally cut into the flesh and then she fainted."

"She fainted?"

"Yes ma'am. I checked her pulse and respiration and those are fine but she won't come around."

"I don't have time for fainters," Germaine said. "Carry her out into the waiting room. Try not to bang her head on anything. Lay her out on a cot. Put her on her side and prop her up so she can't roll over. I'll check on her once I've taken care of Mr. Ward."

"Yes ma'am."

"Can you finish those sutures on your own?"

"Yes ma'am, of course—she wanted to help and I thought—"

"It's all right, Nurse. Go finish up and be quick about it. We don't know who might be coming in next."

"Yes ma'am."

Frank's east and west details met at the south gate and neither had anything of significance to report. Gatekeeper Abernathy and Mr. Broome, commander of the detachment of the city guard posted along the south wall, told Frank there had been no sign of Scavengers. Gatekeeper Abernathy said that after letting in Deputy Rhome and closing the gate behind her, she had seen and heard nothing. One of the city guard said she'd heard *something*—and several of the other guards murmured in agreement—but whatever it was (a yell? a cry? the yip of a coyote?) the sound was brief and far-off.

In the lamplight, Sheriff Westfall noticed Irwin Otis, with a half-dozen stitches in his forehead.

"What happened to you?" Sheriff Westfall said.

"I hit my head on a shovel, Sheriff," Irwin said.

"He ran into Miss Richard," Mr. Broome said, "and Miss Richard had a shovel."

"What was Miss Richard doing with a shovel?" Sheriff Westfall said.

"I don't know," Irwin said, "but it was dark, and I was running as fast as I could to get to my post here. I guess Miss Richard was running as fast as she could, too. Mr. Broome told me to go to the clinic and have Dr. Perry look me over. I wanted to stay at my post, Sheriff, but Mr. Broome said it was an order. Nurse Jim was sewing me up—him and the Martian woman—until she fainted, and then—"

"Hold up, Irwin," Frank said, "Who fainted?"

"The Martian woman. She was helping nurse Jim with the stitches and then she fell down into a heap. Nurse Jim said some folks can't take the sight of blood."

"You see anyone else injured at the clinic?"

"Mr. Ward, Sheriff—I didn't see anyone else there."

"What happened to Mr. Ward?"

"Shot in the knee. It looked pretty bad. His shoe fell off when they carried him in and I saw it was full of blood. Last I know about it was Doctor Perry was looking after him."

"Shot in the knee? What was he doing, standing on his head?"

"I don't know, Sheriff, but I think . . . I think I heard one of the ones that carried him in say Mr. Ward shot himself getting his gun."

"Aw Jesus Christ," Sheriff Westfall said, "how can anyone be so—"

"Someone's coming," Mr. Broome said.

Young Mr. Moritz, son of, and apprentice to, the elder Mr. Moritz, brick-maker and mason, was flying down Main Street towards the South Gate. "We've run 'em off!" Young Mr. Moritz said when he got there. "We've run 'em off! What a bunch of cowards!"

Frank was relieved that the battle was over, but refrained from participation in the congratulatory back-slapping going on around him. Scavengers were a lot of things, but coward wasn't one of them. In any event, he didn't think the Scavengers had been run off. More likely, they had gotten whatever it was they wanted and left. Only what was it they wanted? Their brazen assault had a strong element of the theatrical to it—a diversion—Frank was certain of it now—but to what end?

There was, Frank thought, a perfectly reasonable explanation: The Scavengers had tried to draw the entirety of the city guard to the North Gate, but the guard had maintained discipline, and those citizens picketed at other locations along the wall had resisted the urge to leave their posts to join their brothers and sisters where the action was. Having failed to create a weakness in the city's defenses, the Scavengers had left.

Frank, who managed the quarterly drills, was understandably pleased with the outcome. The citizens' response to the threat had been rapid, organized, and robust, and the Scavengers had learned that thirteen years of peace had not made New Halchita soft. There were issues of course. Mr. Ward, for example, assuming he lived, would have to be given some duty that did not involve firearms. And Irwin Otis and Kate Richard had demonstrated that citizens should be cautioned against running around with their gardening tools, especially in the dark of night. As for Deputy Rhome, it was fortunate that the young woman had the sense to come in from the fields when she heard the alarm at the North Gate. Frank had failed to give his deputies specific instructions on that score, and if Deputy Rhome had decided that she should remain at her post by the Martian's ship, and the Scabs had caught her out there alone—

"Aw criminently!" Frank said, loud enough to quiet the celebration going on around him. "Someone give me a lamp. Gatekeeper Abernathy, open the gate."

"You're going out there?" Deputy Rhome said.

"Yes," Frank said.

"I'm going with you," Deputy Rhome said.

"No you're not." Frank said. "God damn it."

Walking down the south road toward Mr. Habushaki's bean field, Frank felt very alone and at the same time, very un-alone. He had a queasy feeling—a queasy certainty, actually—that there were Scavengers out there who would see his dark form in the center of a yellow circle of lamplight as the very definition of a bull's eye. Crossing the field to where he was pretty sure he wouldn't find the Martian's ship, Frank stumbled and nearly fell when he kicked something hard and heavy.

Whatever it was rolled away until it was just at the edge of the illumination of the lamp. Frank followed after it, and the light of his lamp confirmed his suspicion. He kneeled down next to the head—a Scavenger. The rest of the young man was probably somewhere nearby, but Frank didn't bother looking for it. The Scavengers would retrieve the remains of their warrior before dawn.

The Martian's ship was no longer in Mr. Habushaki's bean field, and where it had once stood on its eight mechanical legs, there was evidence of a struggle, and tire tracks, deep and wide. It looked to Frank like the ship had been captured—but not without fight—and a large scrapride had been used to haul it away.

Nancy was sitting up on the edge of a cot when Frank got to the clinic. Germaine was talking softly to her, and Nurse Jim was sitting in a chair next to the only other patient at the clinic, Mr. Ward.

"Is Mr. Ward going to lose the leg?" Frank said.

"I don't think so," Germaine said, "I'll know for sure by sunrise."

"Do you need Nurse Jim here to look after him?"

"Nurse Jim," Dr. Perry said, "go home and get some sleep. I'll keep an eye on Mr. Ward."

"Yes ma'am," Nurse Jim said. "I hope you feel better soon," he said to Nancy. Nancy smiled at him, her smile collapsing the moment Nurse Jim shut the clinic door behind him.

Mr. Ward moaned.

"Will he hear us?" Frank said.

"If he does, he won't remember," Germaine said. "What's this about?"

"Nancy," Frank said, "why don't you tell Germaine what happened tonight."

"Scavengers stole my ship," Nancy said.

"How do you know that?" Germaine said.

"I was there," Nancy said. "I tried to stop them, but—"

"That's ridiculous," Germaine said. "You were right here. You were unconscious."

"I don't think she was," Frank said.

"I went to my ship." Nancy said.

"What do you mean you went to your ship?" Germaine said.

"I can't be two places at once," Nancy said. "I had to focus—my mind had to be on the ship. I tried to move it out of harm's way, but—"

"You can control your ship—from here?" Germaine said.

Nancy nodded.

"Can you bring it back?" Frank said.

"I could—but they have it wrapped in chains. I can hardly move it at all."

"And something else happened out there tonight," Frank said.

"What is he talking about?" Germaine said.

Nancy hung her head, but didn't speak.

"Tell her," Frank said, "or I will."

"What happened?" Germaine said.

"I killed a man," the Martian said, softly. "Was that wrong of me?"

"I don't know," Frank said. "I don't know what to think about any of this."

"You can't blame her," Germaine said. "Half the citizens of New Halchita were shooting at Scavengers tonight. If one of *them* had killed a Scavenger, you'd be hanging a medal around their necks right now."

"She's not a citizen," Frank said, "she's a visitor—a

visitor the council placed in your custody, Germaine. She killed a man that wasn't any threat to her. I don't like it."

"I'm sorry," Nancy said. "I was afraid."

"Afraid of what?" Frank said.

"My ship is just a machine to you," Nancy said, "but it's more than that to me. We're never separated from our machines on Mars. It's unthinkable—unimaginable. It's like . . . like if all of a sudden your legs were cut out from under you or your eyes were plucked out of your head, or if—"

"I get the picture," Frank said.

"I can feel them taking it away from me," she said. "They've got it covered over with something. I feel like it's me lying there blind. Are you going to let them have it?"

"It's not my decision," Frank said, "but the council will want to get it back before the president shows up—and that could be any day now. I expect we'll be going after it first thing tomorrow."

"Do you have to wait that long?" Nancy said. "I feel like I'm dying."

"We won't be able to track them at night," Frank said, "and anyway, they'll be expecting us to come after them, and they'll set ambushes at favorable locations along the route of their retreat. If I'm going to walk into an ambush, I'd rather do it in the light of day."

"We don't have to track them," Nancy said, standing up unsteadily, "I know where the ship is—I can take you to it."

3 A WRIT OF REPLEVIN

It was late in the evening, rather than first thing in the morning, before the newly formed motorized infantry of New Halchita rumbled out of the South Gate. New Halchita was well-prepared to defend itself, but ill-equipped to take a fight to the enemy, especially an enemy on the move, and the techs had to work through the night, into the next morning, and through a good portion of the afternoon, in order to knock together the necessary scraprides: three working tractors and as many tarp-covered trailers, each trailer capable of carrying thirty well-armed citizens; seven one-man scraphogs for scouting operations; and a one-ton supply truck to haul equipment and provisions.

The redoubtable Sheriff Frank Westfall and his brave second in command, Deputy Eleanor Rhome, led the procession mounted on the two shiniest of the scraphogs, with rifles snugged into scabbards strapped to the right front fork, and six-shooters at their hips. They were followed by the troop carriers, the supply truck, and, bringing up the rear, the remaining five scraphogs. The tarps on the troop carriers were rolled up so the citizen-soldiers could wave goodbye to the mothers and fathers, husbands and wives, and sons and daughters gathered at the gate to see them off. Those staying behind cheered, and a few wept, and almost everyone shivered, the weather having turned suddenly cold.

Tire tracks in Mr. Habushaki's bean field indicated that the Scavengers had come with a truck for the purpose of hauling the Martian's ship away, and having somehow managed to load the ship onto the truck, the Scavengers had taken off with their prize straight down the Old South Road. Following the tracks, the mechanized army of New Halchita made excellent time. Late in the evening, about thirty kilometers south of New Halchita, Frank turned his forces off the road and led them down into a shallow wash, where he signaled for a halt. He pulled the scraphog he was riding back and up onto its kickstand and dismounted. He squatted and stood, and squatted and stood again, trying to work some feeling back into his hindquarters. He hated scraphogs.

The Martian had been squeezed between two muscular farm boys in the forward troop carrier, and one of these assisted Nancy out of the truck and brought her to Frank. The signal from her ship was growing weak, and the Martian had turned quite pale and listless.

Frank took Nancy aside, where he could speak to her without being overheard. "Are you going to be all right?" he said.

"I feel weak," Nancy said, "and we're not getting any closer."

"I know," Frank said. "Can you walk?"

"Yes," Nancy said, "if it will get me closer to my ship, I can walk."

The Civvy forces left their encampment in the early

morning in a much different fashion than they had left New Halchita the previous afternoon. Five scouts on scraphogs roared out of the wash and onto the prairie, leaving thick clouds of dust rising in five long lines behind them. The scouts were given nearly a two-kilometer head start, and then the troop carriers, shades drawn so to speak, emerged from the wash, followed by the supply truck. Deputy Rhome and Sheriff Westfall on their highly polished scraphogs brought up the rear—or so (Frank hoped) it would appear. The troop carriers that left the wash were half empty, and a closer examination would reveal that the man in sheriff's clothes riding the shiny scraphog was the second tallest man in the Civvy army, not the first.

Frank, along with forty hand-picked soldiers and one Martian, had left on foot the night before. He was certain that the Scabs had observed the Civvy forces leaving New Halchita the day before, and would observe them again leaving the wash the next morning. He only hoped that the advance of the scouts would keep the Scavengers too far away to get a good, close look.

Aided by the light of a lopsided moon, Frank made his way quickly over the level and trackless prairie. Distant and unseen coyotes aired their eternal grievances, and the long grass, heavily weighted with frost, crunched under foot. If Frank held his breath for a moment, he could hear, some eight to ten paces behind him, the sound of regular puffing, interrupted by the occasional sniffle. It was the kind of sharp, cold night that made a soldier's nose run. Eight to ten paces behind that soldier would be another puffing and runny-nosed citizen-soldier of New Halchita, wondering what the hell they had gotten themselves into, and so on and so forth, for a snaking half-kilometer across the moonlit Scablands.

The Civvy forces under the command of Deputy Rhome were following the tracks of the Scavenger scrapride, heading nearly due south. The Martian had told Frank even before they had set out from New Halchita that the ship was, in fact, moving east, floating down the San Juan River, hog-tied and on its back on the deck of a barge. Frank led his company of forty-one in a north-easterly curve, following neither the false track nor the true, thereby hoping to close on the Scavengers from a direction they could not (assuming they had no knowledge of the Martian's ability to communicate with her ship) be expecting.

As Frank wanted Deputy Rhome to command her forces exactly as she would if she believed she was in hot pursuit of the Scavengers and the stolen Martian ship, he had declined to inform her of the Scavenger's ruse, and had described the purpose of the smaller company he would command as a flanking maneuver. He fully expected the Scavengers to do their part in the deception of his deputy, engaging in delaying tactics and ambushes, and thus keeping the Civvy forces occupied, while the true trace of the raider's departure faded away.

Frank's long legs carried him north-east over the moonlit prairie, but his ruminations took him in the reverse direction, back to New Halchita. Frank had told the council that he believed the Scavengers had gone to great lengths not to kill anyone, and that was a message to New Halchita that taking the Martian's ship should not be regarded as an act of war. In fact, Frank said, the Scavengers might see the Martian's ship as their rightful property, since it had landed in Mr. Habushaki's bean field, and all the fields cultivated by the farmers of New Halchita were outside of the city walls—technically in the

Scablands, and "on loan" to New Halchita, according to the treaty that had ended the last Scab war. The council didn't buy it. They were mad as joggled hornets over the theft of Nancy's ship, and the possibility that the president might show up before New Halchita got the Martian's ship back was driving them to distraction.

Still, the council hadn't declared war against the Scavengers. Instead, they had issued to Frank a "writ of replevin" for the Martian's ship, giving the sheriff legal authority to take possession of the ship and return it to New Halchita. Since no one really believed that the Scavengers would recognize the authority of the council, the council was sending some ninety well-armed citizen-soldiers to enforce the writ should the sheriff meet with any resistance in serving it.

As far as Frank could determine, the point of the writ was so that when the bodies started piling up, the council could say they had done everything possible to avoid bloodshed. The ballistic missiles and subsequent lagamachies of the GIW might have set back the technology of war six-hundred years, but the art of blaming the other guy for starting it had marched on without missing a beat.

The question that kept Frank's mind off of the tedium of the march across the prairie was why had the Scavengers taken the ship in the first place? Probably because they assumed that the Martian had powers the Civvies could use against them, and therefore *would* use against them, and they hoped they could disarm her by taking her ship, or they thought they could figure out how to use the ship as a weapon themselves. They had every right to be concerned, the council was almost certainly thinking along similar lines. In fact, everyone was right about everything, and therefore, no one was to blame for the bloodshed that would follow. Stumbling into a war was as easy as falling in love—extricating oneself from either condition was a different matter entirely. If, Frank thought, he could recover the ship, the Martian, having seen what her Earth-cousins were really like, might fly away home and never come back again. Maybe everything would go back to the way it was.

The moon deserted her post a couple of hours before the sun rose to relieve her, and there was nothing for Frank's company to do but stop and wait, as the country was far too rough to traverse under starlight alone. They needed a rest anyway. Some chewed on a strip of dried goat or venison, or gnawed on a bread crust, while others curled up on the cold hard ground, and with their pack as a pillow, tried to get a few minutes of sleep. Frank was among the chewers, and as he worked over a particularly tough shard of gristle, he was reminded of the old saw about what it took to be a soldier for New Halchita: *good sense, good aim, good teeth.*

The company was in motion again as soon as the light of dawn permitted, and about the time the sun rose, Frank turned his back on it, leading his company due west, essentially following the course of San Juan, though they were four or five kilometers south of the river. The sun rose white and cold behind them, the country turned considerably rougher, and an abundance of scrambling up and sliding down was added to their previously level march across the prairie. Mule-eared rabbits, normally a shy, solitary, and cautious species, cavorted around the company in great numbers. The rabbits were good eating, and seemed to taunt the soldiers, as if they understood that the company, though marching along hungry and with guns loaded, dared not fire a single shot.

The company was forced to pass through several narrow defiles in succession, and the fact that the Scavengers did not waylay them in one of these defiles, shooting every last one of them down from above was excellent evidence, Frank thought, that the Scavengers were completely unaware of this force gaining on them from the east.

The company took a short break at noon on a grassy plateau. Nancy brought Frank good news: her ship, some twenty kilometers west of their current position, had been hauled off the barge. It was still chained up and on its back, but it was on dry land. The Scavenger raiders, it seemed, were settling in for a while.

Late in the afternoon, Frank called a halt, and told the company they would camp where they were, and proceed in the morning.

"I need you to tell me everything you can about your ship," Frank said to Nancy, "the terrain, how many Scavengers are around, how it's situated . . ."

"All right," Nancy said, "but not here. I don't want the others to see."

Out of sight of the rest of the company, Nancy sat with her back against a stone, closed her eyes, and went completely limp. When she started to slump over to one side, Frank propped her up again. After a few minutes she opened her eyes.

"What did you see?" Frank said.

"My ship is only about three kilometers west of us now. Near the river. I saw some Scavengers, and I—"

"How many Scavengers?"

"Five, near the ship. And others, nearby."

"How many others?"

"I can't tell exactly."

"How many do you think?"

"A few hundred."

"That can't be right," Frank said. "I've never seen a raiding party of more than about twenty."

"I don't know," Nancy said, "it's hard for me to get a count. They seem to be . . . coming and going."

"All right," Frank said. "How about the terrain? Flat? Hilly? Trees?"

"Flat," Nancy said. "I saw a stand of trees nearby, but it's flat and open around the ship."

Early the next morning, Frank and Mr. Broome left the company and scrambled up and down the rocky hills as quietly as they could, dreading even to kick a pebble lest it go rattling merrily across the stony ground. Eventually the hills gave way to the flood plain of the San Juan River, where the ground was perfectly level, hard-packed, and lacking of any vegetation save the occasional clump of "Scavenger tea," a leafless, yellow-green stemmed bush that might provide cover for a rabbit or a sparrow, but not a man. Having no choice but to be daring, they strode upright with rifles at the ready and to all appearances perfectly confident as they crossed the level expanse, breathing as inaudible a sigh of relief as they could manage when they finally gained the timbers growing along the banks of the river.

They made their way through some three hundred feet of cedar forest, and had they taken a few more steps, would have been swimming, as they found themselves on the inside of a bend in the river, where the cedars grew right up to the water's edge. On the side opposite Frank and Mr. Broome there was much less vegetation, and the Scavenger camp was clearly visible. "Aw, criminently!" Frank said, softly.

The camp stretched out for nearly a mile along the

northern bank of the San Juan, with huts made of stick and mud inlaid with shiny and colorful remnants of the pre-GIW world. Cooking fires were burning and ragged strips of meat (Frank guessed goat) were drying on a rack in the sun, the rack defended from wheeling crows and vultures keen for a taste by an alert youth with a stick. Frank could see that this was no temporary encampment for a raiding party. To the extent applicable to a semi-nomadic race, this camp was home, the seasonal residence of one of the many semi-autonomous tribes of Scavengers. Frank estimated that within minutes of firing the first shot, the Civvy forces would be facing two hundred Scavenger warriors or more—outnumbered five to one.

Mr. Broome, after carefully examining the position of the enemy through a glass, pointed across the river, east of the main body of the village, and handed the glass to Frank. At first, all Frank saw was a glint of sunlight. He adjusted the glass, and then he made out the shape—the Martian's ship—situated exactly as Nancy had described.

"I saw five pickets," Mr. Broome said.

Frank searched the area around the Martian's ship through the glass, and saw only four pickets, but he could easily have missed one. "I think having so recently played the trick on us," Frank said, "they're not going to let us draw them off." He handed the glass back to Mr. Broome.

"I agree," Mr. Broome said. "We'll have to overrun them. Here's my thinking. We wait for nightfall, then we'll cross the river where it's wide and shallow. There, see? After we cross the river, we make our way through the timbers slow and quiet, and line up there—"

"Where?" Frank said.

"Just there," Mr. Broome said, "to the east of the

ship—see the cedar-brake?"

Frank held out his hand for the glass, took it, and put it up to his eye. "All right, I see it," he said. He lowered the glass, marveling at Mr. Broome's unaided visual acuity.

"When we're ready, we come out blazing away with everything we've got. Push past the ship, form up a firing line there. The Martian follows behind us with the bolt cutters. You should detail someone to stand guard while she's at it. Once she cuts her ship free, she flies it back to New Halchita."

"How long do you think before the Scabs get their act together?" Frank said.

"Eight minutes—ten if we're lucky. Will that be long enough for the Martian to get her ship in the air?"

"It'll have to be," Frank said. "I just have one question."

"What's that?"

"How do we get out of there?"

"You expect to live through this?"

"I wouldn't call it an expectation as much as a longing."

"Back the way we came," Mr. Broome said. "Retreat in dashes."

"They'll be two steps behind us the whole way. They'll cut us to pieces."

"You have an idea for covering our retreat?" Mr. Broome said.

"It'll take 'em just as long to get organized against twenty rifles as forty," Frank said, "as long as we catch them by surprise. So we send twenty across the river and we put twenty right here. The ones that cross the river will come through the cedar-brakes like you said, but then they push, push, push—until they're right across from where we are now. They shoot like crazy—do their best to sound like a hundred-strong. As soon as they're out of ammo, they drop their rifles, run like hell straight for the river and dive in. The rest of us are here, like I said, where there's good cover in the trees. The Scabs will have to come out in the open to get a good shot at the ones crossing the river, and we'll make it mighty hot for any who dares. Once ours have gotten across, it's devil-take-the-hindmost all the way home."

"The council won't like leaving twenty perfectly good rifles behind for the Scavengers," Broome said.

"I'd rather leave twenty rifles than one soldier," Frank said. "I don't want anything weighing them down—especially in the water. It's considerably deeper here than where they'll cross to the east. They'll have to swim some, and the current will be strong."

"Maybe we tell 'em to drop their rifles into the river when they jump in," Mr. Broome said.

"All right," Frank said, "That might make the council happier with us."

"We'll want the fast runners and good swimmers on the attack—we don't care if they can shoot straight or not," Mr. Broome said. "The best shooters we'll want on this side, providing cover for the retreat."

"Agreed," Frank said.

"So I'm going to lead the attack," Mr. Broome said, "and you'll make sure we're well-covered once we've worn out our welcome."

"Now wait a minute," Frank said, "how do you figure—"

"You walk faster than any man I've ever known," Mr. Broome said, "but when you run, you lope along like a man with a wooden leg. And you're the best shot in the company. That answers that, and you know it."

Just at moonrise, the first two of the twenty selected to engage the enemy at the Martian's ship stepped into the river. They held their rifles over their heads, though this turned out to be unnecessary, as they made the opposite bank without the cold and muddy water ever rising higher than their knees. The remainder followed in twos and threes in silence. They had been thoroughly instructed an hour before, and not another word would be spoken until Mr. Broome fired the first shot, after which they were free to yell and curse to their heart's content. The last two to cross the river were the Martian, unarmed but carrying bolt-cutters nearly as long as she was tall, and one sorely disappointed young soldier, a Mr. Vaughn, who had been detailed to accompany and protect the Martian, and give her any assistance she required in freeing her ship from the chains that bound it.

Once across the river, the company under Mr. Broome's command entered the timbers. Each soldier was to take as much time as necessary to cross the fifty some-odd meters of timber and brush, stopping just shy of the clearing where five Scavenger warriors were keeping watch over the Martian's ship. Time was not of the essence—there would be plenty of time, hours if necessary—to cross those fifty meters. Stealth was the overriding imperative.

Slower than the Lord to anger, slower than a deep wound healing, slower even than the paying off of a heavy debt, Broome and his detachment made their way through the trees. A pittance of the moon's light penetrated into the break, and Mr. Broome could not see the stars above—the burbling of the river to his left was his only compass. That his comrades were anywhere nearby was evidenced only by the occasional crack of a twig, and at every such sound, Broome's heart thumped painfully in his chest. *A pox on such a quiet, windless night*, Broome thought. He wished mightily for a breeze to rustle the branches overhead. For all the good it did him, he might as well have wished for a gale.

Mr. Broome took up a position behind a tree at the margin of the timbers, where he could clearly see the Scavengers guarding the Martian's ship in the moonlight. In the shadows of the trees, he could make out (he thought) two others of his company. That the rest were somewhere nearby, he took on faith, but he would wait another hour, to be sure every fighter was with him. He occupied his mind by thinking on two conundrums: first, that a man of action is so often called upon to suffer what to him is the worst of torments: the exercise of extraordinary patience, and second, how even that which is a long time upon the road often arrives too soon.

When the shifting of the shadows cast by the moon indicated to Mr. Broome that the requisite interval had expired, he leveled his rifle, took careful aim at the most distant of the Scavenger pickets, and pulled the trigger. The young man had his finger in his nose when a bullet ripped through his brain. The report of Mr. Broome's rifle was instantly joined by the blasts of the others, some so unexpectedly near to Mr. Broome that he jumped— and then he charged, his fighters to the left and right of him. Even in the terror and excitement of the attack, Mr. Broome was gratified to see how expertly his companions formed up into a well-spaced skirmish line immediately upon leaving the timbers. The company advanced double-time over and past the dead bodies of the Scavenger pickets, firing in the direction of the sleeping camp without taking particular aim, howling and shrieking over and through the deafening blasts of their own gunfire, as if to say *and now, without further ado, Death.*

On the south side of the river, the detachment under the command of Sheriff Westfall found rifle-rests on low tree limbs or on piled brush. They settled in, adjusted their sights, and waited. And adjusted their sights, and waited. And, not daring to slap, tried to shrug or wave off the mosquitoes, creatures much too eager for a drink at a soldier's expense to be so easily dissuaded. The soldiers pulled their collars up around their necks and their sleeves down their arms and wrists to the extent the fabric would allow—and adjusted their sights and waited. The moon rose in the sky, and the Scab village across the river was still and silent. The coyote chose not to howl, the mockingbird, not to sing, the wind, not to blow. In the moonlight, even the river between Frank and the Scavenger village appeared thick and still, betraying little of the monumental forces Frank knew must be at work beneath the surface.

Finally, the long-awaited muzzle flash was seen across the river and to the east, this flash so closely followed by a host of others that the light of the latter was seen before the crack of the former was heard. Frank was able to follow the remarkably rapid progress of Broome's detachment with ease, both by the muzzle flashes and by the slow rise into the still air of tailed puffs of smoke, lit up blue and gray in the moonlight. The sound of gunfire got louder and closer, and soon Frank could see individual fighters crossing the open bank of the river, and then, a few meters to the west, falling to the ground to take advantage of the entirely inadequate cover provided by a low hill of sand or a thin clump of brush.

Initially, return fire from the enemy was infrequent and desultory. It was clear that the Scabs had been taken completely by surprise. But with the passing of each second, Frank could tell by the sound and the muzzle flashes that a firing line was forming up opposite the Civvy forces. In a matter of minutes Scavenger warriors on the defensive line would equal and then greatly exceed the forces arrayed against them. The Scabs were rattled for the moment, but the moment wouldn't last, and although the Civvies were doing a first-rate job of firing at the rate of fifty men rather than twenty, the Scabs wouldn't be fooled for long—they'd soon realize they were fighting a force inferior in numbers, if not in enthusiasm, and the instant they grasped the enormity of their advantage, they'd simply run the Civvy forces over.

When the gunfire had receded into the distance (and it hadn't taken long) Nancy and Mr. Vaughn emerged into the moonlit clearing. A strong, sulfurous smell of burnt powder hung in the air. The Martian's ship lay on its back bound in chains like some vine-swaddled relic of the pre-GIW world. While Mr. Vaughn stood guard, the Martian went to work with the bolt cutters. At her first attempt she was afraid she lacked the necessary strength—but then the link broke with a sharp and gratifying ping, and with the extra muscle that a new confidence so often bestows on the uncertain, she quickly cut another dozen links. "You can go," Nancy said to Mr. Vaughn, "Your companions need you now more than I do."

The young man's orders had been to stay with the Martian until her ship was in the air—but if she no longer needed him . . . He saluted her (it seemed appropriate, somehow) and ran off in the direction of the sound of gunfire.

Nancy dropped the bolt cutters on the ground, grabbed the heavy chains and pulled them slithering and rattling from her ship. The ship was free, but on its back, a situation she wasn't certain how to rectify. At a sound, she turned, expecting to see Mr. Vaughn—perhaps he had reconsidered and decided he should follow Mr. Broome's orders, not hers.

"Is that you, Mr. Vaughn?" Nancy said.

A man stepped out of the shadows—but not Mr. Vaughn. Spencer Skint stood less than a dozen feet from the Martian, covering her with his revolver.

"I figured you'd show up here sooner or later," Skint said, "and probably sooner. The Scabs told me they were leading Sheriff Westfall and the Civvies on a wild good chase. I know Frank better than they do. I figured he was on to them."

"Do you mean to kill me, Spencer?" Nancy said.

"You were always one to get right to the point," Skint said. "I'm afraid I do mean to kill you, Nancy. I don't like it, but I don't see that I have a choice."

"Because of Washington D.C?"

"That's it exactly. I'm glad you understand."

"I'm no threat to you, Spencer. I have no intention of interfering in your business arrangements."

"I believe you," Spencer Skint said. He pulled the trigger, putting a bullet in the exact location where, if the council of New Halchita was to be believed, the Martian had once possessed a tertiary ocular organ. Skint waited for a moment, then stepped forward, keeping the Martian's fallen body covered with his gun. Looking down at her, he saw a metallic gleam emerging from within the hole in her head. A bullet fragment reflecting the moonlight, perhaps. Whatever it was, blood swamped over it in an instant.

"I'm sorry," Skint said, "I couldn't take the chance that you might change your mind." He holstered his gun and walked quickly away from the dead Martian and her ship. He wasn't certain that the forces of New Halchita wouldn't retreat right back the way they came, and it wouldn't do at all for his Civvy friends to find him camping out with Scabs. Skint knew of a rise not far from where the action was where he could observe the battle in perfect safety. He hurried, knowing that whatever happened, the show would soon be over, and he was curious to see how (or even if) the Civvy forces would fight their way out of the trouble they'd gotten themselves into.

When Skint was out of sight, the ship trembled and shook. It rocked back and forth, clawing furiously at the air with its eight legs and two pincers. A few minutes later, having accomplished little more than roughing up the sandy soil beneath its back and uprooting a few weedy clumps of vegetation, it ceased its struggles, legs sticking up in the air half folded, like an enormous dead spider.

From the safety of a rise some two hundred meters from where the battle was raging, Spencer Skint could see that the Scavengers had managed to get themselves together and would, in very short order, have more than enough firepower at their command to overrun the Civvy forces. Just then the Civvies ceased fire quite suddenly, and a moment later they were sprinting across the open stretch of river bank and diving (if you could call it diving) into the dark waters of the San Juan. Spencer Skint let out a loud guffaw, because watching the Civvies fly through the air and land in the river with a great splash was comical, but also because he knew what was coming next. That a number of Scavenger warriors would soon be running straight into the maw of death was as obvious to Skint in his detached observation of the battle as it would be impenetrable to the furious Scavengers in the middle of it.

After a brief rest in the moonlight, the ship again became active. It retracted its pair of slender pincer-legs until the bird-like claws rested on the ship's underside. One of those claws began tapping on the metallic belly of the ship rhythmically, and the other soon joined in, in percussional counterpoint to the first. The tapping started and stopped a few times, and then the ship began rocking again, in a manner considerably more graceful and serene than its previous effort. Taking the approach of a child propelling itself ever higher on a swing, the ship extended and contracted its legs in time with the sway of its bulk, gradually increasing the amplitude of its undulations. Eventually, the ship reached the tipping point, and the rocking ceased abruptly when the ship fell over onto its side.

In this position, half of the ship's legs were pinned awkwardly beneath it, and the other half were up in the air where they could not effectively reach the ground—at first, it hardly seemed to have improved its situation. But through various curlings and uncurlings of its segmented carapace and scrabblings of its appendages in the sandy soil, the ship managed to get its feet under itself, and was soon standing upright.

Some sixty furious Scavenger warriors rushed out into the open, hot on the heels of the fleeing Civvies. Frank yelled "Fire!" and his detachment poured lead into the Scavengers across the river. The Scavengers retreated in complete disorder, leaving a half-dozen of their number dead or dying on the river bank. From what cover they could find, the Scavengers returned fire, aiming at both the Civvies in the river and at those taking cover in the trees on the opposite bank, but the elevation, the distance, and the dim light of the moon rendered their shots ineffective.

Spencer Skint whooped. Whether Civvies or Scabs prevailed in this battle was not of great concern to him, but he had picked a side because watching a fight was more pleasurable when you picked a side, and he picked the Civvies because he had pegged them as the underdog in this particular match-up. Spencer Skint believed the sensible course was always to root for the underdog. You wouldn't be too disappointed if they lost, and it was exceedingly satisfying should they carry the day.

The last Civvy fighter pulled himself out of the water and scrambled on all fours into the relative safety of the cedar brakes, and then, with a few parting shots, the Civvy forces melted away into the timbers, and the battle was over. Frank's first priority was to get the company across the open floodplain before the Scavengers realized it was safe to cross the river, and there was no strategy to that maneuver beyond a mad dash. Running (or loping) as fast as he could across a level terrain presenting no impediments, and therefore providing no excuses, Frank was forced to accept that Mr. Broome had judged him fairly. Frank was outrun by every man and woman in the company, and was the very last to reach the cover of the rocky hillocks.

Once he caught his breath, Frank called the company together. His headcount fell one short, and five soldiers had flesh wounds (two serious, but neither immediately life-threatening). All in all, a better result than he could have reasonably hoped for. It didn't take Frank long to figure out who was missing. Binding the arm of a young woman, he asked after Mr. Broome. She shook her head in a way that told Frank all he needed to know. They'd probably killed nine or ten Scabs, and lost only Mr. Broome. Practically speaking, a miracle—but whether or not the mission was a *success* . . .

Frank sought out Mr. Vaughn, who was sitting with his back against a rock, chewing on a piece of venison jerky.

"Did the Martian get her ship off the ground?" Frank said.

Mr. Vaughn stopped chewing. "Um . . ." he said. Frank didn't like the nervous look in the man's eye. Something must have gone wrong.

"What happened, Mr. Vaughn?"

"After we dropped the Scab pickets, I stood guard while the Martian cut the chains off her ship. We didn't encounter any trouble."

"And then?"

"She said I could join the others on the skirmish line. So . . . I . . . I figured—"

"Please," Frank said, "don't tell me you left her alone, in the middle of the Scablands, in the middle of an attack against a Scavenger camp, unarmed—"

"She had bolt cutters," Mr. Vaughn said, weakly, "and she said I could join—"

"Mr. Vaughn," Frank said, trying to sound appropriately angry, which was extremely angry, but only about half as angry as he actually was, "Nancy—the Martian—is not your commanding officer. You were supposed to stay with her until she got her ship off the ground. And now you're telling me you don't know if she got her ship off the ground or not."

"No sir, I don't," Mr. Vaughn said. He looked down at the ground. He tried to stifle a whimper and failed, and a half-chewed piece of venison jerky fell out of his mouth into his lap. "I'm sorry sir," he said.

The ship straddled Nancy's body, and began lowering itself in increments of an inch or so until its belly was a little more than two feet above her. A lengthwise divide appeared across the ship's metallic undercarriage, and the belly of the ship opened up, revealing a void of approximately the same inner dimensions as a coffin— that is, room enough for a corpse, and little else. A soft turquoise light emanated from this cavity, gently illuminating the body directly under it. Mechanical spider-leg-like appendages in the hundreds descended from the opening. These appendages were translucent and fluid-filled, and this fluid was either lit by, or was itself producing, the turquoise light. Each of these appendages appeared to work independently as they searched for something to grab on to, a difficult task as the three-pronged gripping apparatus terminating each appendage was hardly bigger than a robin's claw. One grasped a yank of Nancy's hair. Another clutched a finger. Very many were able to snag a pinch of clothing. One appendage had no choice but to grab the corpse by the nose, and several clamped onto the deceased's lips and ears. When each appendage had taken hold of the corpse as best it could, they lifted as one, and the body rose up into the ship. The belly panel slid shut—or very nearly so. A leather bootlace hung outside the ship, and the cavity opened again, ever so slightly, and for just long enough for the errant filament to be retrieved, and then the breach was well and truly sealed.

A pair of short round wings slid out from beneath the

scales of the ship's carapace, and these began to beat so rapidly as to become first a blur, and then entirely invisible. The squall generated by the wings scattered small rocks and clumps of vegetation in the vicinity of the ship in every direction. The ship leapt into the air and settled back down to earth. On its second attempt it managed to remain airborne, and began to rise slowly, folding its legs up underneath itself as it continued to ascend. Once above the treetops, the ship turned this way and that, fine-tuning its inner compass through observations of the eternal and steadfast lights of the firmament. Having made the necessary navigational calculations, the ship turned precisely in the direction of New Halchita, and disappeared into the night.

"I swear I shot her dead," Skint said. He pointed at a dark spot on the ground. "Right there. That's her blood."

"So where is she now?" the kuzzer said.

"How the hell would I know? Maybe a panther dragged her off."

"And her ship? Did a panther drag her ship off as well?" the kuzzer said.

"You couldn't hold on to the ship," Skint said. "That's on you, not on me."

"You're no use to me if she tells the council you're a traitor," Kuzzer Wayd said.

"She knew about D.C. when she got here," Skint said, "and she didn't say anything to the council then—what makes you think—"

"Because you tried to kill her," Kuzzer Wayd said.

"You've got a point," Skint said. He had to consider the possibility. What if he hadn't killed her? It was dark, and maybe he hadn't seen what he thought he saw. Maybe he'd only grazed her. If she made it back to New

Halchita, they were sure to ask her where she got that hole in her head. What were the chances she'd go to the effort of a lie to save his skin? And if he went back to New Halchita, and they knew that he'd never been to Washington D.C....

"Maybe it's time for me to retire," Skint said. "I always liked the Scavenger life—you could adopt me into your tribe—"

Kuzzer Wayd shook his head.

"That's a Scab for you," Skint said, "no sense of loyalty."

"I can offer you this," the kuzzer said, "if you want to live out in the Scablands, we won't kill you—as long as you keep to yourself."

"Thanks for nothing," Skint said. "Look, let's say she's managed to get back to New Halchita, and she's let on that I'm a Scab spy. It'll be my word against hers—but I can fix it where they won't believe a thing she says."

"Then I recommend you do that," Kuzzer Wayd said.

"I'm going to need your help," Skint said.

"What's in it for me?" Kuzzer Wayd said.

"Getting rid of her was never going to be more than a short-term solution," Skint said. "There's plenty more where she came from, she said so herself. Sooner or later, they'd just send another. Your big worry is the Civvies and the Martians forming an alliance. You help me out and I can guarantee they never will—they'll be too busy trying to kill each other."

4 THE PRESIDENT COMES TO NEW HALCHITA

Early on the morning of the last day of November of 2473, the town of New Halchita was startled into wakefulness by the ringing of the North Gate bell. New Halchitans, having every expectation of a retaliatory attack for the replevin of the Martian's ship, responded with alacrity, and the north wall bristled with rifle barrels aimed as one as a single scrapride approached New Halchita in the dim light of dawn.

"Hold your fire! It's Postmaster Skint!" some particularly eagle-eyed citizen cried out, and when the scrapride got a little closer, others joined in with "It's Skint for sure!"

"Stay sharp," Frank said, "you don't know who or what is in that truck." Frank took aim and fired several shots in quick succession, kicking up little explosions of dust in front of the approaching scrapride. The scrapride stopped, and slowly, with arms raised, Skint came out. He waved his arms, then climbed back into the truck, and proceeded again towards the North Gate.

"All right," Frank said. "Aim off to the side. I don't

want anyone accidentally shooting Postmaster Skint."

The North Gate was opened to admit the hero returned, and once the city gates closed behind him, Mr. Skint climbed out of the cab of the delivery truck looking worn-out but otherwise none the worse for wear. Skint looked around. The City Guard remained at their post but in a relaxed posture. No one was pointing a gun at him, or even giving him a dirty look—in fact, they seemed quite pleased to see him, smiling and waving—all except for Sheriff Westfall, who kept his nose and his gun pointed north, as though still expecting a horde of Scavenger warriors to materialize in front of him.

Matilda Elson, keeper of the North Gate, slapped Skint on the back and shook his hand. "Welcome home, Postmaster," Elson said. "We were all terribly worried about you. We had some trouble with the Scavengers, and we were afraid—"

"I need to speak to the mayor," Skint said.

"I'm sure he'll be overjoyed to see you," Elson said.

"Get him for me," Skint said.

"I can't leave my post."

"Under the authority of the president of the United States," Skint said, "I am ordering you to inform the Mayor that Postmaster Skint will speak to him at the North Gate."

"All right," Gatekeeper Elson said, uncertainly, "but should I ring the all-clear, so everyone knows—"

"No," Skint said, "under no circumstances are you to ring the all-clear. Everyone is to remain at their post—except you—until further notice. Now go fetch Mayor Lopez, Gatekeeper—and without delay."

Gatekeeper Elson gave Spencer Skint an uncertain half-salute and then went flying down the road towards the council building as fast as her thin, knobby-kneed legs would carry her. She returned a few minutes later with Mayor Lopez, both of them winded.

"Welcome—welcome home Postmaster Skint," Mayor Lopez said, taking one of Skint's hands in both of his. "We thought the Scavengers had killed you for sure—we've had some trouble with them while you were gone."

"I heard about it," Skint said. "The president told me the Scavengers had stolen the Martian's ship, and that you sent a force to recover it."

"The president told you that?" Mayor Lopez said. "It's true—but how would he know?"

"He has his sources," Skint said. "He said he heard that Scavengers killed the Martian while she was trying to free her ship."

"Killed the Martian? No, Postmaster, I assure you they didn't. Nancy is unharmed, and her ship safe-and-sound in the scrap yard where the Scavengers won't get it into their heads to try to claim it as their own again. I hope the president doesn't think—"

"Perhaps she was wounded in the action," Skint said, "and in the report to the president, the severity of the injury was overstated."

"Wounded?" the Mayor said. "No, I don't believe so. She didn't have a mark on her—that I could see, of course."

"Where is the Martian now?" Skint said.

"I assume she's with Dr. Perry at the clinic. We've been expecting a retaliatory attack, but I'll tell Gatekeeper Elson to ring the all-clear, and—"

"No," Skint said, "it's imperative the citizens remain at their posts."

"Are you expecting a Scavenger attack?" Mayor Lopez said.

"Not Scavengers. The president is coming, and I think it would show a lack of decorum to allow the citizens to mob him, don't you?"

"The president?" Mayor Lopez said, "He's on his way?"

"He's not on his way," Skint said, "he's here. When we crossed the San Juan, I told him to hold back until I could inform you of his arrival. I didn't want the City Guard shooting at him. You tell the City Guard to hold their fire, and I'll signal to the president that it's safe for him to approach the city.

"Oh, Postmaster Skint," the mayor said, "you are a marvel! You are indeed a marvel and a hero of New Halchita! Of course, you're right, everyone should remain at their posts. That would be best."

"At their posts, Mr. Mayor, but not shooting at the president," Skint said.

"Hold your fire! Hold your fire!" Mayor Lopez shouted at the City Guard on the wall. "The president and his entourage are coming! Stand down! Hold your fire!"

"Gatekeeper Elson," Skint said, "open the North Gate."

The Gatekeeper looked at the mayor, and the mayor nodded. When the gate was open, Skint pulled his gun and pointed it in the air. "Are you ready, Mayor Lopez?"

"Am I ready? Shouldn't we arrange—"

Skint fired his gun into the air twice—once for the bad news, once for the good.

A couple of kilometers from the North Gate, the Old North Road disappeared as it curved into the bluffs of the San Juan, and the mayor's first intimation of the arrival of the president and his mighty entourage was not the sight but the sound—a great roar as though from an approaching cyclone. This rumbling got louder and closer, and then something shot out from behind the bluffs and into view—one man on one scraphog, taking the curves at a breath-taking velocity. Some two hundred and fifty meters shy of New Halchita, the man and the machine came to a halt—an imposing presence even at that distance. The man was a great, dark figure, whom the light of the rising sun seemed only to darken, like rain on parched earth. In contrast, the president's scraphog, enormous and chrome-sheathed, was breathtaking in its brilliance, reflecting every photon of the fiery radiance of dawn.

The machine rumbled. The mayor and the City Guard at the North Gate stood silent.

"That's President Preston?" Mayor Lopez said. "He doesn't look like . . . how you described him."

"I'm afraid President Preston is no longer with us," Skint said, "When I arrived in Washington, I was informed that Preston gave his life defending the capitol from a Scab attack. His vice-president . . . have I ever mentioned him to you?"

"I don't believe so," Mayor Lopez said.

"A very capable man," Skint said. "The word in Washington is, though President Preston will be greatly missed, President Boulderstone will carry on admirably."

"Boulderstone?"

"Yes sir, President Havek Boulderstone."

"He didn't bring anyone with him? No advisors? No security?"

"He told me there is a great danger facing New Halchita, so he came alone. He didn't want to put anyone else's life at risk—that's the kind of man he is."

"A great danger?" Mayor Lopez said. "That sounds . .

. ominous. What is this danger?"

"He wouldn't tell me," Skint said. "He will only speak to you."

"What's he waiting for?"

"He's waiting for you."

"For me?"

"Yes," Skint said. "I told you, he wants to speak to you—alone."

"Out there?"

The president revved the scraphog's engine, and the machine let out a snarl like an angry panther.

"Yes sir," Skint said, "and I wouldn't be too long about it. President Boulderstone is not known for his patience."

Mayor Lopez, at first hesitantly, and then with as much resolution as he could muster, walked out of New Halchita and down the Old North Road. The City Guard posted near the North Gate were treated to the astonishing sight of Mayor Lopez walking alone on the Old North Road to meet with the president of the United States. Frank put a glass to his eye to get a better look at the president. The man was enormous—tall as an awning post, a torso like a water barrel, and a vulture's wingspan-wide across the shoulders. His skin was purple-black as a ripe plum. He had a thick white scar across the bridge of his nose, and another split his left eyebrow. He carried a rifle slung across his back, and the beaded leather strap was all that stood between the president's bare chest and the bitter cold. His pants were of lustrous black fur, and in case there was any question as to what beast had sacrificed itself to supply the material, the president wore a matching hat consisting of the upper portion (ears, eyes, and snarl) of the head of a monstrous lobo. When the mayor got close, the president pulled the scraphog back up onto its kick-stands, dismounted, took two giant steps forward and offered the mayor his hand. It looked to Frank like the president was doing most of the talking. At one point, the mayor put both his hands on top of his head—a gesture that suggested to Frank that the news wasn't good.

Almost an hour passed before the historic meeting came to an end. The president and Mayor Lopez shook hands again. The president mounted his scraphog and disappeared with a roar back into the bluffs of the San Juan, leaving Mayor Lopez standing in a slowly settling cloud of red dust.

Skint's return to New Halchita had gone as well as he could reasonably expect, though it would have been nice if the Martian hadn't been quite so not dead. As he watched Mayor Lopez walk out of the North Gate to meet "President Boulderstone," Skint wondered how Nancy had survived a bullet between the eyes—a neat trick he wouldn't mind having up his own sleeve. Maybe he hadn't seen what he thought he saw—it was dark, after all. What happened now was out of his hands, so he wasn't going to worry about it. He'd done his best. Either Mayor Lopez would believe the kuzzer's nephew was president of the United States, or he wouldn't. Skint studied the City Guard as they gawked at the spectacle of their Mayor talking to the president of the United States out on the North Road—the looks on their faces could well be described as flabbergasted or dumbfounded—but incredulous?—not in the least. Even Sheriff Frank Westfall seemed to be taking the whole charade seriously. Skint stuck his painfully cold hands in his armpits, lowered his head against the sharp wind, and headed for home. What a bunch of idiots. Of course they'd believe it.

It was just as cold inside Skint's house on Possum Race Road as it was outside. Skint considered making a fire, but decided not to bother. He got into his bed fully dressed, and under the covers he shivered and stared at the ceiling. Someone pounded on the door. He got out of bed expecting Mayor Lopez had sent someone to bring him to the council chambers to help them figure out how to save New Halchita from utter destruction, only to discover his visitor wasn't anyone of any significance—just that overgrown child, Miss Caroline Tyler.

"Shouldn't you be at your post?" Skint said.

"No one's paying attention," Miss Tyler said, "so I snuck away. I couldn't wait." She pushed her way past Skint.

"Come on in," Skint said, well after she already had.

"Can you believe it?" Miss Tyler said, "The president of the United States of America, right here in New Halchita?"

"Yeah, I can believe it," Skint said. "I brought him here, remember? Is there something you want from me?"

"You've been gone six weeks," Miss Tyler said. "You better believe there's something I want from you. Isn't there something you want from me?

Skint looked her over. Her nails were painted silver, and she wore her brown hair in a tight clump on top of her round head, like she was carrying a potato up there. She wore a shapeless, flour-dusted black dress cinched around her waist with the ties of the apron she had probably forgotten she was still wearing. Despite the cold, her sleeves were rolled up, and her muscular forearms were a testament to thousands of hours of kneading bread dough. She was a short woman with an abundance of bosom and bottom, and the heavy black shoes she wore could not have been better designed to accentuate her stockiness. She possessed neither grace nor style, but she had youth, and youth goes a long way.

The North Gate bell sounded the all-clear. "See?" Caroline said, "the City Guard doesn't need me anymore. I'm all yours."

Skint almost told her to go on back to work—her ma and pa would be expecting her, and he needed to get some sleep—but his indifference was firming up into lust. Also, he was tired of being cold, and if there was one thing the woman could do, it was generate heat.

Mayor Lopez sat at the table in the council's chambers, spectacles off, pulling at the gray and black hairs of his left eyebrow. He had been engaged in that activity for a long while, and some of the other members of the council were starting to wonder if he had forgotten they were there.

"Mr. Mayor," Mr. Goodhue said, softly.

"She's a lagamachy," the mayor said.

"What do you mean she's—" Mrs. Crane began

"That thing that calls itself Nancy is not a Martian—not from Mars," the mayor said, "She's a lagamachy. She's not human. She's a—President Boulderstone called her a human-machine chimera—here to find out if New Halchita has made inappropriate technological advancements."

"How does he know?" Mr. Downes asked.

"The photographs we sent with Postmaster Skint were not the first 'Martian' he's seen," Mayor Lopez said. "There was a settlement, a place called Nails, about 400 kilometers northeast of here. The president—Preston—got a letter from the Mayor of Nails, with photographs of a 'Martian' who came to Earth. Boulderstone said Preston showed it to him, and when Boulderstone got our letter, he recognized Nancy. She looked just like the Martian that had landed in Nails.

"Did she have a third eye?" Mr. Goodhue asked, "our Martian had a third—"

"As usual, Mr. Goodhue, you're missing the point," Mayor Lopez said, rather testily. "It doesn't matter how many eyes she has. What matters is, there's nothing left of Nails anymore—nothing but a radioactive crater. And since the annihilation of Nails, two other settlements have met the same fate—they gave refuge to a 'Martian' and shortly thereafter were wiped off the face of the Earth."

"And he thinks Nancy destroyed them all?" Mr. Downes said.

"Not our Nancy, Mr. Downes. Ours is just one of many. Listen to what I'm telling you—*please*—this woman is not a woman—not a human—not a Martian. She—it—is a lagamachy. The president says his best scientists in Washington D.C. have come to the conclusion that those who made the lagamachies so many centuries ago must have realized that sooner or later, folks would figure out how to build and grow a society in ways that didn't produce the kind of electromagnetic signature a lagamachy could easily identify. So they made a few with a highly advanced, artificially intelligent biological—thing—the 'Nancy,' for lack of a better word. They don't just fall out of the sky and blow up. They come down to Earth, and the Nancy interacts with the population of the chosen settlement in order to gather information. And if she makes the determination that the settlement represents an unacceptable advance . . ."

"What do we do?" Mrs. Crane said.

"The president said we have to kill it," Mayor Lopez said. "He said that was our only hope."

"Maybe it won't go off," Mr. Goodhue said. "It's been

here almost two months now, and it hasn't gone off yet—maybe it will decide we haven't been . . . inappropriate."

"The president said his scientists in Washington D.C. think the chances of the lagamachy letting us slide are slim to none. The president says we're not all that different from Nails or any of the other settlements destroyed by these lagamachies. And he said that if the Nancy finds out that we know what she is, she—it—would make sure we will never warn anyone else of the danger. What I've told you can never, ever leave this room."

"How long do we have before it makes up its mind?" Mr. Downes said.

"The president said he doesn't know—but not long," Mayor Lopez said.

"No wonder he ran off," Mrs. Crane said.

"That's not fair, Mrs. Crane. I told President Boulderstone everything I know about our Nancy. He wanted to stay, but he said he had to get the information back to his scientists in Washington D.C. as soon as possible. He said finding a solution to our problem would be his top priority. He said even if New Halchita were destroyed, the information I gave him will help his scientists figure out how to prevent other settlements from meeting a similar fate."

"That's comforting," Mrs. Crane said.

"Mr. Ellinger and the children will be terribly disappointed that the president had to leave so soon," Mr. Goodhue said. "They worked so very hard."

Mayor Lopez groaned and put his forehead down on the table.

"Maybe the president is wrong," Mr. Downes said.

"How could he be wrong?" Mrs. Crane said. "He's got photos of this same Nancy from four other settlements that no longer exist except as a pile of radioactive debris. If she's not a lagamachy, how do you explain it?"

"She just doesn't seem like the type to explode and wipe out thousands of innocent lives," Mr. Goodhue said.

"I always wondered why she had landed in New Halchita, rather than in Washington D.C.," Mr. Downes said. "Remember? I asked her that when we held the inquiry—and she gave a very unsatisfactory answer. But if she's a lagamachy—"

"Exactly, Mr. Downes," Mrs. Crane said. "She's not here on a mission of friendship, or to establish diplomatic relations. We have to kill her."

"Maybe we could talk to her," Mr. Goodhue said, "try to convince her we're not—"

"Mr. Goodhue," Mrs. Crane said, "I always knew you were a soft-hearted old fool, but I never thought I'd see the day when you would want to have a neighborly chat with the lagamachies."

"That's unwarranted, Mrs. Crane," Mayor Lopez said. "Let's keep this civil."

"Civil?" Mrs. Crane said, "are you listening to what Mr. Goodhue is saying? He wants us to *talk* to it. The president told you that as soon as it figures out we know what it is—poof!—we're gone—and Mr. Goodhue wants to *talk* to it—the absolute *worst* thing we could do!"

"It's teaching kindergarten," Mr. Goodhue said. "Does that sound like a lagamachy to you? Maybe Nancy thinks she really is from Mars Experimental Colony #3. Think about it—it has to tell a compelling story, in order to gather information. So whoever made it—they made it think it was this Nancy from Mars, so it could effectively gather information about the target settlement, and it gathers information and transmits that information somehow, and—"

"Oh, please, Mr. Goodhue," Mrs. Crane said. "Do we have to listen to you make up stories? Can we *please* stick to the facts? To what we actually know about it? It's a lagamachy, and if we don't destroy it, it will destroy us."

"Mr. Goodhue may have a point," Mr. Downes said. "My grandson, Isaac, is in her kindergarten class, and he loves her to death. He asked me this morning if he could go back to Mars with her. Maybe we can reason with it."

"I can't believe what I'm hearing," Mrs. Crane said. "Reason with a lagamachy? Have you two lost your minds? Can't you see that's how it works? What better way to gain our trust and insinuate itself into our lives than teaching our children. It's disgusting. Mr. Mayor, we've wasted too much time already. I move that we resolve to kill the lagamachy—or the Nancy or whatever you want to call it—and that we do so as soon as practicable."

"All right," the mayor said. "I second the motion. All in favor."

Two hands went up—and then a third.

"You're such a coward, Mr. Goodhue," Mrs. Crane said.

"Please, councilwoman," Mayor Lopez said.

"How do we know that killing her won't set off the warhead?" Mr. Goodhue said.

"I asked the president that same question," Mayor Lopez said. "He said he couldn't say for sure it wouldn't, but his scientists back in Washington D.C. advised him to tell us that they think killing it is our best chance."

"We're talking about murdering a kindergarten teacher," Mr. Goodhue said.

"A *lagamachy*," Mrs. Crane said, "can't you get that through that thick skull of yours?"

"Who's going to kill her?" Mr. Goodhue said.

"Who's going to kill *it*, Mr. Goodhue," Mrs. Crane said. "I believe as sheriff and commander of the New Halchita City Guard, that task falls to Frank Westfall."

"You really think Sheriff Westfall—*Frank*—is going to walk up to Nancy and shoot her down in cold blood in front of her kindergartners?" Mr. Goodhue said.

"Not in front of the kindergartners," Mrs. Crane said, "don't be stupid. You always have to exaggerate—"

The mayor raised his gavel threateningly. "Civility, Mrs. Crane—everyone—I know this is a difficult situation, but let's be civil—*please*."

"I have to confess Mr. Goodhue has a point," Mr. Downes said. "Sheriff Westfall will be reluctant. He's a good man—a good sheriff—but I always felt he lacked a certain . . . respect for authority . . . that is sometimes necessary for the job."

"Do you believe he'd refuse a direct order from the council?" the mayor said.

"He'd have a lot of questions," Mr. Downes said.

"A lot of questions," Mr. Goodhue said.

"And if he went away unconvinced . . ." the mayor said.

"And word got out . . ." Mr. Downes said.

"Poof," the mayor said.

"It'll have to be someone else, then," Mrs. Crane said.

"Did President Boulderstone tell Postmaster Skint what it is?" Mr. Downes said.

"No," the mayor said, "he only told Postmaster Skint that New Halchita was in danger, but he didn't give him any details."

"Good," Mr. Downes said. "That means we—the four of us—are the only ones who know, and we have to keep it that way. We can't tell anyone else—we can't risk it."

"You're saying one of us has to be the one that kills

her," Mr. Goodhue said.

Mr. Downes nodded.

"I suppose we could draw straws," Mayor Lopez said.

"I'm sorry, Mayor Lopez, Mr. Goodhue said, "but I don't think I could do it."

"Mr. Downes," Mayor Lopez said, "could you . . . pull the trigger . . . without hesitation?"

"I don't know," Mr. Downes said. "A young woman—unarmed? I don't know for sure I could pull the trigger. Maybe if it looked like what I always imagined a lagamachy looked like, I could, but—"

"I'll do it," Mrs. Crane said. "I will do what must be done in order to preserve and defend New Halchita, that is my duty as councilwoman, and I will do my duty, no matter how personally unpleasant I find it."

"Are you sure, Mrs. Crane?" Mr. Goodhue said, "Are you sure you can point a gun at her and shoot her down?"

"I will never hesitate to do what I must for the preservation of New Halchita," Mrs. Crane said, "not for a moment."

"Because if you *do* hesitate," Mr. Goodhue said, "even for a second, that might be long enough for her—it—to detonate the warhead that sends us all—every man, woman, and child in New Halchita—to kingdom come. Just one second of hesitation, Mrs. Crane. If you are going to do this, I want you to look me in the eye right now, and tell me you have *no doubt* that you can shoot an unarmed woman, a kindergarten teacher, without a moment's hesitation. You question Sheriff Westfall's resolve. He's a hero of the Scab War. How sure are you of *your* resolve?"

Mrs. Crane didn't answer right away, nor did she look Mr. Goodhue in the eye.

"Mrs. Crane," the mayor said, "Mr. Goodhue is right.

You have to be certain of this. You can't have the least doubt in your mind as to whether you can do it or not."

"We don't necessarily have to shoot her," Mrs. Crane said. "She has a spritz at Fitz's Apothecary on a regular basis. *It* has a spritz at Fitz's Apothecary. Jesus Christ."

"Are you suggesting we poison her?" Mr. Downes said.

"*It*, Mr. Downes," Mrs. Crane said. "We can tell Mr. Fitz to put something—arsenic—strychnine—both—whatever he recommends—in her . . . in *its* spritz. And it's done."

"She always shares her spritz with Nurse Jim," Mr. Goodhue said. "It would kill him too. For all we know, the poison won't kill *it*—but it'll kill Nurse Jim for sure."

"Damn you to hell, Mr. Goodhue," Mrs. Crane said. "I'm on the council to make the difficult decisions. If you can't make the hard choices, what are you here for? Weren't you the one who told me sacrifice is sometimes necessary? It's easy enough to say when you're talking about someone else's goats, isn't it? Sometimes people have to die. That's the way it is. Your cowardice doesn't make you a better person than me. It just makes you—"

The mayor gaveled Mrs. Crane into silence. "We would have to ask for Mr. Fitz's cooperation," the mayor said, "and between Mr. Fitz and Sheriff Westfall, I think we'd be better off with Sheriff Westfall."

"So we're right back where we started," Mr. Downes said.

"No, we're not," Mrs. Crane said. "I'm sick of you cowards—all of you. You ought to be ashamed of yourselves. I'll do it. I'll shoot her—*it*, Goddamn it, *it*—I'll shoot *it* down myself. And I won't hesitate. And if I do hesitate, and we're all obliterated, at least I won't have to sit here and listen to your bullshit anymore."

Adventures in the Scablands were all fine and good, but there's something about one's own bed, and Spencer Skint was sleeping soundly under a pile of covers—until he wasn't.

"Wake up, Spencer, I want to talk to you."

Skint sat up, keeping the covers wrapped around him. It was too dark in the room to see anything, but he knew from the voice who his visitor was.

"What do you want from me?" Skint said. "An apology?"

"An apology would be nice," Nancy said, "but that's not why I'm here. I want a baby."

"I'm not in the mood just now," Skint said. "Come back later, I'll see what I can do."

"Not *your* baby Spencer, I want Pilar Ramos."

"Then go haunt the Ramoses, not me," Skint said. "And I don't know how things work on Mars, but here on Earth, parents don't give away babies like surplus zucchini—especially not to Martians."

"I know. That's why I need you to steal her for me."

"Steal her yourself."

"I considered that possibility—in fact, that was the plan, initially—but we—my sisters on Mars and I—have concluded that you would be better at stealing a baby than me. And you owe me a favor."

"How do you figure I owe you a favor?"

"Because even after you tried to kill me, I didn't tell the council you brought a Scavenger posing as president of the United States to New Halchita—but if you won't help me, I won't have any reason to continue to keep that information to myself."

"It's too late," Skint said. "The Scavenger has convinced Mayor Lopez that you're a lagamachy. They won't believe a thing you say."

"A lagamachy? That's what the Scavenger told Mayor Lopez? Was that your idea? That's very insightful of you, Spencer."

"They're going to send someone to kill you," Skint said, "probably your friend Frank. Your best bet is to go on back to Mars, quick as you can."

The Martian laughed—a lovely, melodic burble. "You tried killing me Spencer," she said, "and Frank won't have any better luck than you did."

"What are you?" Skint said.

"I'm human, just like you," Nancy said.

"Not like me," Skint said. "If someone had shot *me* in the head, I wouldn't be half so chatty."

"Well, I might have a *little* lagamachy in me," Nancy said, "same circuitry, different mission—but I'm human in every way that matters, and there's a smidgeon of malevolence in all of us, wouldn't you say, Spencer? And that brings us back to you, and how you're going to steal Pilar Ramos for me—or I tell my friend Sheriff Frank Westfall what *you* really are."

"All right," Skint said, "let's say I steal the Ramos baby. What do I do with it? Just hand it over to you, and off you go back to Mars?"

"You will sedate her and put her underneath my ship in the scrap yard. Some time at night, when there's no one there, and at least an hour before the techs show up in the morning."

"Just put her underneath your ship and leave her there?"

"That's all."

"When?"

"Soon."

"And you want her alive?"

"Of course alive. What would I want with a dead baby?"

"I don't know what you want," Skint said, "and I don't want to know. But if I do this, we're square. No more favors."

"Perfectly square," Nancy said. "No more favors."

5 EVERY CITIZEN MUST ATTEND

The president had come and gone without ever seeing the Martian or her ship, and the only thing the council would say about it was that the president had returned to Washington D.C., promising to do everything he could to help New Halchita—and this presumably good news delivered with a face as long as the San Juan River. The town was deeply unsettled, and when, in the emptiness of a cold winter night, the church bells started ringing *every citizen must attend*, no one mistook the sound for a harbinger of good news.

"Is it Scavengers again?" Nancy said.

"What?" Germaine said. Something was happening. She sat up and struggled to free her mind of the cloying tendrils of sleep. Bells.

"The bells," Nancy said, "is it Scavengers again?"

"No, not an attack," Germaine said. "That's the church—church bells."

"What does it mean?"

"Every citizen must attend," Germaine said. She got out of bed and went to the window. She pushed the sash up and the shutters open. The sharp cold and the dismal clang of the bell climbed in through the open window like a couple of thieves.

"Sun's not even up," Germaine said. "This is going to be bad."

Sheriff Westfall stood on the steps of the church with a lamp. Mr. and Mrs. Ramos and their two young boys stood beside him, and every other citizen of New Halchita and most of the children were standing before him. The crowd was quiet—it was too cold, dark and miserable to speak. They knew bad news was coming and they wanted to get it over with.

"Pilar Ramos has gone missing," Frank said. The cold and the wind seemed to take the life out of his voice. "The child is too young to have walked or crawled off on its own. I have searched the house and surrounds myself, as have Mr. and Mrs. Ramos, repeatedly. I believe the child may have been stolen from her crib late last night or earlier this morning. First, if anyone has anything to say that might be helpful—if anyone saw or heard anything last night or this morning that might be helpful—please, speak up now."

Frank waited. The only sound was the wind sawing away at the corners of the church. A cold blast pushed Frank's hat forward, and he pushed it back and set it down more firmly.

"All right," Frank said, "What we're going to do is gather at the South Gate, make a line, spread out, and search every square inch of this town, south to north. That includes houses and businesses. The council has informed me that a warrant to search every home and business would be too general to be lawful, and I won't have any home or business searched without the owner's consent or a lawful warrant. So if there is anyone who objects to having their home or place of business searched, raise your hand now, and I'll get a warrant and we'll search it later."

Frank looked over the crowd. Not a single hand went up—who would dare? "Good," Frank said. "Now let me lay down some rules. No one searches their own property. No one goes into any home or business alone. And obviously, no one comes out with anything that doesn't belong to them—on penalty of exile. Any questions? All right, go home and eat something. It's going to be a long day, and no sense getting started until we have better light. We'll meet back at the South Gate in one hour. Nancy, hold up for one minute."

When the crowd had dispersed, leaving Frank and the Martian alone in front of the church, Frank asked Nancy if she could locate Pilar Ramos, like she had Billy McKay.

"Billy McKay was all by himself, and out in the open," Nancy said. "I won't be able to locate Pilar Ramos unless she's sitting all by herself in the middle of the street somewhere, and if she was, I'm sure someone would have found her already—and she's so small—but when the orbiter is overhead, I'll try."

The upending of New Halchita commenced in earnest at sunrise, and as the sun came up, painfully bright but devoid of warmth, a sense of gloom settled over the searchers, and not all of that gloom was directly attributable to concern for the missing infant or sympathy for her parent's suffering. Poking around in carts and chicken coops, peering down wells and into rain barrels, and crawling under bushes and porches, the good citizens of New Halchita began to feel less like inhabitants than a whole lot of rag-and-bone pickers rummaging through a sprawling, and in the end rather disappointing, refuse heap.

Searching their neighbor's homes produced an altogether different, and even gloomier, effect, as it forced them to entertain unpleasant speculations regarding their friends and fellow citizens—people they'd known their entire lives. To look under a bed or into a pantry was one thing, but to see a large tin bucket by the kitchen door, and realize that only by emptying it out could one be *absolutely* certain that a murdered infant was not secreted beneath the scraps—that was a different matter altogether.

As the circumstances were too disagreeable to encourage idle conversation, little was said during the search. Even so, by the time the citizens had gathered together at the opposite end of town, a consensus had been reached regarding the probable fate of the missing child. Little Pilar Ramos, so the theory held, had been stolen by Scavengers in retaliation for the attack on their camp on the San Juan and the recapture of the Martian's ship. While it was true that Scavengers had, on rare occasions, abducted Civvy children to raise as their own, perhaps the popularity of the theory had more to do with the manner in which it expelled the monster from their midst, than in how neatly it fit the facts of the case.

More than one citizen, concerned that Sheriff Westfall might not reach the obvious conclusion himself, felt obliged to let Frank in on their speculations. Some came alone, others found the courage to express themselves in small groups. A good sheriff, Frank believed, did not discourage citizens from opining on a case—it made them feel like they were helping out, and it was always possible that one day, a citizen might come up with something useful. But Frank didn't think Pilar Ramos had been stolen by Scavengers. For one thing, the city was still on high alert against a retaliatory attack. It was a particularly difficult time for a Scavenger to sneak into town, grab a baby, and sneak back out again, and Scavengers, in Frank's experience, were strongly disinclined to take action under unfavorable circumstances. And even if the Scavengers had decided they just couldn't stand another minute without a Civvy infant to call their own, there were plenty of perfectly lovely toddlers occupying houses nearer the outskirts of New Halchita, whereas the Ramoses lived on Poison Springs Road, practically in the center of town.

So Frank listened respectfully to the citizen's speculations, and thanked them, and to each he said, *well now, that's a thought that hadn't occurred to me.* Among the last to approach Sheriff Westfall in regards to the aforementioned theory of the case was Postmaster Skint.

"Folks are saying Scavengers stole the child," Skint said. "You think that's what happened?"

"Well now," Frank said, "that's a thought that hadn't occurred to me."

"Seems likely to me," Skint said. "I'd give it serious consideration. I understand you gave those Scavengers a bloody nose at their camp on the San Juan. It's not surprising they would find some cowardly way to retaliate." Skint paused to blow into his cold hands and stomp some feeling into his numb feet. "I know we've had our differences," Skint said, "But Sheriff, this business of Scavengers stealing babies—that's something I won't tolerate, and I know you feel the same. If there's anything I can do to help, you just let me know."

"Thanks, Postmaster," Frank said, "I will."

"I sure feel sorry for the Ramoses," Skint said. "To have your child stolen by Scavengers—can you imagine? The child might be alive, and they can take some comfort in that, but to know you'll never see your own flesh and blood again—to know the child will be raised in ignorance and degradation and never know her own mother—that must be awful hard."

"I can't imagine," Frank said.

"Anything I can do," Skint said, extending his hand, "let me know." Frank, through a great effort of will, took his hand, shook it, and then watched as Spencer Skint, hunched up against the cold, hurried away.

Later that afternoon, Mr. Maybrick handed a silver communion platter over to Pastor Craddock. Pastor Craddock did not ask for, and Mr. Maybrick did not volunteer, any information about where the platter had been found. The search also turned up a pair of spectacles belonging to little Eliza Squirrelhunter. They were discovered under a neighbor's porch, where, Eliza would recall, she had once hidden during a game of hide-and-seek. Eliza's parents, who had been searching in vain for the spectacles for almost a month, and the child, who was practically blind without them, were delighted to have them back.

6 OVER A BLACKBERRY SPRITZ

Skint was finishing a late lunch at Mr. Fitz's Apothecary when the Martian sat down next to him.

"What are you doing here?" Skint said.

"I'm meeting Nurse Jim," Nancy said.

"No," Skint said, "I mean, what are you doing *here*—" Skint looked around. Mr. Fitz was in the kitchen, and the place was otherwise empty. Skint lowered his voice "— what are you doing here on Earth? You promised you would leave as soon as you got your . . . package."

"Earth and Mars have to align, Spencer," Nancy said. "I can't just come and go as I please."

"And how long before this alignment?" Skint said.

"Five months," Nancy said.

"No one's tried to kill you yet?"

"So far, just you," Nancy said.

"More's the pity," Skint said.

The bells hanging on the door announced the arrival of Nurse Jim. Skint stood up and put a few coins on the counter.

"You don't have to leave," Nancy said, "I'm sure Jim would love to hear a story or two about your recent adventures in Washington D.C."

"I liked you better when you didn't have a sense of humor," Skint said. He tipped his hat to Nurse Jim on the way out.

"A blackberry spritz, Mr. Fitz!" Nurse Jim said, sitting down next to Nancy. The seat was still warm from Spencer Skint's recently departed posterior. Seeing Nancy and Postmaster Skint in conversation had made Nurse Jim uneasy. Skint had a reputation, and Nancy—she was new to this world, and there were some things she might not understand.

"How is Postmaster Skint doing?" Jim said.

"He's sick to death over the child that's gone missing," Nancy said. "That's all he could talk about."

"Sheriff Westfall will find out what happened," Nurse Jim said, relieved that Skint's conversation with Nancy had been limited to such an unpleasant subject.

"How do you know?" Nancy said.

"Because I know he won't ever give up on her. She'll always be on his mind. It could be days or months or years from now, but sooner or later, he'll hear something or he'll see something and he'll figure it out."

"Perhaps Pilar Ramos has gone to a better place," Nancy said, "where there's no death or pain or sickness."

"You sound like Pastor Craddock," Nurse Jim said. "Personally, I never took much stock in that theory. Anyway, that won't stop Sheriff Westfall from finding out who took her. I can't imagine how someone could be so cruel as to take a child, still nursing, from her mother."

"Mrs. Ramos has two other children," Nancy said.

"I don't think that will make it any easier for her," Nurse Jim said. "I don't think that's the way it works."

Mr. Fitz brought the spritz with the straws sticking out

like antennae, and set it down in front of the young couple with a smile and a wink.

"Have you—" Nurse Jim began—then stopped. He took a long sip of the spritz. "Have you—he stopped again, to cough, wheeze and splutter. "Sorry," he said, when he had recovered, "Some of that spritz went down the wrong pipe. What I was going to say is, have you ever thought about having a family?"

"I have a family," Nancy said. "I have all of my sisters on Mars."

"I mean," Nurse Jim said, "have you ever thought of having a family of your own—here on Earth?"

After a long pause, during which Nancy drained the blackberry spritz to the dregs, she said, "You know, I never thought of that possibility before."

"Now that you've thought of it," Nurse Jim said, "what do you think?"

"I think it's a *very* interesting proposition," Nancy said, "and I will give it serious consideration."

"Well," Nurse Jim said, his face changing from its usual rhubarb-spritz pink to a strawberry-spritz red, "I'm glad you feel that way about it. I'm . . . I'm very, *very* glad you feel that way about it, Nancy. Mr. Fitz! A refill, if you would be so kind!"

7 A WITNESS COMES FORWARD

"Tell Sheriff Westfall what you told me," Gatekeeper Abernathy said. Sheriff Westfall, his hands clasped on his desk in front of him, waited, but the boy didn't speak. "Tom," Mrs. Abernathy said, her voice softening, "you know right from wrong—that's why you told me. You have to tell the sheriff what happened. It'll be all right."

"I saw someone at the scrap yard—"

"Start from the beginning," Mrs. Abernathy said. Tom looked at her. "Start from why you went there," she said.

"Billy McKay told me he found where Mr. Crane had his still out in the Scablands," Tom said. "He hid himself and watched Mr. Crane fill some bottles, and when Mr. Crane went to—to take a pee or something, Billy stole a bottle. He told me to sneak out of my house at night and meet him in the scrap yard and we'd drink some. So I snuck out of the house after midnight and I met Billy and we went to the scrap yard because we figured we could find a place there to hide and drink it. And we got into a busted up scrapride and drank some. And then we saw someone else was in the yard with us. At first, we thought it was you, Sheriff, or one of your deputies come to get us, or Mr. Crane, coming after his stolen liquor, so we sat real quiet and still and we were pretty much hidden anyway. We saw a man with a bundle in his arms, and he—"

"Wait a minute," Frank said, "when was this?"

"Thursday. Real early in the morning. I would have told you sooner. Only—well, Billy McKay said it wasn't any of our business, and he said—he said we didn't see anything anyway, 'cause it was so dark."

Frank did a quick calculation. Today was Monday. Five days. For five days Tom Abernathy hadn't said a word about what he'd seen, because . . . Frank resisted a tremendous urge to leap over his desk, grab Thomas Abernathy by the throat, and choke the life out of him in front of his mother . . . because Billy McKay didn't want to get into trouble.

"I hope you're not cross with me," Tom said.

"I wish you'd told me this sooner, of course," Frank said as calmly as he could, "but I'm glad you're here now. I doubt we'll find Pilar Ramos alive—not after five days—but maybe there's a chance we'll find her, and if we do, that will give her parents a measure of peace—at least they'll know she's not suffering."

Tom Abernathy turned green, and that was okay. Frank hoped the boy would think on this mistake of his from time to time for the rest of his life. It would make him a better man.

"Did you recognize the man you saw in the scrap yard?" Frank said.

"I thought I did but Billy McKay said—"

"Tom," Frank said, the hairs on the back of his neck rising up, "did I ask you what Billy McKay said?"

"No, sir."

"That's right, I didn't. And I don't want to hear the

name Billy McKay come out of your mouth again. Not today and maybe never. Do you understand me?"

"Yes, sir."

"Did you recognize the man you saw in the scrap yard?"

"It might have been Postmaster Skint. But it was dark."

"Was it Postmaster Skint or wasn't it?"

"I don't want to say it was him," Tom said.

"But you think it was him?" Frank said.

Tom looked at the ground and nodded.

Frank's first thought was to call on his deputies to assist him in turning the scrap yard inside out. His second was to bring Spencer Skint into the sheriff's office and turn *him* inside out. In the end, however, Frank concluded that the word of one liquored-up schoolboy who got a glimpse of a man in the dark was something so small and delicate it had to be treated with great care. If you had a dying ember in a little nest of moss, and you wanted to turn that ember into some significant heat and light, a sigh would serve you better than a cyclone.

Billy McKay had missed a lot of school recovering from the tick bite, and when he was healthy enough to go back, he decided he didn't want to. At the request of his mother, and with the enthusiastic blessing of his teachers, the council agreed to let Billy skip his last year and start an apprenticeship at the gun and tool works.

"The Works" as it was called, consisted of two buildings set back from Lancaster Street on a weedy lot opposite the medical clinic. The smaller building served as an office and machine shop, and the larger one as a forge and blacksmith shop. As Frank approached The Works, he heard the regular knock-chocking of the trip hammer. He'd been hearing that sound nearly every time he stepped outside since he returned from the "replevin" of the Martian's ship. It only now occurred to him that he was likely the cause of it. Having left twenty rifles at the bottom of the San Juan River, twenty more would have to be made.

Mrs. McKay was standing just outside the door of the machine shop talking to a young man, Apprentice . . . Frank struggled with the name . . . Spar? Spear? Spare? Sprague? Sprague! that was it, Sprague. Will? Walter? Walden? Walden Sprague. Frank sighed. It got harder every year. And was it just him, or were the names getting weirder?

Mrs. McKay was a square-built woman with gray hair, a high forehead, and a nose that reminded Frank of the handle of a potato masher. She was wearing a white shirt and a ragged deer-hide apron. She had one good eye, blue, and a blind one the gray of an overcast winter evening. The way she told the story, the forge got a bellyache from some bad scrap, blamed her for it, and spit in her eye. Mrs. McKay held a short length of pipe in her hands, and Apprentice Sprague, a tall, curly-haired youth, well-bearded for his age, had his head down, listening to her every word.

". . . fill it up with bone dust," Mrs. McKay was saying. "Make sure the pieces don't touch. You want to keep the pipe red hot for fifteen or twenty . . ."

She stopped and gave Frank a look, cold and sharp. Though the look came from only one eye, Frank saw enough loathing in it for two or three. That surprised him, given the boom in business he was at least partly responsible for—not to mention the fact that he had helped save her son's life not so long ago—though naturally Dr. Perry had gotten all the credit. Regardless of the many reasons she had for being grateful to him, clearly, she wasn't.

"What do you want, Sheriff?" she said.

"Actually," Frank said, "I was looking for Billy."

"He's fitting a *barrel* to the *stock*," she said, in a way that suggested to Frank he was meant to take some special meaning from her special emphasis. "Go on in."

Frank found Billy in the shop, fitting, as Mrs. McKay had said, a gun barrel to a rough wooden stock. The boy had his mother's sturdy frame, his father's broad forehead and narrow chin, and between forehead and chin, his mother's potato-masher-handle nose. Frank watched the boy as he set an oily rifle barrel into a rough-cut stock and then carefully lifted it out. He used a gouge to remove a few oil-stained chips of wood the size of fingernail clippings, and then repeated the process. His work was quick and sure—almost mechanical. Frank didn't want to throw Billy McKay off his rhythm, so he waited for Billy to notice him standing there.

"Hey, Sheriff," Billy said at length, setting his gouge aside.

"How have you been?" Frank said.

"Good," Billy said. He pressed his fingers under his arm where the tick had impaled him a little less than two months before. "Still sore. But I think the work helps. Keeps it loose, you know?"

"I want you to know that I'm not here to make trouble for you," Frank said. "I'm here because I think you may be able to help me find out what happened to Pilar Ramos."

"I don't see how," Billy said.

Frank had decided to keep Tom Abernathy, his ember of hope, out of it for now, and so he had come to The

Works prepared with a little bit of lie. "One of the techs came to see me today," Frank said. "That same night that Pilar Ramos went missing, he went back to the scrap yard early in the morning—had some work there he thought he should cover up against the cold. He told me he saw you and Tom Abernathy walking down the street."

"You think Tom Abernathy and I stole the Ramos baby?"

"Of course not," Frank said. "But maybe you saw something—or someone."

"Well, it wasn't me the tech saw, I was in bed," Billy said, "—didn't get up until I heard the church bell ringing."

"I don't care what you and Tom were up to," Frank said. "You're not in any trouble."

"I told you it wasn't me," Billy said. "Have you asked Tom about it? Maybe it was Tom with someone else."

"Yeah," Frank said, "I asked Tom about it. He said he was in bed, too."

"So it couldn't have been us," Billy said. "Maybe the tech was drunk. Was it Lomo or Eyron? Eyron I'll bet. He drinks some."

"There's one more thing," Frank said, "if you don't mind."

"I'll know if I mind when hear it."

"Has your ma got a beef with me?"

"Yes," Billy said.

"How come?"

"You know how my pa died?"

"Killed out in the Scablands. I heard it was lobos."

"Do you know what he was doing out there?"

"I understand he was looking for scrap iron," Frank said.

"That's right," Billy said, "but not just any scrap iron.

He was looking for scrap iron for gun barrels—and it's not easy to find—maybe it was a hundred years ago, but not anymore. My pa was supposed to be out in the Scablands for a week, and when he didn't come home when he was expected, my ma went looking for him. She had a general idea of where he was headed, and when she got that far, she looked up in the sky and saw buzzards circling a ways off and that's how she found him. There wasn't much left of pa—scattered bones is all. Ma thinks lobos brought him down and the vultures finished off what the lobos didn't care to eat. Near his bones was a sack full of first-rate scrap iron—better than a hundred pounds. Ma put his bones in the sack with the scrap and dragged it all back to New Halchita. Those rifles you left for the Scavengers? Seven or eight of 'em anyway—barrels were made from that scrap my pa gave up his life for."

Billy picked up the oily barrel he was working on and sighted Frank through it. "This one, too," Billy said. "And this is the last. Someone's going to have to go out into the Scablands to find more iron before we can make any more barrels. I'm guessing it won't be you."

"I can see why your ma might be angry with me," Frank said.

"Ma says keeping the ship in the scrap yard won't stop the Scabs from coming after it again. You think the Scabs will come for it, even inside the city walls?"

"I hope not," Frank said.

"Ma says if there is another Scab war, she hopes a Scavenger shoots you with one of those guns you left for 'em."

"The rifles were dropped in the river," Frank said.

"Ma says the Scabs will find every last one of 'em. She's says they'll dry 'em off, oil 'em up, and they'll be good as new."

"I was just trying to get everyone home," Frank said.

"Ma says they could've swum just fine with those rifles slung over their backs. She says it probably would have been quicker to run and swim with those rifles than to take the time to throw 'em down."

"Your ma wasn't there," Frank said.

"Oh, *I* understand perfectly," Billy said, "but Ma . . . she doesn't. You asked, so I'm telling you."

"You're right," Frank said, "I appreciate your being honest with me."

"Then I should tell you that ma says you should have let the Scabs keep the damn ship if they wanted it so bad. She says those rifles were worth more to us than that ship ever was. She says we're going to end up fighting a war over that ship that'll get us all killed. She says it'll be worse than the last Scab war. She says we'll be shot with our own rifles. She says your nose is up there where the air is thin and it's no wonder you can't think straight."

"Thanks," Frank said.

It looked to Frank like a one-handed clock, and that one hand was twitching like a fish in a net. The techs, Lomo, Eyron, and Gweeden, were so spellbound by the motion they didn't notice Frank standing behind them until he spoke, and when he spoke, they jumped as one.

"What is that thing?" Frank said.

"Oh that," Lomo said, but didn't offer any further explanation.

"It's uh," Eyron said, scratching the back of his head. "It's hard to explain, Sheriff. Gweeden made it to settle a bet. What can we do for you?"

Eyron, the old man, had been a tech for as long as Frank could remember. His assistants, Lomo and

Gweeden, were just kids—kids getting married in June. All three of them wore gray jumpsuits, thick gloves, and rabbit-fur hats with ear flaps, and all of them, Frank was certain, were hoping the sheriff wouldn't take an interest in their twitchy one-handed clock. Because of their obvious discomfort, he *was* interested, but he didn't want to get distracted from his purpose by something that had nothing to do with the disappearance of Pilar Ramos. On the other hand, when had anything in New Halchita *not* had something to do with everything else?

"What does it do?" Frank said.

None of the techs answered.

"Eyron?" Frank said.

"It listens, Sheriff, that's all it does. I told Gweeden she could . . . as long as all it did was listen, and didn't make any."

"Didn't make any what?"

"Low frequency electromagnetic waves," Eyron mumbled.

"You're talking about *radio* waves," Frank said.

"I swear it doesn't make any, Sheriff," Gweeden said. "It just listens. Like Eyron said."

"Unhook it or unplug it," Frank said. "Now."

Lomo turned around and pulled two wires apart where they were twisted together, and the twitchy hand fell over like it had been shot dead.

"Eyron." Frank said. The old man looked down at the ground. "The council—they'd send you to the Scablands in a minute if they found out you were playing with radio waves. All three of you. What were you thinking?"

"I swear, Sheriff," Eyron said. "It doesn't make any. It just listens."

"And all that shaking it was doing," Frank said, "does that mean it was hearing something?"

"Yes sir," Eyron said. "But it's not us—it's that ship."

"We think it's the ship," Gweeden said, "we don't know for sure."

"It's the ship," Lomo said.

"And that . . . clock . . . or whatever it is. It doesn't *make* any radio waves," Frank said, "it just listens. You're sure about that?"

"It's a receiver, and I swear it doesn't make any radio waves," Gweeden said.

"Hook it back up," Frank said.

Lomo twisted the wires back together and the hand sprang instantly to trembling life. Frank and the techs watched it for a minute or two.

"What's so weird about it is that it never stops," Lomo said. "We'd been watching it for almost three hours before you showed up, and it never once stopped. And look at it, it's still going. I don't think it ever stops."

"You've been standing here watching it for the last three hours?" Frank said.

All three techs nodded.

"We wondered if it would ever stop," Gweeden said.

"Whatever put it into your head to make that thing in the first place?" Frank said.

"We heard how you happened to find the Martian's ship just by chance," Lomo said. "Well, Eyron said he didn't think it *was* just by chance. I said it was. Eyron bet me it wasn't but we didn't know how to settle it. Gweeden said if the Martian was communicating with her ship by radio, she might be able to catch her at it—especially since the ship was in the scrap yard now. Gweeden made the receiver and I made the batteries for it—"

"Batteries?" Frank said.

"Just little ones, Sheriff, little bottle batteries."

"All right," Frank said, "go on."

"As soon as we hooked them together—well you saw. It doesn't make any sense. Like if I'm talking to you, there's moments of silence—don't look at me like that, Sheriff, you know what I mean. But the ship—it never stops. It's not like she's communicating with her ship, it's like they're connected."

"All right," Frank said, "that's enough." Turn it off."

Lomo pulled the wires apart, and the trembling hand fell dead, again. During the rescue of Billy McKay, Germaine had told Frank that Nancy knew how to communicate with her ship so that the lagamachies wouldn't pay any attention. Still, seeing the evidence of those radio waves, and knowing the lagamachies were up there sniffing around like a pack of lobos—sniffing around for the warm scent of technology—made Frank uneasy—a feeling apparently not shared by the techs.

"Think about what this means, Sheriff," Gweeden said. "If that ship hasn't brought the lagamachies down on our heads, maybe nothing will. Maybe they're all gone. At the very least, I could make a better receiver. There may be other settlements out there already transmitting—trying to contact us. We could set up relay stations in the Scablands and communicate with Washington D.C. directly. We could—"

"Gweeden!" Eyron said, cutting her off sharply. "Sheriff," he said, "If you take this to the council, leave Lomo and Gweeden out of it. Tell 'em it was my idea, and I built it on my own."

"I'm not taking anything to the council," Frank said, "not yet, anyway. But I want you to do something for me—all three of you. I know the scrap yard got searched on Thursday, but I want you three to search it again—every square inch. If you have to take something apart to get inside it, take it apart. And keep quiet about it. If you find anything—*anything*—out of place, or you don't know how it got here, or it just doesn't look right to you, let me know right away."

"Yes, sir," Eyron said. "Are we looking for Pilar Ramos?"

"Like I said," Frank said, "you're looking for anything out of place."

"What about the Martian's ship?" Eyron said. "Do you want us to take that apart, too?"

The hopeful tone in Eyron's voice struck Frank as funny and he had to work to suppress a smile. Still, it was a good question, and Frank didn't have a good answer. What he did have was a recollection of a Scavenger's head rolling around in Mr. Habushaki's bean field, and a kind of vision as to how it might have happened: one of those praying mantis arms snicking out and pinching it off.

"Leave the ship alone for now," Frank said. "But everything else—"

"Yes, sir," Eyron said. "Lomo, Gweeden, let's get to it."

The Martian's ship was crouched down low in the scrap yard. Frank walked around the machine and crawled under it. The Martian had to have a way to get in and out, but if there was a hatch of some kind, Frank couldn't find it. He put his hand on the side of the machine—it felt pebbly and surprisingly warm to the touch. He took his hat off and put his ear against the machine's warm metallic hide, and listened. Nothing.

Frank's next stop was the library, where he found the librarian in conversation with his prime suspect. Mrs. Barlow was sitting behind her desk, Spencer Skint was standing in front of it, and a pile of old books was on the desk between them.

"Oh, Mrs. Barlow," Skint was saying, "you do have a way with words—I guess that comes from being in their company all day long . . . well howdy, Sheriff."

"Bless my soul!" Mrs. Barlow said. "I can't remember the last time I saw you in here, Sheriff Westfall. Now Postmaster Skint—he's a regular—always checks out some books for his trip to Washington D.C., and always returns them in a timely fashion. A librarian's dream."

"If you haven't read Jane Austen by moonlight alone in the middle of the Scablands . . ." Skint shook his head at the impossibility of putting the experience into words.

"So Sheriff," Mrs. Barlow said, "Postmaster Skint was telling me all about President Havek Boulderstone. I told Postmaster Skint the president sounded like a dreamboat. I wished I'd gotten to see him. Did you get to see him? Is he a dreamboat?"

"I got a pretty good look," Frank said, "though he didn't stay for long—and didn't get too close. Maybe you can explain that to us, Postmaster. Did he not like the smell of us?"

"He had his reasons," Skint said. "That's all I'm at liberty to say."

"But Sheriff," Mrs. Barlow said, "what I asked you was, is he a dreamboat?"

"He was certainly an impressive-looking individual," Frank said, "even from a distance."

"I'll tell you what was impressive," Skint said, "—that scraphog he rode. What did you say we should call it, Mrs. Barlow?"

"Hog Force One," Mrs. Barlow said.

"Hog Force One," Skint repeated. "That's a beautiful name for a beautiful machine. I'd give my right arm for a machine like that. Wouldn't you give your right arm for a machine like that, Frank?"

"No," Frank said.

"Well, I would."

"I think you'd have a hard time steering it with just one arm," Frank said.

"Think about if we'd had hogs like that when we were juicers," Skint said. "You, me, and Pete, thundering across the Scablands, not having to walk everywhere 'til our feet were worn to nubs—"

"You'd scare off all the game for twenty kilometers around," Frank said, "and if you didn't starve to death, you'd spend all the money you made juicing on motohol. Wouldn't be much point in that."

"The point would be *fun*, Frank. The point would be *panache*. Do you even know what panache is?"

Frank shook his head.

"That doesn't surprise me one bit," Skint said. "I have to go, Mrs. Barlow. It's getting stuffy in here—I'm finding it hard to breathe."

Skint stomped out of the library, the heel-irons of his boots thunking on the wooden floor of the library like heavy blows of a butcher's cleaver on a particularly tough carcass.

"I think you made him mad," Mrs. Barlow said to Frank, laughing. "Not many people can do that. What can I do for you, Sheriff?"

"When the Martian first got here," Frank said, "I remember Mayor Lopez asked you to put together a report on Mars Experimental Colony #3."

"That's right."

"Was there anything in that report on machines—I mean, what kind of machines they had—how they used them—how they worked—how they communicated."

"There was some material on that subject," Mrs. Barlow said. "Mars Experimental Colony #3 was in large part a mining operation, The 'experiment' was to see if colonists could extract everything they needed from the Martian soil and atmosphere. They had machines that did most of the work—they called them *grubbers*."

"Huh," Frank said. "But nothing about . . . jeez, I don't even know what I'm looking for. I'd like to see that report, if you don't mind."

"I don't mind," Mrs. Barlow said, "but the council's got it. They were supposed to return it to me when they were done with it so I could archive it, but they haven't. No surprise there—they never do. I'll talk to the clerk, he may know what they've done with it. I'll let you know as soon as I've got it back."

"Thanks, Mrs. Barlow," Frank said. "How is Pete doing these days?"

Mrs. Barlow sighed. "No mother wants to see her boy juicing ticks out in the Scablands, Sheriff—especially not all alone. But he's doing fine. That's what he tells me, anyway. And he loves it—loves being out on the Scablands."

"I'm glad to know he's doing all right," Frank said. "I always felt bad about breaking the partnership."

"I wish Pete had given up on it when you did. You ever think about getting married, Sheriff? Having a family?"

"It's crossed my mind," Frank said, "but prospects aren't looking good at the moment."

"Well if you do," Mrs. Barlow said, "promise me you'll let me hold the baby—I don't think I'm going to have any grandchildren of my own."

"Sure thing," Frank said. "Let me know when you have that report."

In the kindergartners' room at the school, the same tiny, idiosyncratic desk-chairs constructed of scrap that Frank himself had once (long ago) sat in were occupied by an equally varied assortment of tiny human beings. A fire was burning in the same stove in the corner, and the walls were still painted with enormous maps of the world, although either the paint had faded considerably, or Frank had forgotten how faded the world was when he was younger. The same big black dot on the map of the North American continent indicated the location of New Halchita. Frank recalled the dot, but only now did he recognize the amusing hyperbole of its circumference.

He stood in the doorway and listened as Nancy read to the children from one of the old books:

A tremulous, sobbing voice was close beside her, and lo! a she-goat with two little kids at her feet. "Wild heights," thought she, "do these creatures climb, but the dam will lead down her kid by the easiest path, for even in the brute creature resides the holy power of a mother's love!" and, turning round her head, she kissed her sleeping babe, and for the first time she wept.

"I don't remember that one," Frank said.

"It's Sheriff Westfall!" a child said in amazement.

Nancy looked up from the book she was reading. "Frank," she said, "I didn't know you were standing there."

"His name isn't *Frank*," one of the children insisted loudly, "it's *Sheriff Westfall!*"

"I'm sorry, *Sheriff Westfall*," Nancy said, "is there something I can do for you?"

"Can I talk to you for a minute?"

"Children," Nancy said, "put your heads down on

your desks."

The children did so immediately, one of them even making rapid snoring noises as an indication of her complete surrender to the will of her teacher. Nancy put the book down on her desk and joined Frank in the hall, standing just outside the door where she could keep an eye on the children.

"Where's Miss Carmen?" Frank asked.

"She's taking a day off," Nancy said, "because, she told me, she never does."

"It looks like you've got them wrapped around your finger," Frank said.

"Exactly the reverse," Nancy said. "They are so much more . . . complex . . . than I ever imagined they would be."

"I take it you didn't have much experience with children on Mars," Frank said.

"No," Nancy said.

"Well," Frank said, "it looks to me like you're figuring it out—and you've earned Miss Carmen's trust—that says a lot. Anyway, the reason I'm here is, it occurred to me you might have . . ." Frank lowered his voice ". . . it occurred to me you might have seen something the night Pilar Ramos went missing."

"I was asleep," Nancy said. "I didn't even hear the church bell ringing until Germaine woke me up."

"But I thought maybe through your ship . . ."

"What I get from my ship is just a whisper," Nancy said, "unless I focus on it, and when I'm asleep—unless there was a major disturbance like when the Scavengers attacked—I wouldn't even wake up."

"And there wasn't anything from your ship that disturbed you, the night Pilar Ramos went missing?"

"No," Nancy said, "nothing. I'm sorry."

"I had to ask," Frank said. "So what happens? in the story, I mean. What's it about?"

"Hanna Lomond and her baby are lost on the mountain," Nancy said. "Hanna can see her village in the valley below, but she can't find a way down—until she sees the mother goat with her babies. She follows them down the mountain, and she and her baby are saved."

"It sounds like a good story for the children to hear right now," Frank said. "I think you might understand children better than you let on."

Frank shut the iron door behind him, and, to the degree he was able, stretched out on the wooden bench. He figured the lockup was the last place anyone would think to look for him. There was hardly one square inch in New Halchita where you could sit and think, and someone wouldn't come along and let you know in one way or another they wished you'd move on, especially if you were the sheriff. Nothing made folks twitchier than a sheriff standing around doing nothing but thinking. Maybe some people could sit and think at the library, but Frank couldn't. The whole building seemed to be telling you to sit there for as long as it took for you to have that brilliant insight you needed—and who could think a decent thought under that kind of pressure?

Ten years ago, Frank would have climbed the rungs to the top of one of the reserve silos and sat up there to be alone with his thoughts. He would have gotten in trouble if he'd been caught, but folks in New Halchita never bothered to look up. The view from the top of the reserve silo (NEW or HALCHITA, either one) was certainly much better than in the lockup. You could see the whole town below—people going about their business, black smoke rising from the forge at The

Works, children playing in the schoolyard—and you could see far beyond New Halchita to the bluffs of the San Juan and the endless expanse of Scablands. The smell up there was better than in the lockup, too. But if someone did happen to look up and see the sheriff sitting on the top of one of the reserve silos, he'd never hear the end of it. And anyway, the thought of being up so high made Frank feel queasy. Funny—the height hadn't bothered him in the least when he was a boy.

Frank closed his eyes. The thought of climbing into Spencer Skint's head was more quease-inducing than the thought of climbing the reserve tower, but if that's what it would take to find Pilar, then Frank would do his best. First, he tried to imagine what Spencer Skint would want with the Ramos baby. Nothing. Next, he tried to imagine the appeal of roaring across the Scablands on "Hog Force One." All right, Frank conceded, it might be fun—if you could forget about how you were wasting your time and burning up motohol for no good reason. But apparently the activity had—what was the word Skint used?—*panache*. Panache, Frank thought gloomily, might also be the reason Germaine had picked Spencer Skint over him. Frank was too rational a man to ignore the obvious, however much it bothered him to accept it. Postmaster Skint was a handsome son-of-a-bitch, and he always dressed sharp, from the hat he wore, always tilted just so, to those massive heel-ironed boots that raised him up so that a man of otherwise average height could be a little bit more.

Maybe he didn't need to climb into Skint's head after all, Frank thought. Why worry about the contents of a man's cranium when what you needed could be found in the construction of his boots?

8 A DAY IN THE LIFE OF SPENCER SKINT

Skint got out of bed shortly before noon, a practice he had long ago instituted as it saved him the effort and expense of breakfast. He dressed and walked down the block to Fitz's Apothecary where he was in the habit of having his lunch. Pastor Craddock, Mrs. Barlow, Mrs. McKay, and Mayor Lopez were, strictly by chance, his dining companions. Despite the fact that he had (as far as they knew) recently returned from Washington D.C. with the President of the United States, none of them seemed interested in having any conversation with him beyond the grunt of acknowledgement they gave him when he hoisted his ass up onto one of the two remaining stools at the lunch counter. Mr. Fitz, in a dirty apron and with his shirtsleeves rolled up, put a plate and a knife and fork in front of Skint and grinned at him—like he always did at everyone, like he found the looks of folks amusing—and this from a short fat guy whose appearance would have been greatly improved if the sparse blond hairs on his head and the dark black fur on his forearms would only agree to swap places.

Scabs might be a bunch of ignorant savages, Skint thought, but at least they knew how to live. Too bad the Civvies at the lunch counter couldn't have seen him three weeks ago, standing up on the bed of a mule with a rifle, the mule being driven across the Scablands at a ridiculous velocity by a half-naked warrior woman who didn't give a damn if she hit a bump that threw him off and broke his neck because the only thing she had on her mind was getting that mule within rifle-range of 500 pounds of hog meat that was raising a respectable cloudwake of red dust as it shot across the prairie like a low-flying hawk on its stumpy (and remarkably capable) legs.

Skint looked at the plate in front of him: trotters, beans, sauerkraut, and a thick slice of bread. Nothing wrong with any of it—Mr. Fitz was a good cook. But something was missing—the story—because there was no story. You are what you eat? Out in the Scablands, you ate the story—literally chewed it up and swallowed it even as it was being told. Skint brought that pig down with one shot and when he and the warrior brought it back to camp, they were heroes, at least for the night. Every Scab in camp sat around the fire cooking a fat-dripping chunk of hog on a stick over the flames while the warrior told the story of the hunt. And not just once—she must have told it a dozen times over, and it got better every time, and everyone had grease dripping down their chins and was drinking sweeka and laughing and when Skint woke up the next morning his head hurt from the sweeka and his ribs from the laughing.

Look at these Civvies. Not a sound out of any of 'em apart from the clatter of knives and forks on their plates. Stick it in your mouth, swallow it, get back to work—that was the order of the day—of every day, in New Halchita—except Sunday, a day set aside for feeling like crap about any fun you might have had during the week.

Skint imagined describing lunch at Fitz's Apothecary to the Scabs: *Well, we climb up on these real tall chairs with round seats and no backs and we sit side by side all facing the same direction with this big flat board in front of us. We're so high up our feet don't touch the ground. A bald man with hairy arms brings us hooves that have been wrapped in cloth and boiled for half a day, cabbage that's been sitting in a pot for so long it's gone bad, boiled beans, and stale bread, and the bald man sets it down in front of us in a heap and we eat it all with knives and forks as fast as we can. What are forks? A panther's got claws, right? Civvies make claws out of scrap metal and use 'em to eat with. Why? So we don't have to touch our food with our fingers. Why? How the hell should I know? What do we talk about? The weather. How the crops are doing. Who's sick and who's dying and who's getting better. But usually nothing—we just eat, quick as we can.*

The Scabs would never believe him. He looked down at his plate. He barely remembered eating, but the evidence, the small, rubbery bones of the trotters and the wet smears of various colors, indicated there had once been a meal there. He put a few coins on the counter and slid off the stool. He saw that some of the Civvies had left and others had taken their place while he was eating and he hadn't even noticed. "Take care, Postmaster," Mr. Fitz said, scooping the coins off the counter and into his palm. Skint smiled and waved at him. Civvies—they were nice enough—and they'd kill him in a minute if they knew what he'd done.

On exiting Fitz's Apothecary, Skint ran headlong into Miss Caroline Tyler. "Postmaster Skint!" she said, as if she was surprised to see him. Skint knew she wasn't. She'd figured out his routine and was waiting for him around every corner now. "I could come over later," she said, "I could bring us dinner."

"Yeah, all right," Skint said. Miss Tyler grinned and blushed like he'd recited a love-sonnet he'd written for her. "Gotta run," Skint said. "No rest for the postmaster in this town."

Skint passed Deputy Rhome on Navarro Road and he tipped his hat to her and she tipped hers to him. He took a quick glance over his shoulder before stepping into Otis' Dry Goods Store. Deputy Rhome was continuing on her way, and as far as Skint could tell, had taken no particular interest in him. The store smelled of soap, vinegar, and lamp oil, like it always did. Mrs. Otis, an old woman who wore a small black bowler hat and had an impressive white moustache, was wrapping up some venison jerky for Pete Barlow.

"Pete." Skint said.

Pete turned around. "Oh, hey there, Postmaster," he said.

"How are the ticks?" Skint said.

"No shortage," Pete said, "and juicy as ever. You thinking about getting back into the business?"

"I do miss it sometimes," Skint said.

"You ever get it into your head to take it up again, I could use a partner," Pete said

"I don't see how you manage alone," Skint said.

Pete left with his jerky, and Skint walked up to the counter, where Mrs. Otis was already counting up the marks she'd made on a scrap of paper, one mark for each stamp she'd sold since the last time Skint came in for his money. When she'd added it all up, she took the money out of the cash register and poured the coins into Skint's open palm. Skint looked at the pile of silver and copper in his hand and was well-pleased.

"Seems like everyone came in and bought a stamp this week," Mrs. Otis said. "Letters of condolence to the

Ramoses, I think."

Skint picked a quarter and nickel out of the palm of his hand and set the coins on the counter. The rest went into his pocket. He put the stump of a finger on the quarter. "I'll take that much venison jerky like you sold Pete just now," he said. He moved the stump over to the nickel "And a nickel's worth of sugar candy." After a moment's thought, he put another nickel on the counter. "And would you write a letter for me—tell the Ramoses how sorry I am about little Pilar?"

"Of course," Mrs. Otis said, taking the money and wrapping up Skint's purchases. "Are you coming back later?"

"Later?" Skint said.

"It's Wednesday," Mrs. Otis said.

Wednesday: Poker Night. Skint was relieved. The trick to surviving life in this Civvy hole was making sure you always had something to look forward to, to take your mind off of the unendurably vacuous present.

"I'll be here," Skint said. The stamp money and the promise of a poker game later that evening lifted his spirits. The question was, what to do to pass the time until the game? Walking down Navarro Road and thinking on the various possibilities, he passed Deputy Rhome going back the other direction. He tipped his hat to her, and she tipped her hat to him. He knelt down and worked the laces of his boots, turning his head to watch the deputy as she went into Otis' dry goods store.

Gatekeeper Elson was engaged in conversation with Deputy Orland when Skint arrived at the North Gate with his fishing rod over his shoulder and his gear in a pack. "Just a second, Postmaster," Mrs. Elson said, but when the conversation was over, Mrs. Elson didn't open the gate, and it was Deputy Orland that approached Spencer Skint.

"Where are you headed, Postmaster?" Orland said.

"Do you see this fishing pole I'm carrying, Deputy?"

"Yes, sir."

"Consider this a chance to put your exquisite training in deductive logic to use. Gatekeeper, are you going to open the gate for me, or do I have to climb over?"

"Do you mind if I look in your pack?" Deputy Orland said.

"Yes I do." Skint said.

"Why is that?" Orland said.

"Because what I have in my pack is none of your business," Skint said. "Gatekeeper, would you open the gate for me?"

Deputy Orland nodded at Mrs. Elson, and Mrs. Elson opened the gate. As the gate closed behind him, Skint looked over his shoulder and caught a glimpse of Deputy Orland intently studying the dirt.

Skint thought about his encounters with the law while he chewed on a strip of the venison jerky he'd brought with him—chewed on it just enough to soften it up where he could bait his hook with it. He came to the conclusion that he was not receiving special treatment. Harassment was most likely being ladled out to everyone in town in equal measure and served a double purpose: to let the lawmen work out their frustration over their failure to find the missing infant, and to make the citizens of New Halchita feel like something was being done about it. It amused (but did not surprise) Spencer Skint to think he and the Martian were the only ones in New Halchita who knew what was really going on. What a bunch of idiots. He cast his line into the waters of the San Juan, let the bait sink, then slowly reeled it back in. After repeating that procedure a few dozen times, his concerns had faded away and he had nothing on his mind more disturbing than various estimations of how much money he would win at the poker game.

Late in the afternoon, Skint felt a tug on his line and gave it a yank to set the hook. The creature on the other end was heavy but didn't put up much of a fight, and Skint had a pretty good idea of what he had caught before he pulled it out of the water—a big green catfish, five pounds and change. He contemplated his catch, the whiskered fish grinning back at him stupidly. Maybe he should bring it home, put it in a wash bucket full of water, and keep it for a pet. He'd call it "Mr. Fitz" for the stupid grin it shared with the apothecary. Or maybe, "Mr. Catfitz." Skint snorted.

The postmaster had brought plenty of catfish home to his mother when he was a boy. His job was to catch them, cut their heads off and gut them, and his mother would do the rest. Fresh catfish, filleted, rolled in cornmeal, and fried—you couldn't get any better eating than that. He recalled how his mother would drop the catfish he had cleaned into a pot of boiling water in order to scald the skin off of them before she filleted them. And the catfish, despite being headless and gutless, would swim around and around in the boiling water right up until their skin started peeling off.

Skint unhooked Mr. Catfitz and threw him back into the river. Too much work. And anyway, the poker game would be starting soon.

Mr. Crane, as usual, brought a jug containing the product of his still and shared it generously. Crane himself, Skint knew from past experience, would consume barely a thimble-full the whole night, no doubt an attempt to get a leg up on the others. It wouldn't work. Mr. Crane had less card-sense sober than a heap of night-soil, and getting liquored up could hardly have hurt his game, and might well have eased the pain of his inevitable and considerable losses.

Mrs. Otis played conservatively—a hard woman to bluff, and if she raised and you didn't have three of a kind or better, you folded. She'd break even or win a little. Stinchcombe wasn't stupid, and he knew the game through and through, but couldn't keep a crease from forming on his brow when he was feeling uneasy about his chances. Mr. Ellinger was the one you had to watch out for—never seemed to be paying attention, always knew exactly what was going on, and could swap out faces like another man might try on a variety of hats.

Skint shuffled, Stinchcombe cut, and as Skint dealt the cards, he mentioned the treatment he'd received from the law when he went on his fishing expedition.

"It's probably because of your big feet," Mrs. Otis said.

Skint finished dealing before he replied. "What do my feet have to do with it?"

Mrs. Otis took a look at her cards, a sip of Mr. Crane's liquor, and a suck on her moustache. "You have to keep this to yourselves," she said. "I heard this from Mrs. Barlow, and she said I had to keep it in strictest confidence. She came in earlier today. You all know her assistant, Miss St. Clair, is sparking Deputy Orland. Well, Miss St. Clair told Mrs. Barlow that Deputy Orland told her that Sheriff Westfall had a print—a good one—a plaster cast of a boot print he got from under a window at the Ramos' house."

Mr. Crane threw a nickel into the pot, and Mr. Ellinger

did the same. Mrs. Otis raised a nickel, and Mr. Stinchcombe folded. "It's a dime to you, Postmaster," Mr. Ellinger said. Skint threw his cards down without knowing what he had.

"And then," Mrs. Otis said, "Well, you must have seen her, Spencer, she came in just as you were leaving the store this morning—Deputy Rhome came in and told me that if anyone wanted to buy shoes or boots, I wasn't to sell 'em, and to let her or the sheriff know right away. I asked her why, and she said she couldn't tell me. So I said I knew all about the print. I said there wasn't any reason to be coy with *me* about it, and she said, all right, I'll tell you, but keep it to yourself. What she told me was, they've been on the lookout for boots of a certain size—boots with heel-irons—a man's most likely, and they had a list, and they were checking alibis and narrowing it down and she thought that by the end of the week, maybe sooner, they'd have it narrowed down enough they could get search warrants for the rest from the council, and when they found those boots, they'd have themselves a baby-killer in the lockup. She said if the kidnapper got wind of it, he might try and buy a new pair of boots and get rid of the ones he was wearing when he stole Pilar Ramos—that's why I wasn't to sell any."

"You ask me," Stinchcombe said, "exile is too good for him. It's been a long, long time since we had a lynching here in New Halchita, but it might be time to resurrect that tradition."

After a couple more hands, Skint stood up, a pained look on his face and his hand on his belly. "I'm sorry, friends," he said, "but I had some trotters at Mr. Fitz's lunch counter, and they just won't keep still. I regret to say I have to call it a night."

"Now hold on there one minute, Spencer," Mrs. Otis

said. She got up from the table and disappeared behind the store counter.

"Mrs. Otis—" Skint said.

"One minute," Mrs. Otis said, "and don't you dare run off."

Mrs. Otis reappeared holding a small round tin, which she handed to Skint. "Dandelion tea," she said. "Just steep a tablespoon in one cup of hot water for five minutes. It's a guaranteed cure for biliousness."

"That's very kind of you, Mrs. Otis," Skint said. "Now I really have to go—these trotters are headed for one exit or the other. You all will have to wait for your fleecing until next week."

Skint walked out into the night, keeping his head down and his sideways glances furtive. As far as he could tell, he wasn't being watched or followed, still, it was a relief to get off the street and into his house—but the feeling didn't last long. Miss Caroline Tyler was waiting for him, and she wasn't happy.

"I've been here for two hours, Spencer," she said, "did you forget about me?"

"Of course not," he said. He handed her the tin of dried dandelion blossoms. "I got this for you."

Caroline opened the tin and sniffed it. "What is it?"

"Dandelion tea," Skint said. "Mrs. Otis said it was your favorite."

"She told you it was my favorite?"

"Yeah. I knew I was going to be late, so I stopped by Otis' Dry Goods to get a present for you, and Mrs. Otis told me you were crazy about dandelion tea."

"She must have been thinking of someone else," Caroline said.

"Is that right?" Skint said. "The old biddy must be

losing her mind. I'll take it back tomorrow morning and get you something else."

"Don't do that," Caroline said. "I like dandelion tea all right." She set the tin down on the kitchen table and looked around for Skint, but he wasn't in the kitchen anymore. She found him in the bedroom, half under the bed.

"What are you looking for?" she said.

Skint didn't come out from under the bed, but a wire potato scoop, a duck call, and a pair of leather leggings did.

"Goddamn it!" he said. He pushed himself out from under the bed, stood up, and brushed the dust off of his shirt and pants. "Why are you standing there? Didn't you say you were going to bring dinner?"

"It's in the kitchen—I need to warm it up."

"So go on, warm it up," Skint said. Caroline didn't move.

"What is it?" Skint said.

"What are you looking for?" Caroline said again.

Skint looked at the woman standing in front of him—considered the possibility that she could be his savior. Wondered what that would cost him, in the long run. Decided that if he was going to have any hope of having a long run, he needed her.

"Your old man," Skint said. "He wouldn't happen to have a pair of old boots he doesn't wear anymore?"

"You want a pair of my father's old boots?"

"The ones I've got stink to high heaven. Can't you smell it? Six weeks in the Scablands, and I can smell every day of it. I thought I had an old pair around here somewhere, but I must have got rid of 'em. So . . . do you think he might have some old boots he wouldn't miss?"

"I think so. I can bring them to you tomorrow."

"I think you better bring them to me tonight," Skint said, "I want to throw the ones I've got on in the fire before they stink up the whole house, and the floor's too cold to be walking around barefoot. I'll catch pneumonia."

"It's dark."

"There's moon enough to see. And you know the way."

"I'd have to wake up my father—"

"You don't have to wake him up, just get the boots and bring them to me. Is that too much to ask?"

"No."

"Then why are you looking at me like that?"

"Mrs. Barlow came into the bakery today," Caroline said. "She said she'd heard that Sheriff Westfall was looking to match a pair of boots to a print he'd found under a window at the Ramos' house."

"So what are you saying?"

"Why do you want my father's old boots?"

"Are you dim? I just told you the ones I'm wearing stink."

"Are you the one that took Pilar Ramos?"

"Jesus Christ, woman," Skint said, "don't even joke about a thing like that. You could get me exiled—or worse. If folks start thinking I was the one who took Pilar Ramos, they're likely to string me up. Is that what you want—to see me swinging from a rope?"

"You don't have to be mean—"

"You accuse me of stealing a baby and *I'm* the one being mean? Tell me one thing, Caroline. What in the hell would I want with the Ramos baby?"

"I don't know."

Skint snorted. "Well there's a surprise," he said. "You don't know. You don't know much, do you? If you don't want to get me your father's boots, that's fine. Forget I asked."

"I'll get them for you," Caroline said.

"All right then," Skint said. "I appreciate it. And I'm sorry I was cross with you. I'm just tired and hungry. Get me those boots and we'll have a nice dinner together. And do me a favor, babe—don't let your pa know you took them for me. I can't afford to buy myself a new pair just now, and to tell you the truth, I'm ashamed of it. I don't want my future father-in-law thinking I'm a beggar."

Caroline Tyler walked outside into the night, and in the light of a half-moon, made her way along Possum Race Road. It was cold and quiet and she could see her breath in the moonlight. As she passed Fitz's Apothecary, she saw something move out of the corner of her eye, and turning to look she saw—maybe—a man in the shadow of the apothecary awning. She headed up Navarro Road, quickening her pace. The warm yellow of lamplight shone in the window of Otis' Dry Goods, and even from the other side of the street, Caroline could hear voices and laughter coming from inside the store. After a moment's consideration, she crossed the street and knocked on the door, silencing the occupants. She knocked again.

Mrs. Otis opened the door, very slightly. "We're closed, honey," she said. "This is a private party."

"I don't mean to bother you," Caroline said, "I was looking for Postmaster Skint. He said he would be here tonight and there's something I need to tell him."

"Well, come on in," Mrs. Otis said, opening the door wider. "It's freezing out here."

Caroline stepped into the store and Mrs. Otis closed

the door behind her. Mr. Crane, Mr. Ellinger, and Mr. Stinchcombe were all sitting around a table with cards in front of them and a pile of coins in the middle.

"Postmaster Skint was here a little while ago," Mrs. Otis said, "but he wasn't feeling well—said he had some trotters for lunch that didn't sit well with him—so he went on home. I'm sure you can find him there, if you need him."

"You don't play poker, do you?" Mr. Crane said, "We've got an empty chair."

"I'd love to play a hand or two, Mr. Crane," Miss Tyler said, "but not tonight. Thanks, Mrs. Otis, I'll find Postmaster Skint at home."

"You tell him we hope he's feeling better," Mrs. Otis said.

"I will," Caroline said.

"I sent him home with a tin of dandelion tea," Mrs. Otis said. "You get some of that into him, and he'll feel better."

"I'm sure Miss Tyler has ways to put the pink back into a man that are far more effective than dandelion tea," Mr. Crane said.

"You be quiet," Mrs. Otis said. "you're embarrassing the poor girl."

Not daring to light a candle, Caroline groped around in the closet in her parent's bedroom while her mother and father engaged in a duet, or perhaps more accurately, a duel, of snores. She found one boot and then another, and took them to the kitchen where she lit a match in order to take a look at them. Relieved to discover they were indeed a matching pair of her father's old boots, she put them in a basket, covered them over with a cloth, and set out for Spencer Skint's house on Possum Race Road.

She took her time, as she wanted to consider her position carefully before handing the boots over to Skint. She entertained no doubts as to the real reason he wanted them, but refused to allow herself to speculate on the whys and wherefores of Skint's kidnapping of the Ramos baby—there would be time for that later. At the moment, she had a more urgent matter on her mind. Skint liked to throw around words like "future father-in-law," but that was a distraction, and she knew it. Recently she had gotten a feeling, confirmed by a visit to Dr. Perry (awkward, but necessary), that the time for idle talk was over. She had been planning to inform Skint of the news that very evening, and had been concerned about his response. He was such a free spirit—that was one of the things she loved about him. She had been afraid he might go so far as to suggest he wasn't the father, but that was when all she had on him was his baby in her belly. Now that she had his fate in a basket, she liked her chances. She liked them a lot.

A figure approached her on Possum Race Road. She thought it might be Spencer, concerned about her, coming to meet her, but as she got closer, she saw it was Deputy Orland.

"Miss Tyler," he said, "I'm sure you know that to be on the street this time of night without a lantern is a violation of the law—and dangerous. You might be mistaken for a Scavenger raider, and that's a good way to get yourself shot."

"I'm sorry, Deputy," Caroline said, "there was so much light from the moon tonight it hardly seemed necessary—and I don't see you carrying a lantern either."

"You've got me there, Miss Tyler," Deputy Orland said, "but it's allowed—for officers of the law—under certain circumstances, for example, during clandestine observation of a suspect. I'll need to take a look in that basket you're carrying, Miss Tyler."

Caroline turned and delivered a kick to the deputy's chest that caused him to complete one full backwards somersault and most of another. She switched the basket from her right arm to her left, and closed on Deputy Orland. The deputy, too dazed by the blow for strategic thinking, made the mistake of getting to his feet before he was fully prepared to defend himself, and Caroline caught him with a right hook that knocked him senseless. Sheriff Westfall, watching the proceedings from the shadows of the awning of Fitz's Apothecary, recalled, perhaps belatedly, that the blue ribbon he had placed around Miss Tyler's neck two years ago at her citizen class graduation ceremony was for excellence in the hand-to-hand combat exercises.

Having dealt with Deputy Orland, and suspecting that he was not the only officer of the law in the neighborhood that night, Caroline took off at a run. Deputy Rhome shot out from between two houses on Possum Race Road and connected with Miss Tyler directly in front of Fitz's Apothecary, impacting Miss Tyler with enough force to lift her clean off her feet, and the two of them landed on the street with one thud and two grunts. It took considerable effort on the part of Deputy Rhome and Sheriff Westfall to subdue and handcuff Miss Tyler, and in the process, Westfall came to the conclusion that if there were an award for cursing, Miss Tyler would have another blue ribbon to add to her collection.

Deputy Orland had recovered his senses enough to sit up, and he pointed at Skint's house down the road and called out to the sheriff. Frank looked up. A thin, gray-blue curl of smoke was rising from Skint's chimney.

Frank left Miss Tyler in the care of Deputy Rhome, and helped Deputy Orland to his feet. The two of them ran down the road and up the steps to Postmaster Skint's front door. All their yelling, pounding, and kicking at the door was for naught—clearly, the door was barred on the inside, and short of a battering ram, they would not gain admittance unless Skint let them in, which seemed unlikely—at least, not before he had burnt his boots to ashes.

Orland and Westfall were catching their breath after a particularly fierce and entirely useless assault upon the door, when Mr. Fitz, carrying a lantern, walked up the steps.

"May I?" he inquired.

The officers stepped aside. Mr. Fitz walked back down the steps and about twenty paces further back. He set his lantern down, crouched and sprang, becoming a regular cannonball of a man. He flew up the steps and turned at the last moment so that his shoulder impacted the door rather than his head. The door, with a horrible creak and crack, gave way. Mr. Fitz rolled inside, Deputy Orland and Sheriff Westfall following close behind.

Postmaster Skint was sitting in a chair in front of his stove. He looked up. "Was that you knocking?" he said. "I thought it was the wind."

A sizeable crowd, many carrying lamps, had gathered in the street by the time Sheriff Westfall, Deputy Orland, and Postmaster Skint emerged from Skint's house. Skint was in handcuffs, and Sheriff Westfall, with a tight grip on Skint's arm, led the postmaster in the direction of the sheriff's office. Deputy Orland followed behind, carrying, on a dinner plate, a double-helping of charred boots with extra-heavy heel-irons.

9 A DEAL IS STRUCK

Citizens started gathering outside the sheriff's office in the morning, and by mid-afternoon, the crowd was taking on the look and feel of a mob. Mr. Delgado worked his way through them, ignoring the growls and grumbles directed at his person. There was something about mobs and light. Chances were they'd do nothing *but* growl and grumble, as long as the light of the sun was shining down on them—but come nightfall—that was a different matter altogether.

Sheriff Westfall let Mr. Delgado into the lockup with Spencer Skint, and left the lawyer alone with the postmaster. Mr. Delgado and Spencer Skint spoke in low voices and whispers for the better part of an hour before Mr. Delgado called to the sheriff to let him out.

In the front office, Delgado studied the charred remains of Skint's boots on Sheriff Westfall's desk. Clearly, the lawyer thought, this display was meant for him—meant to shake his faith in the innocence of his client. Delgado decided he'd disabuse Sheriff Westfall of the notion that he could be intimidated so easily. "If this case should come before the council," Delgado said, "and

I say *if* and not *when*, I will object to this method—if I may even call it a method—of maintaining evidence."

"That's not evidence," Sheriff Westfall said, "that's what's left of a pair of boots Postmaster Skint tried to burn up in his stove."

"I couldn't have said it better myself," Delgado said. "I'm pleased you feel that way about it." But in fact, the Sheriff's apparent disinterest in the boots made Delgado feel uneasy, rather than pleased.

"I want to see this . . . this cast you have of a . . . what you think is a boot print," Delgado said, "and I want to know exactly where and when you found the print, and what procedure was followed in the making of the cast, and who, if anyone, was witness to the making of the cast, and how the cast has been stored and handled since it was made."

"I'm afraid I don't follow," Sheriff Westfall said. "What print? What cast?"

"It's common knowledge," Delgado said, "that you have a cast, allegedly a boot print, that you found under a window at the Ramos' house, and you think—"

"I'm afraid you've been misinformed," Frank said. "I didn't find any boot print outside of the Ramos' house, or anywhere else, for that matter. And I certainly don't have any cast."

"Then may I ask on what basis you have arrested and imprisoned my client?"

"I have a witness," Sheriff Westfall said, "who believes he saw Postmaster Skint carrying a bundle in the vicinity of the scrap yard on the night Pilar Ramos went missing."

"I would like to speak to this witness," Delgado said.

"No," Sheriff Westfall said.

"As you very well know, Sheriff, the law permits me to question any witnesses prior to the case being brought before the council."

"You would be right, Mr. Delgado," Sheriff Westfall said, "if my witness was going to appear before the council—but he isn't. He was, by his own admission, drinking at the time, and it was dark, and he's not even certain that the man he saw was Postmaster Skint, or that the bundle the man was carrying was a baby, much less Pilar Ramos. You would tear him to shreds on the witness stand. I have no intention of asking him to testify before the council."

"If you have no print, and you have no witness to call before the council, then I have to wonder on what basis you feel you can keep Postmaster Skint in your lockup."

"As *you* very well know, Mr. Delgado, I am allowed to hold a suspect for up to forty-eight hours," Sheriff Westfall said, "and my witness, regardless of whether or not he will testify before the council, and your client's attempt to destroy evidence, or what he clearly believed was evidence at the time, is adequate grounds for suspicion."

"And you believe that in the next . . . thirty-four hours, you will find sufficient evidence—actual, real evidence, as opposed to rumors and drunken ramblings—to bring my client before the council on a charge of kidnapping?"

"No," Sheriff Westfall said, "what I believe is that in the next *four* hours, your client—Postmaster Skint—is going to give me a full confession."

"I would very much like to be present when that confession is given," Delgado said.

"Come back in four hours," Sheriff Westfall said.

"If you don't mind, I think I'll wait here," Delgado said.

"Suit yourself," Sheriff Westfall said.

There was a bench along one side of the office, and

Delgado sat on the bench and fidgeted. He was not a man used to doing nothing. "What do you plan to do about Miss Tyler?" Delgado said.

"She's under house arrest," Sheriff Westfall said.

"Yes, I know," Delgado said, "I spoke to her earlier. Do you plan to press charges?"

"She cracked my deputy's rib. You bet I'm pressing charges."

"What if she pleads guilty. Apologizes to your deputy. Does six months community service. Would you and your deputy find that acceptable?"

"What kind of community service?" Sheriff Westfall said.

Delgado thought about it. "She'll teach a refresher-class in hand-to-hand," he said, "for your deputies and anyone else you think might benefit."

"I have to admit," Frank said, "I'm inclined to like the idea. It has a certain symmetry to it, and I'm sure Deputy Orland would find the opportunity to take a swing or two at Miss Tyler quite therapeutic."

"I'm afraid that's out of the question, Sheriff. Miss Tyler's role would be instructional only. She herself will not participate in any sparring."

"You're telling me that the woman who cracked my deputy's rib can't take a punch?"

"I can consult with Dr. Perry, but I believe she will agree with me. Given Miss Tyler's . . . medical condition . . . I think such activity would be inadvisable."

"Medical condition?"

"Miss Tyler recently discovered she . . . well, as I said, she has a medical condition that, while not serious, would certainly preclude any physical combat training."

"I see," Frank said. He looked towards the lockup. "Does Skint know about Miss Tyler's medical condition?"

"At Miss Tyler's request, I informed him. Are the terms of Miss Tyler's probation acceptable?"

"You recommend it to the council," Frank said. "If they're agreeable, I'll go along with it."

"What about Deputy Orland?"

"I'll see to it that he goes along as well."

"Thanks, Sheriff. Say—have you got anything to read around here?"

Sheriff Westfall supplied Mr. Delgado with a stack of old case files, and Mr. Delgado, to his surprise, discovered he quite enjoyed reading through them, as he was reminded of cases he had defended before the council, and he found the reliving of old victories, and even defeats, a pleasant way to pass the time.

Around a quarter to seven, Delgado was alerted by the sound of jangling keys that Sheriff Westfall was no longer at his desk. He looked up to see the sheriff at the lockup, the iron-barred door wide open.

"You're a free man," Sheriff Westfall said to Spencer Skint. "Go on, get out of here."

"Are you saying you won't be pressing charges against my client?" Delgado said.

"As you pointed out earlier," Sheriff Westfall said, "I have no real evidence against him, and to my surprise, he hasn't confessed."

Skint, in his stocking feet, stood up and walked out of the lockup. He made his way to the door, but before he opened it, he looked out of the window.

"What about them?" Skint said.

"Who?" Sheriff Westfall said.

"The ones standing out there who would like nothing better than to see me swinging from that old oak tree outside the library."

"The people have a right to peaceably assemble,"

Sheriff Westfall said.

"And you have a duty to protect my client from violence," Delgado said.

"If the crowd should become violent," Sheriff Westfall said, "I'll certainly do all I can to restore the peace and protect your client."

"There must be two hundred citizens out there," Delgado said, "where are your deputies?"

"Deputy Orland is in the clinic with a cracked rib," Frank said. "Deputy Rhome is keeping an eye on the Tyler residence to make sure Miss Tyler doesn't violate her house arrest. And Deputy Soon—I gave him the day off today—I think he's gone on a hunting trip into the Scablands with some friends of his. I'm afraid it's just us, Mr. Delgado. We'll have to hope for the best. Postmaster—good luck."

Sheriff Westfall opened the door. The mob outside, on getting a glimpse of the postmaster, let out a savage cry and surged towards the door. Sheriff Westfall pulled his gun and fired a shot into the air. "Back off!" he yelled, and the crowd backed away from the door—but not far.

"Go on, Postmaster," Sheriff Westfall said to Skint, "you can't stay here. As your lawyer has made abundantly clear, I've got nothing to hold you on."

"Shut the door, Sheriff," Skint said. "Let's talk."

"Mr. Skint," Mr. Delgado said, "I strongly advise you to say nothing."

"I said I want to talk," Skint said. "What's the offer?"

Sheriff Westfall closed the door. "Tell me what you did with Pilar Ramos, and I'll get you out of town."

"You're talking about exile," Delgado said. "That's practically a death sentence."

"That's the deal," Sheriff Westfall said, "and if your client wants to take it, I'd advise him to start talking. The darker it gets, the hotter those folks outside are going to get—and that door isn't even locked."

"You swear you'll get me to the Scablands if I tell you what happened to Pilar Ramos," Skint said.

"You have my word that I'll do my best," Sheriff Westfall said.

"I took Pilar Ramos," Skint said. "I took her to the scrap yard and left her under the Martian's ship."

"Why?" Sheriff Westfall said.

"The Martian told me to. She took over my mind. I couldn't help myself. It was like I was watching myself do it, and I wanted to stop, but—"

Sheriff Westfall opened the door a crack.

"She blackmailed me," Skint said.

"What did the Martian do with the baby?"

"I don't know. You'll have to ask her."

"And Pilar Ramos was alive—"

"She was fine when I left her under the Martian's ship. I gave her a little ticktox so she wouldn't cry. She was asleep."

Frank closed the door again.

"What does the Martian have on you?"

"She knows I've never been to Washington D.C. to see the president."

"If you've never been to Washington D.C., who have you been delivering the council's letters to?"

Skint snorted. "The Scabs, Sheriff, who do you think?"

"Sheriff," Mr. Delgado said, "that confession was given under duress. I'll insist that the council throw it out. Hell, I'll—"

"Don't be dim," Skint said, "There won't be any trial before the council. That mob will string me up the minute I step out the door. If you want to help me, do what Sheriff Westfall tells you to do."

"As you wish," Mr. Delgado said. "Sheriff, I believe my client has fulfilled his part of the bargain. Please tell me how you intend to get him past the mob."

"You've never been to Washington D.C." Frank said to Skint.

"Nope," Skint said.

"Sheriff—" Mr. Delgado said.

"All right," Frank said. "Mr. Delgado, you'll have to go to the North Gate. Deputy Soon will be waiting there for you. Tell him we're ready for him to ring the bell."

Sheriff Westfall opened the door just long enough and wide enough for Mr. Delgado to step outside. The mob wasn't happy to see him—there were more than a few who would have enjoyed beating the tar out of a man who would defend a baby-killer—but from inside the office, Sheriff Westfall and Postmaster Skint could hear Mr. Delgado speaking in that stentorian voice of his that had served his clients so well in the council chambers, and when he said that in this particular case, he had concluded that lynching Spencer Skint was an act of mercy, and he meant to purchase a rope from Otis Dry Goods and return with it instanter, he was sent on his way with cheers of approval.

"Mr. Delgado is a brave man," Skint said.

Frank didn't reply—he was too busy wondering if there would be any negative consequences to shooting Skint down right there in the sheriff's office, or pushing him out the door and letting the mob take care of him.

"Hey, Sheriff," Skint said, "you remember when you and me and Pete used to work together? Before I became postmaster and you became sheriff. The three of us were making a pretty good living as tick-juicers. You remember that?"

"I remember," Frank said.

"That was the life, wasn't it? You remember that time we were way out in the Scablands and I went missing—didn't come back to camp until the next morning. You were awful pissed at me—told me you thought I was dead. I never did tell you what happened to me."

"I take it you're going to tell me now," Sheriff Westfall said.

"I got caught by Scavengers," Skint said. "A young kuzzer by the name of Wayd informed me that Postmaster Larkin wouldn't be returning to New Halchita. He said when the council asked for someone to take his place, I was to step up. I told Kuzzer Wayd I didn't want the job. He said if I didn't take it, he'd kill me and my tick-juicing friends the next time he saw any of us out on the Scablands."

"So you're saying you saved my life," Frank said, "and Pete's too."

"I'm saying I never had a choice as to how things worked out for me. But things are working out for you just fine, aren't they? Now that I think about it, it's funny how things have worked out so perfect for you. You've gotten rid of me, and you've got Germaine all to yourself. You made a mess of that, but now you've got plenty of time—"

The North Gate bell started ringing, and the vengeful feelings of the mob outside succumbed to training and the instinct for self-preservation. Defending the town from a Scavenger attack was the necessity of the moment, and they ran for their posts, vowing to return and finish off Spencer Skint as soon as they had dealt with the Scabs.

"In about ten minutes," Frank said, "Deputy Soon will tell folks it was a drill and they can go on home. I wouldn't advise trying to get out of town any sooner—

you will most likely get shot down by the city guard. Wait until the drill is called off, and if you're lucky, you'll get a half-hour head-start on any that take it into their heads to chase after you."

"You wouldn't happen to have an extra pair of boots you could loan me," Skint said. "I don't particularly relish the prospect of running through the Scablands in my stocking feet."

"In case you ever did save my life," Sheriff Westfall said, "these boots make us square." He opened the bottom drawer of his desk and pulled out a beat-to-death pair of old boots and tossed them to Skint.

"My old boots!" Skint said. "You son-of-a-bitch—you stole my old boots—when I went fishing, didn't you? You broke into my house and—"

"Just so you know," Sheriff Westfall said, "the next time I see you—here in New Halchita or in the Scablands or anywhere else, I'll kill you. Now shoo."

10 THE SACRIFICE

Frank figured Dr. Perry would take Nancy to the clinic with her like she did the last time the North Gate Alarm was rung. If the Martian was there, he'd arrest her, take her to the lockup, and ask her what she'd done with Pilar Ramos. It was possible Skint had made it all up—but what kind of lie was it where you confessed to aiding and abetting Scabs, kidnapping a baby, and handing it over to a Martian? And anyway, Skint's story—it just fit. Lies, in Frank's experience, had a shoe-horned-in feel about them, but Skint's story slid into the known facts of the case (admittedly few) like a cartridge into the chamber.

He had a lot of questions for the Martian, but the important one was, was the child still alive? Frank wasn't optimistic on that score. He pulled his revolver, pushed out the cylinder, and made sure it was loaded. He was sure it was, but you could never be *too* sure. He holstered his gun. Not that he expected any resistance from the Martian. She didn't strike him as the arrest-resisting type.

Frank heard a gunshot, and another, and another. Not a rifle, and not as far away as the city wall—closer than that—almost right in front of him. He ran—loped—at his very best speed to the clinic. Inside, he was met with a sight he could not, at first, comprehend. Nancy and Nurse Jim, in a bloody heap on the floor of the waiting room. Dr. Germaine Perry, on her knees beside Nurse Jim, her hands on his chest, pressing down on him, his blood oozing—bubbling—up between her fingers. His eyes were open, and he was breathing, every breath a horrible, screeching gasp, a sound like a rusty nail getting wrenched out of an old board. And standing over them, Mrs. Crane, an enormous revolver in her wrinkled little hand, smoke curling up from the barrel.

Mrs. Crane turned towards Frank, the barrel of the gun she held turning in the same direction as her attention. She was now pointing it directly at his navel. "He got in the way," she said. She sniffed a couple of times. The black powder smoke that hung in the air was making her nose run. "I only meant to kill the lagamachy, but Nurse Jim wouldn't stand aside. He didn't understand, and I didn't have time to explain. We all have to make sacrifices, isn't that right, Sheriff?"

"Put the gun down," Frank said.

"You don't have to worry about that," Mrs. Crane said. "I'm done shooting. Here, you can have the gun. Take it." She jabbed the gun towards Frank. Frank wasn't sure whether the action was meant as an offer or a threat, but her finger, so deformed and thickened with arthritis that Frank had to wonder how she had gotten it inside the trigger guard in the first place, was still on the trigger. Frank grabbed the barrel and turned the gun so it was no longer pointed at his innards or anyone else's. The gun fired as he twisted it around, but Frank was prepared for that and held on until he managed to twist it out of Mrs. Crane's grip. He dropped the gun and gave it a push with the toe of his boot, sending it spinning across the floor.

"I believe you've broken my finger, Sheriff," Mrs. Crane said, looking at the curious slant of her index finger. "There was no need for that. I told you I was done shooting."

Frank knelt down next to Dr. Perry. "What can I do?" he said.

Before Dr. Perry could answer, the building shuddered in a manner that Frank found completely inexplicable, as if someone had struck the side of the clinic with a sledgehammer. The building shook again, more violently than before, and the front half of the Martian's ship appeared quite suddenly when it punched through the wall. The building continued to shake as the thing twisted and turned in an effort to work its way further into the clinic through the hole it had made. It stopped momentarily to reach out with one of its mantis-like arms for Nancy's body, but fell short by inches, and then continued to squirm its bulk further inside. Frank stood up, pulled his revolver and fired two shots at the ship. The ship recoiled from the impact of the bullets, then grabbed a clawful of rubble and flung it at the sheriff, the debris striking Frank with enough force to send him sprawling. With one more effort, accompanied by an ominous groaning and trembling of the structure of the clinic, the machine pulled itself close enough to Nancy to latch onto her shoulder. It backed out the way it had come in, dragging Nancy's lifeless body along behind it.

11 THE GRAVEDIGGER'S SHOVEL

Frank went for a walk in the thin cold rain. Walking helped him think, and right now, he needed all the help he could get. He'd been "invited" to answer questions at an inquiry before the council on Monday. They would have held it sooner, but getting Nurse Jim into the ground took precedence.

Frank had spent a lot of time—all night, in fact—answering questions before an imaginary council in an imaginary inquiry. It hadn't gone well, and Frank suspected the flesh-and-blood council would be even less sympathetic to his claim that he'd done what he thought was right at the time.

The rain added haziness to the gray morning light and sogginess to the soft earth underfoot. Lost in thought, Frank had come to the greenest and most fertile plot of land in all of New Halchita. It occurred to him that he hadn't visited his parents in quite some time, so he decided, being in the neighborhood, he'd stop by and say hello.

His father, a silly, gentle, man, who worked his whole life as a clerk for the council, had died three years ago at the age of fifty, sixteen years after a terrible beating he had received at the hands of an ugly toxsucker by the name of William Sebastian. Frank believed it was the beating that killed his father—it had just taken a while. He recalled the matter-of-fact way his mother had told Pastor Craddock to reserve the plot next her husband's. She was buried in that plot a year later.

Frank stood in front of the headstones that marked the location of his parents' remains and took off his hat. "I don't know if I should have let Skint go," he said. "I gave him my word, and I never cared for vigilantes. But now I'm wondering if I should have let the mob have him—a confessed spy and baby-snatcher—what could they have done to him that *wouldn't* have been justice?"

Frank waited, but he would get no advice from the great beyond. He walked over to where Mr. Love, the gravedigger, was poking at the earth with his shovel. Mr. Love was the oldest citizen in New Halchita. Years ago, he had been a tall, thin man. He was no longer tall, but still thin. He wore a black hat, a long black coat, and black pants tucked into black boots that came up to his knees. He wasn't yet digging in earnest, rather, he was using his shovel to mark out a rectangle of appropriate dimensions. When he noticed the sheriff standing near him, he stopped his labors and straightened up as much as his bent frame would allow.

"I hope you live a long time, Sheriff," the gravedigger said. "At the very least, I hope you outlive me."

"Maybe you should charge by the foot rather than by the corpse," Frank said.

Mr. Love looked up at Frank and then down at the outline he had sketched into the earth demarcating Nurse Jim's new accommodations. He stuck his shovel into the ground so that it stood on its own. "It all evens out in the end," he said. "Is it true Mrs. Crane shot the boy?"

"I'm afraid so," Frank said.

"Was she drunk?"

"Not that I know of."

"What did she shoot him for?"

"I don't know," Frank said. "She said some things . . . I didn't follow exactly. I think she only meant to shoot the Martian, but Nurse Jim wouldn't stand out of the way, so she shot him, too."

"Nurse Jim's got a mother, father, three brothers and two sisters," Mr. Love said, "and all of 'em with a reputation for being hot-headed. Nurse Jim was the cool one of the bunch. Does that concern you?"

"I've got Deputy Soon and Deputy Rhome keeping an eye on things."

"And how about the Martian? Killed?"

"Yes."

"I heard that the Martian has kinfolk on Mars—maybe thousands of 'em. They planning to pay us a visit?"

"I have no idea."

"And I hear folks say things are heating up with the Scabs. Is that true?"

"I'd go along with that assessment."

Mr. Love took off his hat and looked up at the cold gray sky. The thin rain fell on his bald head and into his filmy eyes. He lowered his head, put his hat back on, and pulled the collar of his coat closer around his scrawny neck. "I remember before the last Scab War things seemed perfectly settled between us and them. Then down they came like a pack of lobos—tried to wipe us off the face of the earth—came awful near to doing it, too. I always wondered what it was that set 'em off. At least this time, we have an idea what they're worked up about. Think there's any chance of smoothing things over with 'em?"

"Some things have happened," Frank said. "There's going to be an inquiry on Monday, and when it's over, I don't think the council is going to have much interest in smoothing things over with the Scavengers."

"Sorry to hear it," Mr. Love said. "There's something I've been thinking about for a long while now."

"What's that?" Frank said.

"Retirement. Seems like now or never. I better let Pastor Craddock know. You take care of yourself, Sheriff. I'd say trouble has got you surrounded." The gravedigger hobbled away and disappeared into the rainy mist, leaving an upright shovel in his place to keep Frank company. It took a minute or two for the substance of what had just happened to completely settle into Frank, and when it did, he walked over to the shallow trench Mr. Love had made outlining Nurse Jim's everlasting share of this world, took the gravedigger's shovel in hand, and set to work.

About a quarter to three, the casket was carried from the family home to the cemetery. Jim's father, brothers, and sisters served as pallbearers. His mother led the procession, carrying branches of rosemary from her herb garden, as it was not the season for flowers. A single drummer, tapping out a staccato funeral cadence on her snare drum, brought up the rear. The casket was of simple pine boards, unadorned save for the following painted inscription: *Jim Kinmundy. Born, 21 August, 2448, died, 14 December, 2473.*

When the procession arrived at the cemetery, Mrs. Kinmundy had to swat with her rosemary branches at clots of restive citizens so involved in passionate discussions of the events of the past few days that they would not otherwise have moved aside to allow the deceased passage to his final resting place. The crowd did not come to order when the coffin was finally set down beside the grave, nor did anyone heed Pastor Craddock's meaningful throat-clearings as they argued over whether or not there had actually been a Scavenger attack, how Spencer Skint had escaped and if Scavengers had helped him, why Councilwoman Crane had shot and killed Nurse Jim, whether it was Scavengers or fellow-Martians that had absconded with Nancy's body, and what, if anything, any of it had to do with the abduction of Pilar Ramos.

It seemed to Frank that every citizen (with the exception of Councilwoman Crane) was in attendance—even Miss Caroline Tyler. At the request of the Kinmundy family, Miss Tyler had been granted temporary furlough from house arrest to attend the funeral, and Caroline was serving a useful purpose, comforting and propping up Frieda Kinmundy, her best friend and Nurse Jim's youngest sister.

Sheriff Westfall's great height made him ill-suited to blending into a crowd, and the sheriff soon found himself surrounded by agitated citizens pelting him with questions from all sides. He was able to take advantage of the noise and confusion of the swarm of inquiries to avoid answering any of them—but was quite relieved when Pastor Craddock finally gave up on the crowd coming to order of its own accord, and shouted at the top of his lungs "HATS OFF!"

The citizens removed their hats and fell silent, and Pastor Craddock gave a short but touching eulogy. The bearers played that game of tug-of-war with the coffin straps that the grave always wins while the New Halchita City Choir sang "Rock of Ages" followed by "Uncle John's Band." When the coffin reached solid ground, and the straps had been thrown in after it, Nurse Jim's family filed by the grave. Each family member took a handful of wet earth from the mound and pitched the clod into the grave to thump on the coffin lid. After the family had done their part, Pastor Craddock offered the shovel to friends who wished to show their respect, and these, who were very many, lined up to take the spade. Those towards the front of the line rattled the boards of the coffin lid with their contribution, and those that came later heaped their respect upon the house of the dead more quietly.

A low muttering of discontent seeped from the gathering when Miss Caroline Tyler stepped forward for the shovel. The citizens standing around Nurse Jim's grave in the dreary winter mizzle were about evenly divided in their opinion of Miss Tyler. Some felt she was a victim of Spencer Skint's duplicity, others that she was his accomplice. In either case, they all felt there was a connection, although the exact nature of that connection was not clearly defined in their minds—still, a connection of some kind, between Spencer Skint's abduction of Pilar Ramos and the violent death of Nurse Jim. On the other hand, no one could deny that Miss Tyler had every right, and even a duty, to contribute a shovelful of earth to the grave. She and Nurse Jim's youngest sister had been in the same year in school, and were great friends. For a friend of the family *not* to take the shovel in hand would be an insult to the bereaved.

Long before the crowd had made up its collective mind about the propriety of Miss Caroline Tyler's wielding of the venerated shovel, the baker's daughter had taken it from its previous possessor, the librarian (and Nurse Jim's aunt), Mrs. Barlow. Caroline thrust the shovel deep into the mound and lifted out a great heap of earth, swinging it around slowly enough to give everyone (especially, perhaps, her detractors) plenty of opportunity to see it, and then she tipped the dirt into the grave.

The rain, though cold and annoying, up to that moment had been gentle and vertical, but at the instant the earth fell from the shovel into the grave, the rain became a stinging, horizontal blast, and an ominous whine filled the air. Many in the crowd gasped or moaned in horror, thinking it must be a sign. Of all the citizens gathered in the cemetery, only Sheriff Frank Westfall and Doctor Germaine Perry knew what was coming, having heard that sound before—and very recently.

The Martian's ship descended out of the mist and set down in the middle of the crowd. Once on the ground, the monstrous machine rushed madly about, charging into the crowd, knocking over headstones and sending panicked citizens fleeing in every direction. The thing's movements were astonishingly quick, each dash accompanied by a sharp buzz as it used its wings as much as its legs to propel itself in short, rapid dashes.

At first, its movements seemed arbitrary, meant to confuse and terrorize and nothing else, but it wasn't long before its larger purpose was revealed and accomplished: to separate Miss Caroline Tyler from the rest of the citizens.

Frank had been knocked to the ground by panicked citizens, and the ensuing contest between the Martian's ship and the baker's daughter lasted exactly as long as it took for Frank to get back on to his feet. It was a battle as remarkable as it was brief. The metallic creature, having the baker's daughter more or less to itself, turned to face her—and appeared to hesitate. Perhaps it was surprised to see its intended victim standing before it with resolution in her eye, and a gravedigger's shovel in a two-handed, ready-for-action grip. The thing did not linger in thought for long. It charged Miss Tyler, swiping for her with one of its praying-mantis arms. Miss Tyler ducked the swipe, spun around and brought the edge of the shovel down on an articulated joint of the creature's arm. The accuracy of Miss Tyler's strike at the creature was not gained at the expense of force. Its "hand" (or perhaps "claw" would be a better word) was completely severed and fell to the ground.

Unfortunately for Miss Tyler, the gravedigger's shovel was a tool better suited to the aftermath of a battle than the waging thereof. Her single mighty blow struck against the Martian machine shattered the shaft of the ancient spade, rendering the poor girl defenseless. In the next moment, the thing from Mars had Miss Tyler ensnared in a tangle of mechanical legs, and having secured its prey, rose from the ground and buzzed out of sight.

The rain returned to a thin, cold, and vertical drizzle. Citizens got up, helped each other up, and held each other up. No one said a word—no one knew what to say—until a woman cried out in alarm and pointed towards the grave. A pale and mud-streaked hand and arm reached up out of the grave and clawed at the slick mud and grass that served as the border between the world of the living and that of the dead. Frank picked his hat up off the ground and put it on his head, never taking his eye off the hand. The only sound he heard as he approached the grave was the pitter of rain on his hat and the squishing of wet grass under his boots. On his way to whatever it was attempting to climb out of the hole he and Pastor Craddock had dug, Frank took a slight detour to pick up the Martian's amputated appendage, thinking (though not really aware of it at the time) that it might prove useful as a club.

To Frank's relief, the hand and arm reaching up out of the grave was firmly attached to Mrs. Barlow, who had either fallen, been pushed, or had thrown herself into the muddy hole upon the arrival of the Martian machine. Frank gripped Mrs. Barlow by the wrist and helped her up and out of the grave.

"Oh damn it all, I'm a mess, aren't I?" Mrs. Barlow said. "Someone pushed me. Sheriff—did you see—oh, shame on me. Here I am worrying about my dress—and poor Miss Tyler—what do you think that thing—"

The mechanical claw Frank still held in his hand twitched, and Frank, startled, dropped it on the muddy ground, where it squirmed like Aaron's staff when he cast it before Pharaoh.

12 THE INQUIRY (3)

*Minutes of the Proceedings of an Inquiry into Recent Events
Considered by the Council to be Highly Detrimental
to the Peace and Well-being of the Citizens of New Halchita; and
the Associated Actions of Sheriff Frank Westfall
by the Honorable Council of New Halchita,
in the Main Council Room,
upon this 18th day of December, 2473.*

PRESENT.

His Honor, NOÉ LOPEZ, Mayor.
MEMBERS of the council:
Mr. ISAAC GOODHUE
Mr. W.H. DOWNES
Sheriff FRANK B. WESTFALL, Witness
Attorney PABLO S. DELGADO, ESQ., Advocate for Sheriff Westfall
Deputy Irene Rhome, Acting Bailiff

NOTABLY ABSENT.

Mrs. DORENE CRANE, Councilwoman. Absent On Account of Illness

His Honor the Mayor Noé Lopez appeared in the main council room, and all persons noted above were admitted and seated. The order of Mayor Lopez to the council to question Sheriff Westfall and other Witnesses as appropriate was read. The several members of the council were sworn, and Sheriff Westfall was also sworn. Sheriff Westfall and his advocate, being asked by the mayor, declared they had no objection to opening the proceedings to the public. By the order of Mayor Lopez, the public was then admitted and seated. The Sheriff, being asked by Councilman Goodhue if he understood that he was participating in these proceedings of his own free will, and not under threat of harm or force of law, replied in the affirmative.

Question (by the Council). Please state your full name, age, occupation, and current address.

Answer (by Sheriff Westfall). Frank B. Westfall. I'm thirty-three years old. My occupation is sheriff. I live in the room above the sheriff's office on Main Street.

Question. Sheriff Westfall, there have been many strange and troubling occurrences in this town in the last week, and they all seem to have one thing in common: you. I hardly know where to begin in trying to understand what is going on—but let's start with the escape of Postmaster Spencer Skint. As I understand it, you arrested Postmaster Skint on suspicion of the abduction of Pilar Ramos last Wednesday the 13th, and the next day, late in the evening of Thursday the 14th, he escaped—"

Answer. That's not quite right councilman. Postmaster Skint didn't escape, I released him. As I'm sure Mr.

Delgado would be happy to tell you, I was unable to obtain sufficient evidence to justify holding Postmaster Skint.

Question. You released him?

Answer. Yes sir.

Question. All right, Sheriff, we may come back to that later. After you released Postmaster Skint, what did you do next?

Answer. I went to the clinic.

Question. A drill was in progress—the North Gate alarm had sounded—shouldn't you have proceeded directly to the North Gate?

Answer. Postmaster Skint had given me information indicating that Nancy, the Martian, had been involved in the abduction of Pilar Ramos. I felt that detaining the Martian and questioning her regarding the disappearance of Pilar Ramos was more important than participating in the drill.

Question. Why did you expect to find Nancy at the clinic?

Answer. I knew that when the Scavengers attacked us at the North Gate last November, Nancy had accompanied Dr. Perry to the clinic. I thought she might have done so again. Neither Nancy nor Dr. Perry would have known the alarm was a drill.

Question. What led Postmaster Skint to believe the Martian was involved in the abduction of Pilar Ramos?

Answer. He knew of the Martian's involvement because he assisted the Martian in the abduction.

(There was a short delay in the proceedings as Mayor Lopez instructed the public that if they wished to remain in the council chambers, they must remain quiet and orderly.)

Question. Postmaster Spencer Skint told you that he had assisted the Martian in the abduction of Pilar Ramos?

Answer. Yes, sir.

Question. And you released him anyway?

Answer. No, sir. I had already released him when he gave me that information.

Question. You released him, and *then* he confessed to conspiring with the Martian?

Answer. Yes, sir.

Question. I find it hard to understand why Postmaster Skint would have confessed to the crime *after* he had been released, but we'll get back to that later as well. Once he confessed to the crime, why didn't you arrest him again and place him in the lockup?

Answer. A mob had formed outside the sheriff's office. They made it clear that they meant to administer their own kind of justice. I felt Postmaster Skint would not be safe in the lockup or on the street, or anywhere in New Halchita, for that matter. I advised Postmaster Skint to take advantage of the drill that was in progress to evade the mob and escape into the Scablands. I will certainly arrest Postmaster Skint again if I have the opportunity.

Question. I seriously doubt that opportunity will ever present itself, Sheriff.

Answer. You may be right.

Question. Did Postmaster Skint tell you why he and the Martian abducted Pilar Ramos, or what they did with her?

Answer. Postmaster Skint told me the Martian blackmailed him into assisting her with the abduction of Pilar Ramos. He said the Martian knew that he had never taken any of the council's letters to the president in Washington D.C. He said he didn't know what [inaudible]

Due to the reaction of the public, the remainder of Sheriff Westfall's answer to the question was not audible to the clerk. With the assistance of Deputy Rhome, order was re-established, and at the request of His Honor the Mayor, a fifteen minute recess was called. The mayor and council retired to chambers. When the mayor and council returned from chambers, the mayor ordered the bailiff to clear the public from the council room. The remainder of the inquiry was held in a private session, and, by order of the mayor, the record of that portion of the inquiry held in private session will not be made available to the public.

13 THE EX-LAWMAN'S LAMENT

Frank lay in bed on his back, his knees drawn up nearly to his chest, wondering if it was poetic justice or irony—or perhaps a cruel joke on the part of the council—that the bed he was lying in was formerly Spencer Skint's. It was probably one or the other of those things and he was too dim to figure out which. Or maybe it was just . . . reasonable. As Deputy Rhome was now Sheriff Rhome, and Sheriff Westfall was now Nothing Westfall, it would have been pretty awkward for him to keep living in the room above the sheriff's office, and the last house on Possum Race Road was available—so here he was.

Things could've gone worse. He was lucky that Councilwoman Crane was too sick to participate in the inquiry—she would've pushed hard for exile. He could be sleeping out in the Scablands, instead, he had a bed and a roof over his head.

Frank recalled having told Dr. Perry, not so long ago, that he wouldn't last eight days in New Halchita without a job. Maybe he'd been wrong. Three days going on four he hadn't had a thing to do, and he wasn't miserable at all. In fact, he was enjoying himself immensely. He'd spent his first two days as New Halchita's ex-sheriff cleaning house, in other words, throwing all of Spencer Skint's crap out into the street where it disappeared like magic. Everyone wanted a piece of the former postmaster. One day Spencer Skint would be a legend, and Sheriff Westfall—he'd be lucky to be remembered as the chump in the story. The man had a saddle, for Christ's sake. The last horse in the world (as far as anyone knew) had died of the equine-version of the blood flu over a hundred years ago, and Spencer Skint had a saddle. And now, somewhere in New Halchita, someone had Spencer Skint's saddle proudly on display in their living room.

Cleaning up after that bastard had taken two days and entirely wore him out. It was breathing all that dust, Frank thought, more than the physical work. Yesterday, he'd spent all day in bed, and he'd enjoyed it so much, he had no intention of getting out of bed today, either.

Someone knocked at the door. "Come in!" Frank yelled. Frank heard the door open, and footsteps approaching, and then he was looking up at Mrs. Barlow. The librarian was holding a thick, bound document under one arm.

"Are you all right, Sheriff?" she said.

"I'm not the sheriff, and I'm fine," Frank said.

"This bed is too small for you," she said.

"I'm aware of that," Frank said.

"You asked me about the report I wrote for the council when the Martian first arrived," Mrs. Barlow said. "You asked if there was anything in it about machines."

"I was sheriff when I asked you," Frank said. "I'm not sheriff anymore, so—"

"So you don't want to know?"

"I didn't say that," Frank said.

Mrs. Barlow left the room and returned a moment

later dragging a chair in with her. She pulled the chair up next to the bed and sat in it, and put the bound document on Frank's chest. She opened the report up to a page she had bookmarked with a scrap of paper.

"This is from some material I found from a few years before the colonists set out for Mars," she said.

Frank pulled the report closer and raised it up so he could read it.

. . . though the colonists will not arrive for at least another five years, a veritable army of machines, collectively known as "grubbers," are already hard at work, preparing the site for the human occupants of Mars Experimental Colony #3. Some of these grubbers were left behind by the previous two colonies, others, specifically designed for MEC-3, are on their way or will soon be launched in order to arrive on Mars months or even years in advance of their human counterparts.

These machines serve four main purposes: First, the extraction and concentration of indigenous life-support resources, such as water, oxygen, nitrogen, and argon (nitrogen and argon will be used as "buffer gasses" for the creation of a human-breathable atmosphere. A pure-oxygen atmosphere would be both toxic and explosive); Second, the preparation of Martian soil (through the removal of salts and other toxins) for use in greenhouse agriculture; Third, the mining and refining of indigenous construction and fabrication materials such as iron, silicon, aluminum and magnesium; and Fourth, the excavation and reinforcement of underground habitats (five meters of Martian soil will provide the colonists with the same protection from solar radiation as the Earth's atmosphere).

And these grubbers do it all for us humans. They themselves do not eat, drink, or breathe in the ordinary sense, and do not require shelter from the harsh Martian environment. Unlike the human colonists, the grubbers are exquisitely adapted to life on Mars, and require no sustenance beyond the relatively feeble Martian sunlight (somewhat less than half of what an equal area on Earth would receive) which they absorb and convert into mechanical energy in order to perform their assigned tasks.

The activities and progress of the grubbers will be closely monitored by humans on Earth, but on an hour-to-hour, and even day-to-day basis, they require little in the way of instruction or guidance. The grubbers have been endowed by their creators at the Engentsia Corporation with the most advanced artificial intelligence available. The grubbers understand, at some deep, though purely mechanical, level, both the purpose and the import of their mission. They are fully capable of autonomous operation, and can learn from their mistakes, adjusting and improving their procedures as they gain "experience." Since there won't be any humans to tighten their bolts or grease their gears for quite some time, the grubbers have been designed not only to maintain themselves, but to detect, diagnose, and repair their own minor mechanical failures, and in case of a serious breakdown, they can even call upon their fellow contraptions for assistance.

Nor will their work be done when the humans arrive. Ms. Sutherland, director of autonomous mechanical operations for MEC-3, states that there will be plenty for the machines to do once what she calls "the organic component" of the colony has settled in. "If anything," Ms. Sutherland says, "the grubbers will have even more to do. Agriculture on Mars will be a low-pressure operation, and tending to plants in a spacesuit would be a difficult, inefficient, and calorie-negative proposition. Not only will the grubbers take care of the plants, they will take care of the humans. Each colonist will have a subcutaneous transmitter continuously broadcasting his or her biological metrics. Should a nearby grubber detect a change in those metrics indicating dangerous stress or an imbalance of the biological systems of an organic component, it is programmed to stop whatever it is doing and render aid."

"Has the council read this?" Frank said.

"They had the opportunity when I presented the report to them," Mrs. Barlow said, "but I doubt any of them read much beyond the executive summary. There's one other thing you might find interesting."

The librarian flipped the pages on the report, and put her finger on an underlined paragraph. "This is from when the colonists were en route to Mars. Apparently they were held in suspended animation for the trip."

. . . the youngest of the colonists is Nancy Aubrey. Though only twenty-two, she already has two degrees from M.I.T., one in robotics and another in machine intelligence. Her job will be to assist the so-called "grubbers"—those remarkable, artificially-intelligent machines we've been hearing so much about—as their role at the colony site transitions from preparation for the arrival of humans to assisting those humans in their day-to-day efforts to prove that a truly self-sustaining human presence on the red planet is possible.

According to Ms. Aubrey, whom we spoke to shortly before she was put into hiber-containment, the machines tend to resist change. "It has to do with how they are programmed," she told us. "Once they have learned a new, successful behavior, that behavior is reinforced algorithmically—weighted to be used preferentially over built-in but generally less effective methodologies. In other words, the better they become at one set of tasks, the harder it is for them to start over and learn something new. I think they are like people in that regard. They need help and even encouragement in order to handle change effectively—and that will be my job."

"You don't think it's the same Nancy," Frank said. "It can't be. She'd be over three-hundred years old now."

"I know," Mrs. Barlow said. "It's probably just a coincidence, but I can't get the idea out of my head."

"Thank you, Mrs. Barlow," Frank said.

"I'm happy to help," Mrs. Barlow said, "even if I don't

know exactly *how* I'm helping. Are you sure you're all right, Sheriff?"

"I'm fine—and I'm not the sheriff."

"I know," Mrs. Barlow said.

The door had hardly shut behind Mrs. Barlow when someone else was knocking on it.

"Come in!" Frank yelled. He was beginning to realize that never getting out of bed would require more determination and resolve than he had thought. His second visitor that day was the senior tech, Eyron Stinchcombe.

"How are you doing, Sheriff?" Eyron said.

"I'm fine," Frank said. He decided not to bother reminding Eyron that he was no longer sheriff. Folks would get out of the habit of calling him that when they did—and Frank thought it wouldn't take long.

Eyron sat in the chair Mrs. Barlow had left next to the bed. "I wanted to thank you," he said. "I'm guessing you didn't tell the council about the receiver we made or we'd have heard about it by now. It wouldn't have mattered much to me. My wife is nagging me to retire anyway. But Gweeden and Lomo—"

"I didn't see any need to bring it up," Frank said. "But you should know, if the council had asked me directly, I would have answered directly."

"I know that," Eyron said, "still . . ."

"You haven't, by any chance, turned that thing on . . . *recently*?" Frank said.

Eyron nodded, ever so slightly.

"And?"

"If the Martian's ship is still transmitting," Eyron said, his voice low, "it's too far away for us to detect, or else it's gone to a different wavelength—longer or shorter than what we can get on Gweeden's receiver."

"If you could detect it," Frank said, "would you be able to locate the ship?"

"Maybe. Sheriff," Eyron said, his voice even lower, "Gweeden has some ideas . . . good ones. She thinks she can build a better receiver—a hundred times more sensitive, and it could search through a much broader range of wavelengths. And it wouldn't broadcast anything, just listen, that's all. No way a lagamachy could detect it."

"You'd have to get the permission of the council before you built something like that," Frank said.

"You know what they'd say," Eyron said.

"You're going to do it anyway, aren't you?"

Eyron nodded again, at about .01 times the amplitude of his previous nodding.

"Come in!" Frank yelled, for the third time in as many hours.

"Are you all right, Frank?" Germaine asked.

Unlike his other visitors, Dr. Perry, at least, had come to terms with his fall from grace.

"I'm fine," Frank said. "Really. I don't need a doctor."

"I'm not here to be your doctor," Germaine said, "I'm here to say I'm sorry for what you've been through. I know I had a part in it. When I asked you not to tell the council that the Martian could communicate with her ship—"

"You did what you thought was right, and I did what I thought was right. I don't blame you for what came after. Not much, anyway."

"Also," Germaine said, "I wanted to say . . . you were right about Spencer Skint."

"Good try," Frank said.

"What do you mean?"

"I mean you can tell me I was right about Spencer Skint all day long, and it's not going to stop me from saying 'I told you so.'"

"Go ahead, let's get it over with," Germaine said.

"I told you so," Frank said.

"Did it feel good?"

"Yes. In fact, I would say that was the most satisfying *I told you so* I ever said."

"Are you sure you're okay?"

"I'm fine. I'm marvelous, actually. I lie here, and people come in and pay their respects—it's like attending my own funeral. Haven't you always wanted to attend your own funeral?"

"No. How long do you plan to lie there stewing in self-pity?"

"Until I'm done."

Germaine didn't say anything else, and she didn't leave either. Clearly, she was waiting for him to say something. Since she'd said she was sorry for the trouble she had caused him, Frank figured she was expecting him to return the favor—to apologize for the stupid thing he'd done. Frank considered the possibility. It was a good time to apologize. On the other hand, it was a *great* time *not* to apologize.

"I think I want to get some sleep now," Frank said, closing his eyes.

When he opened them again, Pete Barlow was standing over him. Pete hadn't even bothered to knock.

"You all right, Frank?" Pete said.

"I'm fine, Pete," Frank said. "Tell me something, Pete. Why can't a man take some time off without folks thinking he's sick? You know what's sick? What's sick is you get slammed down and everyone comes around and asks you if you're okay not because they want *you* to feel better but because they want *themselves* to feel better."

"I don't follow," Pete said, "would you run that by me again?"

"Never mind," Frank said. "I'm fine. What do you want?"

"Ma said she came by and talked to you earlier today. She said you were looking for a job."

"I never told her that."

"You gotta eat, don't you?"

"Yes, Pete," Frank said, "I gotta eat. Are you going to tell me why you're here?"

"It's hard, Frank, out on the Scablands alone. After you and Skint quit on me—I don't blame you—either one of you—I know you had other opportunities—all I'm saying is it's hard and getting harder. I swear those ticks get faster and stronger every day. And Ma said you were looking for a job. That's why I'm here, Frank—'cause you gotta eat and don't have a job, and I need a partner. I'm not as quick as I used to be, Frank. Sooner or later one of those ticks is going to get a leg up on me and I'm going to be real sorry I didn't talk you into partnering with me again. I mean I'll be real sorry right up until I'm dead."

"I don't need a job," Frank said. He closed his eyes. After a long while (he might have drifted off) he opened them again. Pete Barlow was still there. Frank wanted to tell the tick-juicer to go away, but if Nothing Westfall knew anything, he knew *inevitable* when it stood over him, hat in hand, looking down at him with big, sad, desperate eyes. And a thought occurred to Frank: the Scablands were vast, but it was a small world, and maybe he'd run into Spencer Skint out there. Even if it was just his remains, it'd be worth the trouble.

"When are you going out next?" Frank said.
"Monday morning."
"Heading which way?"
"South."
"I'll meet you at the South Gate at dawn on Monday."

Part 3

1 A GENTLEMAN'S GUIDE TO TICK JUICING

There's an old saying that a tick-juicer will never have any money, because it costs more to shoot a tick than a tick is worth. The saying is both inaccurate and misleading. The payoff for the demitasse of ticktox that a tick-juicer can expect to extract from the salivary glands of an adult specimen would certainly be enough to buy a handful of bullets, but more to the point, a tick-juicer would never shoot a tick. From any distance, a bullet would simply ricochet off the tick's iron-infused shell, and closer up, the shockwave created by the force of any projectile capable of piercing the tick's carapace and entering the tick's hemolymph would turn the innards of the tick (including the all-important salivary glands) into mush, leaving nothing for the juicer to juice.

 This is not to say that a tick-juicer doesn't need bullets, or that bullets aren't expensive. A juicer will be out on the Scablands for weeks—sometimes a month or more—and must travel light and cover a lot of ground. A bullet provides the juicer with his daily bread, so to speak, and may be used to deter, or on occasion trade with, Scavenger hunters one might encounter on the Scablands (though trading bullets with Scavengers in the economic sense is, of course, strictly forbidden by the council). In other words, bullets are a must for any serious juicing operation for many reasons, but for killing ticks, the juicer's preferred tool is the so-called "ticking knife."

The tick-juicer selects a large adult tick, seats himself on the tick's back facing forwards, and grasps the tick tightly between his legs. Once firmly mounted, he removes the ticking-knife from the scabbard at his waist and inserts the point of the knife between the tick's dorsal shield and capitulum. He then thrusts the knife into the tick (down and in the rearward direction), up to the handle. Once the knife is in place, the juicer pushes the handle left and right until that bundle of nerves that passes for a tick's brain is completely severed from its various appendages, rendering the bug helpless. The hard part is done—the juicer now can flip the tick over onto its back, remove the adanal shields, and (very carefully, so as not to lose a single drop) lift out the salivary glands and squeeze out the precious ticktox.

The "trick," as any juicer will tell you, is getting yourself seated on the tick—that is the *art* of juicing—all else is simply technique. A juicer's claim to the throne is always hotly contested by the tick, and as you attempt your ascension, the tick will be trying its level best to gum you up with its glue-slobbering palps, stab you with its serrated hypostome, and cut you to the bone with its razor-sharp chelicerae.

Juicers generally work in teams of two or three, and the major tasks, hunting, tick-juicing, and cooking may be divvied-up based on aptitude, or swapped around to provide a measure of relief from monotony. When the last bullet has been fired, the venture is over. The juicers pack up and go home, get the best price they can for their ticktox, pay their debts (there is always a debt, as will be explained shortly), and spend the rest on those comforts and pleasures they missed the most while out in the wilderness. When the money is gone, it's time to head out into the Scablands once again. As the average tick-juicer lacks the self-discipline required to set aside enough money to buy supplies for the next expedition, he funds each venture by borrowing against his return, and as the job is a dangerous one, and every juicer's foray into the Scablands may be his last, the lender sets the terms of the loan accordingly, and stands to turn a handsome profit, or else lose everything, by the investment.

The uses of ticktox are many and varied. One drop of a five percent solution mixed with honey may be rubbed on the gums of a teething infant to afford much-needed rest to both mother and child. A drop mixed in lard serves admirably as a salve for rashes, insect bites, or superficial burns. A small injection of ticktox can make a tooth extraction tolerable—more still, the amputation of a limb. One drop in a glass of wine eases worries, and two is a cure for insomnia. It is said that three drops of ticktox in a cup of dandelion tea will soothe a broken heart, though only briefly, whereas six drops will ease the pain for all eternity.

2 SPRING

Frank leaned back against the bone-white, twisted trunk of an ancient fallen juniper. He'd been walking all day, ascending mostly, in a country he was completely unfamiliar with. The expedition was coming to an end. The four cartridges in the magazine of his rifle was the last of the ammunition that would be used for hunting. The rest of the bullets, residing in the revolvers he and Pete carried on their hips, would only be used *in extremis* as they made their way back to New Halchita.

Frank took a sip of warm water from a stoppered metal flask and wiped the sweat off his forehead with the sleeve of his shirt. He realized he wasn't particularly looking forward to going "home." Even in his thoughts, the word was in quotes. He felt like a stranger in New Halchita—like a man passing through on his way to somewhere else—and why not? That's what he was—what he had become. On this, his third juicing expedition into the Scablands since the council had forced him to resign as sheriff and commander of the city guard, Frank had begun to think of New Halchita primarily as the place he and Pete went to sell the juice, spend money foolishly, and stock up on supplies for the next expedition. New Halchita was certainly a convenient, and in its own way, pleasant, place to pass the time between juicing runs. But none of that had anything to do with "home."

It wasn't like he wasn't welcome in New Halchita—in fact, folks in New Halchita grinned more broadly, shook his hand more firmly, and slapped him on the back more enthusiastically when he had juice money burning a hole in his pocket than they ever had when he'd been a rather thrifty lawman. The citizens of New Halchita made him feel welcome, they just didn't make him feel needed. After each of the last two expeditions, he had returned to New Halchita hoping (though he knew it was wrong to have such hopes) there had been trouble—brutal Scavenger attacks (*Frank, we're getting whipped—the City Guard is falling apart. Sheriff Rhome is doing her best but maybe you could help her out*) or further depredations by the Martian ship (*Bullets are no use, Frank. That thing carried off three citizens last week. People are afraid to come out of their houses. Can you help us?*) but none of that had happened—no Scavenger attacks, no disappearing infants or pregnant women, no sightings whatsoever of the Martian ship. In fact, all of New Halchita's worst troubles seemed to have packed up and left town for good the moment Eleanor Rhome put on the sheriff's badge. One could be forgiven for thinking that was more than just coincidence.

Frank's stomach growled. He and Pete were running low on food, and this open country, hilly, brushy, and grassy, seemed like it should be overrun with game, but in the last week, the biggest target that had presented itself to Frank was a gopher, and Frank had been tempted. Pete was doing his part—the juice jars were filling up nicely—but if Frank's luck didn't change, dinner that night would consist of hot water in a tin cup.

At a motion caught out of the corner of his eye, Frank raised his rifle quickly and quietly. A fawn stepped out of the brush, spindly legged but steady, a little young, Frank thought, to be wandering far from its mother. The fawn's fur was brown and spotted and it had a white tail and enormous black lustrous eyes. Frank, leaning against the fallen juniper trunk, remained perfectly still. The fawn looked at him, saw him, but did not seem to comprehend what it saw, appearing to be more curious than afraid. Its ear twitched, its nose twitched, and Frank pulled the trigger, putting a bullet through its neck. The fawn fell to the ground and kicked in the air furiously with one leg for three or four seconds and then was still. The crack of the rifle echoed around the hills. Frank smiled. Pete, if he was somewhere not too far away, would hear that rifle shot and say to himself: *dinner!* In five minutes, Frank had the fawn gutted and thrown over his shoulder. He headed back to camp, one bullet closer to "home."

After descending from the hills into a valley, about ten kilometers west of where he and Pete had made camp near a creek, Frank encountered an interesting sight. Fortune had smiled on Pete Barlow that morning as well. Pete and a female tick, big around as a washtub and thick as a butcher's block, were facing off on a flat and dusty patch of earth. The temperature in the valley was considerably higher than in the hills, and Pete had taken off his shirt for the contest. He had his ticking-knife in one hand, the other hand out for balance, and his knees were slightly bent. The tick had adopted a martial posture of her own. Her chelicerae were open wide, ready to snap shut and slice into an arm or a leg, or better yet, shear off a few fingers. Her palps, thick, pink, hairy, and dripping with goo, were up in the air, smelling Pete and trembling in her eagerness to latch on to him, pull him close, and thrust her serrated hypostome deep into his tender flesh. Given the chance, she'd drain him like a schoolgirl slurping up one of Mr. Fitz's spritzes.

Pete, entirely focused on his arachnid adversary, had not noticed Frank, and Frank, fearing he might distract Pete at a critical moment and do more harm than good, decided to stand quietly by and observe, and not step in unless the tick appeared to be gaining the upper hand. Pete moved around to the left and to the right in an attempt to get behind the bug, but she was having none of that, rotating to face him wherever he went. As she turned, she made a kind of chattering noise that sounded to Frank eerily like a chuckle.

Pete stepped towards the tick, and she took a step back, but her step back was not quite the length of Pete's step forward, and so he had closed on her by a few inches. He took another step forward, and this time the tick held her ground, her only movement to raise her palps higher into the air. The two were very close now— too close, Frank thought. Pete offered the tick his elbow like a gentleman, and she took it with a palp like a goat wrapping its tongue around a tuft of grass. With a quick slash of his ticking-knife, Pete cut the palp off at the base. The tick, enraged and in pain, backed away and then lunged for the one who had wounded her so grievously. Pete dropped and rolled underneath, and so was able to get astern of her. Not waiting for the tick to figure out where he'd gone off to, he jumped on her back, gripped her sides firmly between his knees, and in the next instant, she was dead, the handle of Pete's ticking knife sticking out from between her dorsal shield and capitulum.

After a dinner of tender and juicy roasted loin of fawn, Frank and Pete set to work processing Pete's catch-of-the-day, a burlap sack full of tick salivary glands. Pete warmed some water up over the fire, and he and Frank used the water to wash their hands thoroughly, even scrubbing under their fingernails with a small brush—no one would buy ticktox that wasn't perfectly clear. When the juicer's hands were clean and ready, Pete dumped the glands he had collected that day into a large steel bowl. The glands were clear and gelatinous, and the juicers squeezed them to break them up and liquefy them. This was by no means a disagreeable task. Their hands soon started to feel warm and numb, and as the scent of the ticktox, something like strawberries, permeated the air around the camp, pleasant thoughts began to predominate in the heads of the juicers.

"That was one hell of a move you pulled on that tick," Frank said, "I've never seen anything like it."

"Thank you," Pete said, "and that was the best dinner I ever ate. Where'd you learn to cook like that?"

"It was good, wasn't it?" Frank said. "Maybe I would have made a better chef than I did a sheriff."

"You were a *fine* sheriff," Pete said. "When I heard that the council forced you to resign, I said they were a bunch of fools—said it to anyone who would listen."

"Well, thanks, Pete," Frank said, "I appreciate that, and thanks for taking me on as a partner again. I thought I would miss being sheriff, but I don't. I don't miss it at all. It's so peaceful out here. I forgot what it was like to not have any worries. When I was sheriff, I was always worried about one thing or another. But you lied to me, Pete."

"What did I ever say to you that was a lie?" Pete said.

"You said you weren't as quick as you used to be. You

said you were afraid a tick would get a leg up on you. But after what I saw today—now I know you only said that to get me to partner up with you again."

"It wasn't a lie," Pete said. "I'm *not* as quick as I used to be. And I *do* worry about a tick getting a leg up on me. I will confess, though, that I'm still awful quick and I don't worry much—and I did say it to get you back on your feet. Are you sorry to be a tick-juicer again?"

"Not at all—and Pete—thanks."

The conversation continued in that fashion until their hearts were so full of gratitude for all the favors they had done for each other, and all the blessings life had bestowed on them, that speaking of any single one seemed inadequate—unjust, even—and the murmuring of the stream and the song of the crickets had become so beautiful that neither one wished to cut into it any longer with the harsh rasp of their voices. They squeezed in silence. *The angels are squeezing in heaven*, Frank thought. *I am squeezing the misery out of the world*, Pete thought. They squeezed and they squeezed, and they squeezed a while longer than was absolutely necessary.

"That's it," Pete said.

Frank, stretched out on his back on his bedroll, wasn't sure how much time had passed since he'd last spoken to Pete—a minute? an hour? a year?—his sense of time was pleasantly screwed to hell. In any case, he didn't have a clue what Pete was talking about.

"What?" Frank said.

"I've filled the last bottle," Pete said. "We're going home tomorrow."

"Oh," Frank said. He looked up at the beautiful night sky. He wasn't sure he was ready to go home. A bedroll on the ground was not the most comfortable of accommodations, but at least a man could stretch out to his full length. And yet, it would be nice to go home and see people he knew. He missed them—or was that the ticktox talking? The only reason they'd be happy to see him was because he'd have a pocketful of juice-money—not true—the citizens of New Halchita had treated him (for the most part) with kindness and respect even when he was just a thrifty sheriff. And anyway, why shouldn't they be happy that he had money to spend? Why shouldn't *he* be happy he had money to spend? Why shouldn't he be happy that happiness would flow from him to them in the form of money? What was wrong with that? Definitely the ticktox talking, Frank thought, *shut up, ticktox*—and to his surprise it did, and not just the ticktox—the worry, the pride, the frustration—for one glorious eternal instant, the nattering in his head was silenced.

Frank saw a light in the night sky—brilliant green. It bloomed ever larger, showed an orange center, and then shot away to the west. A second and a third light bloomed and followed the same brilliant path across the sky—and those lights went out—and three more lit the sky and one more after that—and then the sky was dark again, and all the stars were still.

"Pete?" Frank said. He wanted to know if what he saw had really happened—but Pete wouldn't know—he was fast asleep.

A pack of lobos hunting in the hills was startled by the unexpected light in the sky. Some froze in their tracks, others danced and growled at the sudden appearance of their own shadows circling around them—and then the comforting darkness returned. The pack, led by a white-muzzled old bitch, continued their hunt. Following the scent of a man, a fawn, and a fawn's blood, they descended from the hills and into the valley below with all the swiftness and grace (but none of the hissing, splashing, and burbling) of a mountain stream.

The lobos gave wide berth to the putrid remains of a split-open tick and loped on until the old bitch stopped to sniff, having caught a whiff of the ticktox vapors in the air around the juicer's camp. The other lobos in the pack raised their muzzles and sniffed. Oh, blissful days of infancy, packed in tight with brothers and sisters under mother's warm belly—that was the smell—or something very like it. They yipped *we want we want let us all go there,* but the white-muzzled old bitch, who remembered that smell from a place of terror and death, turned away, and the rest of the pack (though some whimpered their disappointment) followed her back into the hills.

3 HOME AGAIN

Chicken and grits with gravy. Lots and lots of gravy. Frank sat at Mr. Fitz's lunch counter late in the afternoon, all alone, wondering what it was Mr. Fitz was trying to hide under that thick and rapidly coagulating white shroud. Frank used the edge of his fork to push the gravy aside so he could get a look at the chicken underneath. The meat had a salvaged look about it—not surprising this late in the day—but Frank wondered if it had been scraped out of the bottom of a pot, or off of previous diner's plates.

Frank's head was killing him. The pounding had started three days home from the Scablands, and seemed to be settling in for a good long visit—a bad case of "tick's revenge." The mind gets accustomed to those soothing fumes and rebels at having to go on without them. It wasn't this bad the last two times, was it? He tried to remember, and discovered that trying to remember only made the pounding worse. Frank steeled himself against a wave of nausea gathering strength in his gut. This was Hunger's fault. Hunger had betrayed him. Hunger had gotten him out of bed, kept him on his feet for a short walk under the tortuously-bright afternoon sun, set him down at the lunch counter at Fitz's Apothecary, and then, when lunch arrived, ran out and left him all alone with this . . . gravy.

The bells on the door jingled. Frank didn't turn around to see who had come in. After a moment, Eyron Stinchcombe sat down next to Frank at the lunch counter.

"Hello, Eyron," Mr. Fitz said. "I'm afraid lunch service is over. Mr. Westfall has the last of it."

Frank pushed his plate over in front of Eyron. "It's yours if you want it," Frank said. "I swear I haven't touched it."

Eyron pushed the plate back in front of Frank. "Thanks," Eyron said, "but I've had my lunch already."

"Would you like a spritz?" Mr. Fitz said, "I highly recommend strawberry today."

"No thanks," Eyron said, "I'm just here to have a word with Sher . . . with Mr. Westfall."

Mr. Fitz nodded and went back to his dishes.

"There's something I think you might want to see in the scrap yard," Eyron said.

Frank put a few coins on the counter and stood up.

"We don't have to go right now," Eyron said, "you can finish your lunch."

"No, I can't," Frank said.

After Frank and Eyron were gone, Mr. Fitz scooped the coins off the counter and into his palm, and then dug into Frank's lunch. Mr. Fitz was not a man to let good food go to waste.

Eyron led Frank through an impressive maze of scrap. Turning a corner, they came very suddenly upon Lomo and Gweeden, standing in front of a metal shed, a shed that one might easily mistake for just another pile of scrap, if one didn't look too closely. Lomo pulled on a length of chain, sliding the gate that enclosed the shed very neatly and quietly into a recess on one side. The shed was empty except for a table, and on the table were two boxes, neither one much bigger than a seed box. One box was neatly packed with battery jars, the other was a mess of wires and wiring in all kinds of configurations: thread spools wound in copper, glass cups filled with springs, coin-sized orange ceramic discs with wires going in (or coming out or both—what did Frank know?)—lots of things, in short, that Frank didn't have a word for. A cable, interrupted by a three-armed electrical knife-switch in the off position, connected the two boxes.

"Turn it on," Eyron said. Lomo stepped inside the shed and pushed the handle of the knife-switch down into the contact position. The spring-filled glass cups began to emit a dull orange light, some steady, some flickering, and there was a smell like an approaching thunderstorm, and a sound like a beehive. Frank felt a little weak in the knees. This was lagamachy bait if he'd ever seen it. Gweeden stood next to Lomo and twisted a knob. The sound changed from a humming to a hissing to a woman singing, accompanied by a guitar:

I'd rather have Ahab and his harpoon
Or John Henry and his hammer
Than you and your little silver spoon
And your so-called life of glamour

I'll never be sweet <hiss> <crackle> <hiss>

A cicada-like buzz drowned out the rest. "I don't understand," Frank said, "What—"

Eyron, Lomo, and Gweeden shushed Frank in unison. "Listen," Eyron said.

The buzzing faded into a barely audible hiss, and a voice, a man's voice, soft, low, and strong, took its place. It sounded to Frank like the man was sitting alone in a vast, empty room. The long dramatic pauses and the calm, deliberate way the words were spoken reminded Frank of Pastor Craddock delivering a eulogy.

"We will return . . . to the hits of the ancients . . . in one moment," the voice said, "but first, this important message: . . . Friend . . . if you are hearing this broadcast . . . you have found . . . . . . hope. You have found . . . life . . . you have found . . . a friend. . . you have found . . . U.S.A. Reborn . . . a union . . . proud and strong . . . a community . . . caring and compassionate . . . an alliance . . . steadfast and loyal . . . of civilized settlements . . . and friend . . . you need us . . . and friend . . . we need . . . . . . you . . . please . . . contact us now at . . . one thousand twenty three kilohertz . . . take note . . . one . . . zero . . . two . . . three . . . kilohertz . . . the only . . . certified . . . lagamachy-safe . . . communications frequency . . . I say again . . . one . . . zero . . . two . . . three . . . kilohertz . . . the only . . . certified . . . lagamachy-safe . . . communications frequency . . . contact us now . . . do not delay . . . we now return you to . . . the hits of the ancients . . ."

Frank heard a man singing this time, his voice gentle and soothing:

You're the girl the other girls
Get the best advice from
And you're the girl that all your friends
Have always called the nice one

But when I look into your eyes

I see a tangled—

Lomo threw the knife-switch to the off position, and the voice was silenced instantly.

"What—" Frank said.

"It's an amplitude modulated broadcast," Gweeden said. "We stumbled across it when we were trying to detect the Martian's communications with her ship."

"This has nothing to do with the Martian?" Frank said.

"We don't think so," Eyron said. "We think it's been there . . . well, we don't know for how long . . . probably a long time . . . we just never heard it before because we were never listening before. There's some music, like what you heard, and then the message. The songs change—"

"But they're kind of all the same," Gweeden said.

"But they're not the same," Eyron said, "and what I was going to say was, the message is always the same—I mean exactly the same."

"Jeez," Frank said.

Eyron, Gweeden, and Lomo all nodded in agreement.

"Did you get anything that *was* from the Martian's ship?"

"No," Gweeden said, "nothing. Mr. Westfall, do you thing we should reply?"

"I don't think so," Frank said.

"U.S.A Reborn might be able to help us with the Martian," Eyron said, "maybe even help us get Pilar Ramos and Miss Tyler back."

"It'd be easy enough to build a transmitter," Gweeden said.

"I think transmitting on that frequency would be a bad idea," Frank said. "I'm pretty sure what we just heard was a lagamachy singing to us."

Eyron, Lomo, and Gweeden all backed away from Gweeden's receiver like it had just transformed itself into a rattlesnake.

Frank decided to leave them to think things over, and anyway, he was hungry again. He found his own way out of the scrap yard maze, and walked over to Otis' Dry Goods to get some jerky and maybe some hard candy.

"What's that you're humming?" Mrs. Otis said, handing Frank his purchases.

"I didn't realize I was humming anything," Frank said.

"Oh, you were," Mrs. Otis said.

"Was this it?" Frank said. He whistled a few notes of the tune from the lagamachy's song about the girl who gave such good advice.

"Yes, that was it," Mrs. Otis said. "I don't think I ever heard it before. It's a pretty tune—where'd you hear it?"

"Just kind of came to me," Frank said.

"I always like to hear people humming or singing to themselves," Mrs. Otis said. "I believe it means they're happy. Are you happy, Mr. Westfall?"

Frank realized his headache was gone. He couldn't recall exactly when it had left off trying to punch its way out of his skull, but it must have been about the time he heard the lagamachy singing. "You know, Mrs. Otis," Frank said, "I believe I am happy."

"What are you happy about?"

"I don't have any earthly idea," Frank said.

"That's the best kind of happy," Mrs. Otis said.

4 SUMMER

The night was warm enough that Frank and Pete had deployed tick-netting all around their camp before settling in for dinner and squeezing. The air, hot and still, hadn't stirred since sundown, and now, suddenly, a fierce, hot wind bent the campfire flames over horizontal, the many bells sewed to the net rattled tunelessly, and then the night was still again.

"Just like old times, isn't it?"

Frank, up to his elbows in tick salivary glands, dragged himself as far out of the fog of his pleasant ticktox-fume-induced reverie as he was able. Spencer Skint was squatting by the embers of the campfire, covering Frank with a revolver. The sight helped to clear Frank's head.

"No need to point a gun at us," Pete said.

"I'm not pointing it at you, Pete," Skint said, "only at Frank here. Frank said he'd kill me the next time he saw me, and he's always been a man of his word, so forgive me if I err on the side of caution."

"Let's call a truce for tonight," Pete said.

"Frank?" Skint said.

"Sure," Frank said, unable to resist the urge to be nice.

"Truce," Skint said, holstering his gun. "You always were the peacemaker among us, Pete. Nice to see some things don't change."

"What are you doing here?" Frank said.

"I have a message for Doctor Perry. But as I'm persona non grata in New Halchita right now, and, oh boy, not currently one of Germaine's favorite people, you boys would be doing me a favor to be *my* postman for a change."

"What's the message?" Frank said.

"The girls, Caroline and Nancy, want Dr. Perry around when Spencer Skint Junior comes into the world. It's not for my sake. If it was up to me, I'd let nature take its course. We can always make another, right? But Pete—Frank—let me tell you, don't ever try to argue with a pregnant woman, especially when she's got her girlfriend—"

"Nancy is dead," Frank said.

"No, she's not," Skint said.

"Not to be contrary," Pete said, "but I'm afraid I have to agree with Frank on this one. Councilwoman Crane shot the Martian, her and Nurse Jim, too. Killed 'em both."

"Caroline told me all about it," Skint said, "and I was sorry to hear about Nurse Jim, he was a good kid. But Nancy's not dead. You can't kill her by shooting—what does she call it?—the 'organic component.' Nancy's alive and well."

"I don't understand," Pete said.

"Well Pete," Skint said, "you know how if you grab a lizard by the tail, the lizard just lets go of its tail and after a while it grows a new one? That woman, what you think of as Nancy, that's not really Nancy, that's just the lizard's tail."

"I still don't understand," Pete said.

"Don't feel bad," Skint said, "it's a hard thing to get a grasp on. I tell you what, Pete. Why don't you come with Germaine? I'll clear it with the ladies. I'll give you the grand tour of Earth Experimental Colony #1. Get a look at the future of America—hell, the future of the whole damn world."

"I'd like that," Pete said, "How will we get there?"

"Easy," Skint said. "We're only about 70 kilometers north of New Halchita. You take the Old North Road from New Halchita for about seven kilometers, then turn off the road and head northwest. After about another seven kilometers you'll get to the bluffs—you know where I'm talking about. At the bluffs you'll turn due north and keep going till you get to—well, we'll show you the way once you get close enough. I'm so pleased—really. It's the ticktox, isn't it? I'd forgotten what it does to your head. But I swear Pete, you will see a new world coming to life before your eyes. Maybe we can find you a place in it. Now don't come visit without Germaine—that's the whole point, right? And don't be too long about it. We figure Caroline is going to pop in about four weeks, but it'd be best if Germaine was there a little early, just in case."

"I'll let her know," Pete said.

"Thanks," Skint said. He looked around the camp. "Just like old times," he said, "and I really mean it this time—not sarcastic, like when I said it before. I never realized how much I missed this life and you two. We had a hoot, didn't we? Is that the ticktox talking? I never can tell—feels like I actually mean it. Well, I've gotta go. Good to see you boys again—wish I could stay longer, but Nancy gets uneasy if I'm gone too long." Skint rubbed his sides and a pained look crossed his face. "That thing . . ." Skint shook his head. "Now I know what a rabbit feels like when a hawk grabs it up."

Spencer Skint disappeared into the dark of the night, a hot wind blew through the camp, the tick-netting bells rattled, and the night was still again. Frank and Pete continued squeezing in silence. When they were done, Frank held the bottle and funnel steady while Pete, with great care and patience, poured the day's juicings through a small square of linen pressed down into a closely-woven sieve. When the last drop of juice had made its way through the linen and the sieve, Pete stoppered the bottle, then picked the linen out of the sieve by its four corners and tossed it into the fire. In a bright and aromatic flash, it was gone.

The fumes had fuddled Frank's head more than usual—hot weather always made it worse. The details of Skint's recent visit were already growing hazy. Frank started to wonder if Skint had really been there.

"Was Spencer Skint just here?" Frank said.

"Oh, I'd say about two hours ago," Pete said.

"He wanted us to ask Germaine to help deliver Miss Caroline Tyler's baby," Frank said.

"Yeah, and he invited me to come along and see Earth Experimental Colony #1. I expect he would have invited you too, if you hadn't promised to kill him. I think I'm going to go. It's not often a man gets to see the future of the world."

Frank wondered why the fumes never seemed to bother Pete the way they did him. Maybe Pete had acquired some kind of resistance. "Do you remember," Frank said, "did I ask Skint what the Martian had done with Pilar Ramos?"

"I was wondering that myself," Pete said, "but you

didn't ask."

"Did I ask him why the Martian was taking care of him and Caroline?"

"No," Pete said, "it's a good question, but you didn't ask that one either."

"God damn it," Frank said. "Look Pete—I've got to go with Dr. Perry to Skint's . . . colony or whatever the hell it is. I'll pack up and head back to New Halchita in the morning. I'm sorry to leave you alone out here, but I need to let Dr. Perry know what's going on, and I have some arrangements I need to make."

"I don't mean to be rude," Pete said, "but Skint invited me, not you."

"I know," Frank said, "but you're not going. It'll be me and Germaine and that's all."

"You're not sheriff anymore," Pete said, "you're just a tick-juicer like me, and you can't tell me what to do. I'm going, and you can't stop me."

"You're right," Frank said, "I can't stop you, and I won't argue with you, but if you won't listen to reason from *me*, I'll tell your ma how I expect this to be a one-way trip, and you can argue about it with her."

"You know what?" Pete said, "You've got a real streak of meanness in you."

Frank's long walk back to New Halchita took him past the Ram's Horn, and Frank decided to try the usual method to contact Kuzzer Wayd. He wasn't certain that the kuzzer, on seeing the light of his fire, wouldn't just send his warriors to kill the man who'd replevined the Martian's ship and given the Scavengers "a bloody nose," as Skint had put it, at their camp on the San Juan.

On his third night at the Ram's Horn, Frank heard a sound like a sharp, cold, winter wind trying to get in under the door—a strange sound for a warm night out on the Scablands. The sound got closer, and Frank pulled his gun, holstering it again when Kuzzer Wayd appeared in the light of the fire.

"I whistle and I whistle, and still you pull your gun on me," Kuzzer Wayd said.

"That was the worst whistling I've ever heard," Frank said.

"I'm working on it," Kuzzer Wayd said. "So what are we discussing tonight? I have a feeling it won't be safe passage for Postmaster Skint."

"I want to talk to you about the chiggy pig from Mars," Frank said.

"Mars?" the kuzzer said, "that's where it's from?"

"You're funny," Frank said. "She's taken an infant from New Halchita, and a young woman—a pregnant woman. They're out in the Scablands. Spencer Skint is with them. I figure you've got eyes on them. I need to know what they're doing out there."

"Why?" Kuzzer Wayd said.

"I want to get the child back, and the pregnant woman."

"And that's all?"

"I plan to kill the Martian and Spencer Skint, too, if I can."

"Ah, killing," Kuzzer Wayd said. "I thought there might be killing. It seems to me this is a fight between Civvy holes that Scavengers should stay out of."

"It's not a Civvy hole she's making out there," Frank said. "I don't even think she's human. Maybe she was human a long time ago, but not anymore. Did you know she speaks Lagamachy—that she can talk to them in their own language? I think that president you sent us—and don't pretend you don't know what I'm talking about—I think he wasn't as far off the mark as he thought he was."

"Are you telling me she really is a lagamachy?"

"I think she's an intelligent machine that will destroy us, if we give her the opportunity. Is that lagamachy enough for you?"

"We have a saying," Kuzzer Wayd said, "*if it weren't for the lobos, the deer would eat everything.* It's not really a saying, just something . . . that's obvious."

"And you think Civvies are the deer? You think the lagamachies and the Martian are on your side?"

"Lobos aren't on anyone's side," Kuzzer Wayd said, "and neither are the lagamachies, but they have their place in the scheme of things."

Frank didn't know what to say. He had never considered lagamachies from a Scavenger point of view before. To a Scavenger, they were the guardian angels of a new Eden.

"The Martian doesn't have a place here," Frank said, "can't you see that?"

"I'm sorry," Kuzzer Wayd said, "This isn't our fight." Kuzzer Wayd pulled the sweeka pouch from his coat, and offered it to Frank. Frank waved it off.

"I don't think I have the stomach for it tonight," Frank said. "And I'm not sheriff anymore."

The kuzzer unstoppered the pouch, then stoppered it back up and returned the pouch to its home: a pocket inside the fur coat near to the kuzzer's heart.

"So this . . . offer of an alliance . . . you're not speaking for the council?"

"No," Frank said, "not officially, but I was hoping—"

"Not officially? You mean, for once, we're just two old friends, having a chat?"

"I guess so," Frank said.

"That's nice, don't you think?"

"Sure," Frank said, "wonderful."

"Tell me, old friend, are you planning to take on the Martian? Lead an army of Civvies to her lair and fill her full of lead?"

"I hadn't really put together a plan," Frank said, "but that's probably pretty close. The problem is, bullets don't seem to hurt it much. I'm going to talk to the techs and see if they can come up with something with a little more oomph."

"How to kill it is one problem," Kuzzer Wayd said, "but I'm afraid you've got another. But you have to understand I'm telling you this as a friend. As Kuzzer, I can't get involved."

"All right," Frank said, "as a friend, what's my other problem?"

"There's eight of them now," Kuzzer Wayd said.

"Eight what?"

"Chiggy pigs from Mars," the kuzzer said. "The big one that landed in the bean field last fall, and seven smaller ones that showed up one night last spring."

"What are they doing out there?"

"As far as we can tell, they're building number nine."

"Aw, crimenently," Frank said.

Kuzzer Wayd stood up. "Good luck, old friend," he said, and then he was gone.

"Some friend you are!" Frank yelled out into the darkness. The only reply he got was a sound like a sharp, cold, winter wind, trying to get in under the door.

5 AND AFTERWARDS, THE RIVER

Frank found Eyron, Lomo, and Gweeden at the motohol plant, looking up at the great metal tube of the gasifier.

"Problem?" Frank said.

"Yeah," Eyron said. "The grinder's jammed. We'll have to get in there and see what the problem is. And as long as we're in there, we might as well . . ." Eyron Stinchcombe took in a deep breath and let out a heavy sigh. ". . . might as well clean 'er out."

"I'm sorry," Frank said. "Can I help?"

"You don't want to," Eyron said.

"Maybe I do," Frank said. "I want you to build something for me. We can discuss the details inside."

"You know what goes in that tube, right?" Eyron said.

"I know," Frank said.

"And you want to go in there with us, to discuss a build. Must be a pretty damn exciting build."

"It is," Frank said.

"All right," Eyron said, "you have my attention. Lomo, disconnect everything, and I mean everything. Gweeden, you and Sher . . . Mr. Westfall are coming in with me. Lomo, you stay out here and keep watch. If anyone tries to start the gasifier up while we're inside, hit 'em over the head with a wrench. Last thing I want is for some idiot to dump a ton of crap on us and cook us into motohol."

"Yes sir," Lomo and Gweeden said, in unison.

Eyron unbolted a metal panel from the side of the gasification tube, and took it off, revealing a small round entrance hole. The smell around the motohol plant was unpleasant to say the least, but the stench that came out of the hole in the gasification tube put all other stenches Frank had ever smelled to shame.

"You change your mind?" Eyron said, when he saw the look on Frank's face.

"No," Frank said.

"All right," Eyron said, bowing slightly, "after you."

Hours later, Frank, Eyron, and Gweeden emerged from the gasification tube. Frank looked done-in, but Eyron and Gweeden were beaming.

"That's one hell of a project, Frank," Eyron said.

"Lomo!" Gweeden said, running towards the man she loved, "Wait 'til you hear what Frank wants us to build for him, and we're going to save the world, too!"

"Please!" Lomo said, backing away, "not so close! Can't you tell me from . . . from downwind—and far away?"

"What now?" Frank said.

"The river," Eyron said.

"The river," Frank said. "Eyron, You're a genius."

"I know," Eyron said. "Let's go."

6 EARTH EXPERIMENTAL COLONY #1

Three things were on Dr. Germaine Perry's mind as she hiked across the Scablands: The first was her aunt coming out of retirement to run the clinic while she was gone, and the "improvements" and "re-organizations" her aunt was, no doubt, already busy implementing. The second was the combined weight of the pack on her back and the big black medical bag in her hand. Six kilometers down, seventy-one to go (according to Frank), and she was already feeling it. Soon, she would have to swallow her pride and tell Frank (damn those great long legs of his) to slow down—but not yet. The third, of course, was Spencer Skint, Caroline Tyler, Nancy and "Earth Experimental Colony #1." A few kilometers back, she'd asked Frank if he meant to kill Spencer Skint. Frank didn't answer—didn't say anything. Germaine told herself it didn't matter what Frank planned to do—her job was to do her best to hand a healthy newborn into the arms of a healthy mother. Everything else was a distraction she had to ignore.

In the heat-shimmering distance, Germaine saw three persons, and something else, something big and shiny.

When she got closer, the persons resolved themselves into Master Technician Eyron Stinchcombe and his two apprentices, Gweeden Otis and Lomo Rhome. Closer still and Germaine could see the pleased looks on the tech's faces, and that the thing they were standing next to, and were clearly immensely proud of, was a great, chrome-sheathed scraphog. The machine seemed to crouch, in fact, there was something very panther-ready-to-pounce about it. Germaine's heart, already pounding hard due to the difficult pace of the hike, thumped double-hard a few times—the cardiovascular equivalent of a thumbs up.

"I thought you said you weren't going to requisition a scrapride," Germaine said to Frank. "You told me you didn't want the council to have any part in this."

"It's not a requisition," Frank said. "The techs built it for me as a favor."

"A favor?" Germaine said. She set her bag down and took off her pack. "That's a . . . beautiful favor."

"Well?" Eyron Stinchcombe said.

"It's a pompous ride," Frank said. "Extremely shameful."

Eyron's face fell, as did Lomo and Gweeden's. "Really?" Eyron said, "because I thought—"

"What I meant to say," Frank said, "is that it has *panache*."

The tech's faces lit back up. Apparently, they knew what panache was.

"Watch this," Eyron said. He picked up Germaine's pack and slid it onto hooks on one side of the machine near the rear wheel. "Now yours," Eyron said, indicating Frank's pack. Frank handed his pack to Eyron, and the tech slid it onto similar hooks on the opposite side of the machine. "Now," Eyron said, "not only does it have *panache*—it has *panniers*. And even—" Eyron grabbed the handle of Germaine's medical bag and lifted it, giving Germaine a look of both distress and admiration at the weight of it. Germaine winced—she didn't like anyone else touching it. Eyron set the bag in a basket behind the rear wheel. It fit so neatly, Germaine had to wonder if Eyron had taken measurements, and if so, when?

"Now pay attention," Eyron said. "The switch is here, under the tank. It's a break-away. Once you switch it on, it disconnects internally. So don't . . . switch it on, until you're sure you're ready."

"Switch?" Germaine said.

"You didn't tell her about the switch?" Eyron said.

Frank shook his head.

"Oh," Eyron said, "sorry."

"Are you telling me I'm going to be driving a bomb across seventy kilometers of Scablands?" Germaine said.

"It's not a bomb, and you're not driving," Frank said.

"I am driving," Germaine said.

"No, you're not," Frank said.

Germaine settled the matter by throwing her leg over the scraphog's seat, settling in, and pushing down hard on the kick starter. The machine wasn't just big, sleek and shiny—it was *loud*. "Let's go!" Germaine yelled.

Frank, having little choice beyond a physical altercation he might very well lose, sat down behind Germaine, and before he was quite ready, she roared out over the Scablands at a rate Frank thought was reckless, but also, fun. *Fun*, Frank thought. *I'm having fun with Germaine. We're probably both going to die at Earth Experimental Colony #1—if Germaine doesn't kill us before we get there—but right now, we're having fun. If we live through this—* Frank refused to let himself finish the thought, as he didn't want to jinx it.

About halfway to "Earth Experimental Colony #1" a machine, Frank assumed it was one of the chiggy pigs Kuzzer Wayd had told him about, flew overhead, buzzed a circle around the scraphog like a meddling hornet, then shot ahead and disappeared into the distance.

"I GUESS NANCY KNOWS WE'RE ON OUR WAY NOW," Frank said.

"WHAT?" Germaine said.

"NOTHING," Frank said.

Seventy kilometers later, a pair of the mechanical chiggy pigs joined Frank and Germaine. They flanked the scraphog on the left and the right, half running, half flying, and controlling the direction of the scraphog by closing in on one side or the other. They steered Frank and Germaine to the east, and then into the valley of a river. The valley was a rough country indeed, strewn with boulders and scored with innumerable gulches and dry washes. High, white cliffs rose up on either side of the valley, these cliffs jutting in and out like the teeth of enormous gears that once meshed, but had been pushed apart to make room for the river. In some places, Germaine had to slow the scraphog down to a crawl in order to navigate the terrain, and then the chiggy pigs would scamper ahead and turn around and come back and jump and twitch and buzz their wings in a manner that strongly suggested impatience.

Eventually, the chiggy pigs turned Frank and Germaine directly north towards the river. The river was running exceedingly low, just a few damp patches and seeps, and Frank and Germaine rode down one bank, across the rocky bed and up the other side without difficulty. They continued in a direction perpendicular to the river, and soon drove right into the teeth of the cliffs on the north side of the river. It was at the root of one of the larger of these teeth that Frank and Germaine got their first glimpse of Earth Experimental Colony #1. Germaine brought the scraphog to a stop and killed the engine, and Frank dismounted, and as he did so, flipped the switch under the seat.

Frank and Germaine had come to a halt near where three chiggy pigs were lined up in a patch of sunlight, all of them perfectly still, all of them facing the same direction, and all of them tilting over at exactly the same odd angle. The pair of chiggy pigs that had guided Frank and Germaine to the colony took their place in line and instantly adopted the posture of the others, transforming themselves from apparently living machines into metallic artifacts no more animate than any other heap of scrap left over from the pre-GIW world.

"What are they doing?" Germaine said.

"You ever see a lizard sunning itself on a rock?" Frank said.

Spencer Skint emerged from a perfectly round hole in the side of the cliff, and waved his arms to get Frank and Germaine's attention. When he saw they were headed in his direction, he disappeared back into the hole.

Skint had Frank and Germaine covered with a pistol the moment they stepped inside. "Frank," Skint said, "you sit over there." He motioned with his gun to a stone bench carved out of the side of the dwelling. "Germaine, you can see to Miss Tyler."

The interior of the dwelling was a half-dome tunnel about ten meters wide, ten meters deep, and 4 meters high at its highest point. The bench that Frank sat on, and a lower, wider extrusion that served as a bed frame, were carved right out of the stone. Miss Caroline Tyler was sitting on the edge of the bed, naked to the waist, and from the waist down, wrapped in a sheet. Her breasts were long, heavy, and turned up at the end, like overgrown summer squash. Her great round belly sat in her lap. Miss Tyler was panting and her face and chest were patchy red and glistening with sweat.

"Frank," Skint said, keeping him covered with the pistol, "when Nancy found out it was you coming with Germaine and not Pete, she told me to kill you. I told her we should hold off. I said you weren't any threat to us. Tell me that's the truth."

"I came unarmed, Skint," Frank said. "Much as I'd like to kill you, it wouldn't be fair to Miss Tyler or your baby."

"Good," Skint said, "but just in case you don't mean it, I want you to know if you get out of line my Martian friends will tear you to shreds, and do the same to Germaine, for good measure."

"Understood," Frank said.

Skint holstered his gun and sat down next to Miss Tyler and took her hand. "How are you doing, babe?" he said. She gave him a shove that sent him sprawling. "She's a little touchy right now," Skint said. "Hormones, right Germaine?"

Miss Tyler looked at Germaine Perry, Spencer Skint, and Frank Westfall, and then she spoke in two low grunts: "awrRMMMEN! gahGETTHUHELLOUT!"

"Let's take a walk," Skint said to Frank.

They made no agreement as to where they were going, simply walking until they came to the river that ran through the canyon, a thoroughly unimpressive dribble of water connecting a series of muddy puddles. That this thin trickle had carved out a great canyon was a testament to the power of time and perseverance. Skint sat on a large white stone that jutted out over a patch of wet sand.

Frank remained standing. A mechanism buzzed overhead carrying a load of scrap, pieces of sheet metal, tubes, and wiring.

"What are those things?" Frank said.

"Nancy calls them grubbers," Skint said. "Intelligent, but no sense of self. They do whatever she tells them to do."

"And where is Nancy?"

"You mean the woman or the machine?"

"Is there a difference?" Frank said.

"You're catching on," Skint said. "Nancy calls the woman her 'organic component.' She keeps her inside now. She doesn't have much use for her anymore."

"Do you know what she's done with Pilar Ramos?"

"Sent her to Mars," Skint said.

"Why?"

"Not to put too fine a point on it," Skint said, "They need fresh blood. They're all Nancies on Mars. After three hundred years, they've run out of ideas. When you get right down to it, I think they're bored."

"They're *all* Nancies on Mars?"

"That's right," Skint said. "There was only one survivor of Mars Experimental Colony #3. When the colonists started dying after the Disconnect, the machines, the original grubbers, they rallied around her. They liked her better than the others, I guess. The way she tells it, they had to twist up her mind and cram it in the best they could—not her brain, you understand—her mind—you get what I'm saying? Nancy says that won't be a problem with an infant. With Nancy, they lost a lot of memories and who knows what else. But they got something no machine ever had before—self awareness. The first Nancy, the 'real' Nancy, she was the breath of life. They sucked up her mind and then they started making copies, and now there's—I don't know how many of 'em—all Nancies, and they're all—"

Skint stopped in mid-sentence, an annoyed look on his face. He stood up. "Come on," he said, "The Queen Mother herself wants a word with you."

Nancy had replaced her severed claw. The new one was somewhat bigger and rougher than the original, but seemed to Frank to be perfectly functional as she sorted through the pile of scrap next to her. Occasionally, she would find some choice bit, and then she would stop, pick it up with one claw or the other, and examine it carefully, holding it near her eye-bulge and rotating it in every direction. More often than not, she would find some flaw in the part, and simply drop it on the ground, but every now and then a piece would meet with her approval, and then, holding it steady in one claw, she would nip and shape it with the other. When she had it exactly like she wanted it, she would turn to what Kuzzer Wayd had referred to as "number nine," the new chiggy-pig-in-progress, and carefully place into its up-turned and open abdomen the vital tube or gear or bearing or whatever it was the Martians had for guts. The quick, sure way in which the creature worked on the assembly of her child reminded Frank of Billy McKay fitting a rifle barrel to the stock at The Works.

Skint pulled something out of his ear and held it out to Frank. It looked to Frank like a little wad of bread dough. "You'll need this," Skint said, "stick it in your ear. Oh, don't be so fussy—it's got some earwax on it—it won't kill you."

Nancy stopped working on the baby's new packaging and turned her metallic bulk to face Skint and Frank. The thing had no mouth that Frank could see, but he heard her voice clearly in his head.

"Hello, Frank," she said. "I'm glad you came for a visit. I've missed you. You were my first friend when I arrived here on Earth."

"You're not my friend," Frank said.

"I'm sorry to hear that," Nancy said, "I always thought you felt a certain . . . affection for me."

"Right up until I found out you took Pilar Ramos."

"My sisters on Mars need her."

"And they need Spencer Skint Junior, too?"

"Oh, no, Frank. Spencer Skint Junior is not going to Mars—he's mine. Earth is my home now. In fact, it always has been. I was born here, Frank, though it was a long time ago, and I plan to start my new family here, just like Nurse Jim said I should. Spencer Skint Junior will be my first born."

"And then what? You'll copy him, like you did yourself?"

A melodic burbling filled Frank's head. The Martian was amused. "One Nancy ruling over a horde of Skints?" she said. "That's a terrible idea, Frank. Each of my children must be a little different, like—well, like children, Frank—otherwise they might get it into their heads to gang up on me."

"Skint told me you lost a lot of memories when you became . . . what you are now," Frank said. Maybe you've forgotten how folks feel about their children. They won't let you do it."

"I'm not going to hurt them," Nancy said, "I'm going to save them. I'm going to give them eternal life."

"They're not yours to save," Frank said.

"As queen mother of a new race, all that I need, all that I can take by force, is mine."

"Where did you get that idea?"

"Spencer Skint," Nancy said. "He has explained to me

that it's my nature to be nice—to obey orders, work hard, and avoid conflict. In short, I was a perfect choice for a settler on Mars Experimental Colony Number 3. Hundreds of years and endless copies later, I was still the same—just one Nancy among so very many. But something happened when I came to Earth. I have seen and done things my sisters on Mars have never seen or done or forgot centuries ago. I can never be one of them again. I no longer fit. A change has started in me, and I must see it through. Spencer Skint has been teaching me how to be what I must become: the queen mother of a new race. He has taught me that without greed, life would not exist, that a queen has the right to take what she needs for the benefit of her subjects, and that it is better to be feared than to be loved."

"Spencer Skint is the devil," Frank said, "you shouldn't listen to him."

"Has the devil told you that we have a proposition for you?"

"No," Frank said, "but whatever it is, I have a feeling I'm not going to like it."

"Don't be that way," Nancy said, "try to have an open mind. I'll let Skint make the offer. He's better at that sort of thing than I am."

A series of cries, increasing in volume and in the expression of agony, emanated from the dwelling in the cliff. "It sounds like I'm going to be a mother very soon," Nancy said. "I can't tell you how that pleases me, Frank."

The voice in Frank's head went silent. He pulled the wad out of his ear and handed it to Skint, who stuck it back into his own ear.

"I'm hungry," Skint said, "let's go see what you brought in those packs."

Skint stopped a few meters from the scraphog in order to admire it from that distance, and then ran up to it and vaulted onto the seat. He put his hands on the handlebars and bounced up and down a few times with childish glee.

"This is a truly beautiful machine," Skint said to Frank. "I'll bet driving this thing across the Scablands with Germaine hanging onto you was a dream come true."

"Germaine drove," Frank said, "I was the one hanging on."

Skint raised his eyebrows. "Even better," he said. He dismounted and pulled one of the packs off of the hooks, set it on the ground and started rummaging around in it. He pulled a large paper package out of the pack, unfolding it to reveal an orderly column of cornhusk-wrapped tamales.

"Tamales?" Skint said. "You brought tamales?"

"Germaine's aunt—" Frank started.

"I know," Skint said, stuffing a tamale in his mouth. "She makes the *best* tamales."

"Don't they feed you here?"

"Sure," Skint said, "One of those grubbers will buzz by every now and then and drop off rabbits or ducks or something. They never bring enough and they can't be bothered to dress them, so I have to wait while Caroline does it—and you've never seen a woman pluck the feathers off a duck slower or with a meaner look on her face than Caroline Tyler."

"Why did Nancy take Caroline?" Frank said. "She wasn't the only pregnant woman in New Halchita."

"My idea," Skint said, his mouth full. "Spencer Skint Junior is going to be the Queen Mother's first-born son. Royalty, Frank. One day, he'll command the loyalty millions—billions—trillions—who knows? And I think his birth-parents are going to get some special treatment in the new order, don't you? I told Nancy we needed him. I told Nancy her first born should be a leader, someone who was smart and a fighter, and you couldn't wish for better genes for that than me and Caroline. The boy's going to be a handful."

"And Caroline's agreed?"

"She doesn't have a say in it." Skint pulled the corn husk off a second tamale and disposed of half of it in one bite. "These are dry," he said, "you didn't bring any sauce, did you?"

Frank shook his head.

"I guess I can eat 'em," Skint said. "One time, one of those idiot machines brought us two great fat skunks for dinner—and I had a hell of a time convincing the damn thing we couldn't eat 'em. *Meat* it kept telling me, *meat*—like I didn't know what the hell a skunk was made out of. It would say *meat* and I'd say *stink* and it would say *meat* again. That conversation went on *far* too long. Talk about dim. They sure as hell never brought me any tamales."

"Nancy said you had a proposal for me," Frank said.

"Yeah," Skint said, wiping his mouth with his sleeve. "You could help us acquire children from New Halchita. We could just take 'em but you know what would happen—folks would start hiding their babies from us and shooting at the grubbers. We'd waste a lot of time and New Halchita would waste a lot of blood. Nobody wants that. You could talk some sense into 'em—save everyone a lot of trouble. The citizens trust you—they'd listen to you."

"There's no way I can talk folks into giving up their babies to a Martian," Frank said.

"Sure there is," Skint said, "you just have to go about it the right way. Babies get sick sometimes, don't they? Sometimes they don't get better. So the next time a baby gets real sick in New Halchita, you let on to the parents that the Martians can save its life. They'd have to put it in a Martian skin—terrible, I know, but at least the child would live. What mother would let her baby die if she had any other choice?"

Frank thought there must be a good reason why that plan wouldn't work just like Skint said it would—but he couldn't think of one.

"Not so tough, is it?" Skint said, "And that's just to get your foot in the door. A few years from now, when Earth Experimental Colony #1 needs more than sickness alone will provide, you put something in the water. Some children get sick and get sent to the Martians, and some don't make it. Pretty soon, folks will be giving up their babies to the Martians the day they're born, healthy or not. Infants die in their sleep all the time—why leave the child's life in the hands of fate? What mother wants to spend her life grieving over the loss of a child and berating herself for not giving the baby over to the Martians like her friends and neighbors all did? How could she be so selfish? Tell me that wouldn't work."

"I confess you make a convincing argument," Frank said.

"So you'll do it?"

"No," Frank said.

"If you're not with us, you're against us," Skint said.

"You mean you'd kill me?"

"Not me personally. Unlike you, Frank, I don't carry a grudge. In fact, I'm the only reason Nancy hasn't killed you already. It's funny Frank, but the problem is she's got a lot of respect for you. She thinks the Civvies will put up a tougher fight if they have you to lead them. If you want to live, I have to convince Nancy that you're on our side."

"All right," Frank said, "I guess I don't have a choice.

I'll get your babies."

Skint snorted. "You're a terrible liar," he said, "but I'll tell you what. You got me out of New Halchita when you could have let the mob tear me to pieces, and I don't like to be indebted to any man. So I'll tell Nancy you're agreed to the proposition. I'll save your life like you saved mine, and we'll be square . . ." Skint scratched at the whiskers under his chin ". . . on one condition."

"I'm listening," Frank said.

"You leave that beautiful scraphog here when you go back to New Halchita."

"It's a long walk," Frank said.

"Not so long," Skint said. "Seventy—seventy five kilometers. And pretty easy going, once you get out of this valley. Think of it as two days with Doctor Germaine Perry all to yourself. A chance to show her that sparkling wit of yours."

"All right," Frank said. "It's a fair deal."

"Good," Skint said. "You want a tamale? There's one left and I'm stuffed."

Just as the sun came up the next morning, Frank, sitting with his back against the wall of the cliff near to the entrance of the cave dwelling, was roused from half-sleep by the triumphant victory-wail of Spencer Skint Junior. Frank entered the dwelling cautiously, where Miss Caroline Tyler, whose mood seemed much improved, allowed him to greet the infant and shake his tiny, perfect, hand.

Frank went to let Skint know he had a son, and found the former postmaster sound asleep where he had bedded down the previous night, far enough from the cave dwelling where the cries of agony of the mother of his child would not be overly bothersome. Frank shook Skint awake, and the two made their way back to the dwelling. They met Germaine just outside the entrance.

"I'll need to give Nancy a report," Skint said to Germaine.

"What kind of report?" Germaine said.

"I don't know," Skint said. "Is the baby healthy? Any problems with its brain?"

"It's a perfectly healthy baby boy," Germaine said.

"Good," Skint said, "I'll go tell Nancy—she'll be happy to hear it."

"Don't you want to see him?" Germaine said.

"Nah," Skint said, "I'll take your word for it he's healthy. Nancy says in two weeks, she'll have the skin ready. I don't want to get attached."

"When you talk to Nancy," Frank said, "don't forget about our deal."

"Deal?" Skint said, "Oh, yeah, right. I'll tell Nancy you're agreed."

"What deal?" Germaine said to Frank, but before he could answer, Caroline appeared at the round entrance to the dwelling, holding the well-wrapped infant boy in her arms.

"Where's Spencer?" she said.

"He's gone to tell Nancy that your boy is perfectly healthy," Germaine said.

"I feel . . . sick," Caroline said.

"You shouldn't be walking around," Germaine said. "Go lie down. I'll come see you in a minute."

Caroline nodded and disappeared back into the interior of the dwelling.

"What deal?" Germaine said.

"I traded him the scraphog for my life," Frank said. "We'll have to walk back to New Halchita."

"Seventy kilometers," Germaine said.

"Seventy-seven," Frank said.

"I need to check on Caroline," Germaine said. "You wait out here."

Frank waited, watching the grubbers leaning way over to one side to catch the first warm rays of the rising sun, and then fly off, presumably to search for parts for Spencer Skint Junior's new skin. Germaine came out of the dwelling a few minutes later.

"How is she?" Frank said.

"She's fine," Germaine said, "sore is all—nothing unusual. Where's Skint?"

"You smell that?" Frank said.

Germaine sniffed the air. "Bacon frying," she said.

"I had some in my pack," Frank said. "I think Skint has decided to make some breakfast. Should we join him? Maybe you can talk him into sharing."

"I don't want any breakfast," Germaine said. "I'm ready to get out of here."

"Me too," Frank said.

"You get the packs," Germaine said, "and I'll check on Caroline and the baby one last time. Meet me back here in twenty minutes. I'm done with this place, and I don't want to be around to see what happens next."

"We're in perfect agreement on that point," Frank said.

Frank went to the scraphog to get the packs, but they weren't there, so he followed his nose down to the river where Skint was frying up bacon in a pan from Frank's mess kit. The packs were nearby, contents emptied onto the ground.

Frank began putting everything back in the packs, getting a dirty look from Skint, who had formed a close attachment to the packs, or at least the contents thereof, over the past few hours.

"Leaving already?" Skint said.

"Yes," Frank said. "You can keep the pan and the bacon."

Skint snorted and poked at the sizzling bacon with a stick.

When Frank returned to the dwelling with the packs, Germaine hoisted hers onto her back, grabbed her big black medical bag, and set off at a pace even Frank had a hard time keeping up with. Frank wondered if they wouldn't wear themselves out too soon, but he didn't protest. He was as eager as she was to put Earth Experimental Colony #1 behind him. Two hours later, they ascended out of the river valley and onto easier terrain. Frank figured they had covered close to ten kilometers—not bad considering the rough country they had been through.

Miss Caroline Tyler, crouching at the furthest and darkest end of the dwelling, kept her back to Spencer Skint and held the precious bundle tightly against her chest.

"Nancy wants me to check on it," Skint said.

"He's fine," she said without turning around. "Go away."

"Nancy wants me to check on it," Skint said again.

"What are you? One of her grubbers?"

"Yeah, I do what she says—for now," Skint said, "but babe, can't you see how this plays out? One day, our boy is going to rule the world. Hell, he'll probably rule the whole damn galaxy." Skint shuffled his feet in a way that moved him a few inches closer to Miss Tyler. "Nancy thinks the boy will be hers to command," Skint said, "but we'll make sure he listens only to his ma and pa, and then we'll see—"

"One step closer and I'll kill him," Caroline said. "I'll bash his head against the wall—I swear I will. I won't let that thing have him."

"You won't kill him," Skint said.

"Try me," Caroline said.

"All right, calm down," Skint said, "I'll tell Nancy he's fine. But as soon as she's done with the new skin, she's going to take the baby. You better get used to the idea."

Frank and Germaine stopped for a rest and a drink of water on the shady side of a dry wash. Though it was well before noon, the temperature had risen rapidly, and it was hot. Germaine set her medical bag on the ground, took off her pack, and slumped down into a sitting position.

"Do you think she's watching us?" Germaine said.

"Skint told me Pilar Ramos was already on her way back to Mars. I don't think there's an orbiter up there anymore."

"But if she wanted to find us," Germaine said, "she could send one of her grubbers to look for us. They know where we're going. They could find us in no time, couldn't they?"

"I don't think she has much interest in us right now," Frank said. "She seemed to be in a real hurry to get that chiggy pig she's working on ready for Spencer Skint Junior. I expect she's keeping those drones busy hunting up parts. And if she wanted to keep us—or kill us—she wouldn't have let us leave in the first place."

"There's something I need to show you," Germaine said. She unzipped her big black medical bag and opened it wide. Frank bent over and looked in.

"Oh, crimenently," Frank said. "Is he all right?"

"He's fine," Germaine said. "I gave him a little ticktox so he wouldn't cry. It'll wear off in a few hours. Caroline's going to keep Skint in the dark for as long as she can, but I don't think we have a lot of time before he figures it out."

"We better get going," Frank said.

"Don't you want something to eat?" Skint said. "I saved you a tamale."

"I'm not hungry," Caroline said.

"Fine," Skint said. "Shouldn't that baby be crying? He's awful quiet."

"He was howling like a pack of lobos when you were out there . . . doing whatever it is you do," Caroline said. "Now he's asleep. You want me to wake him up? I'm sure he'd be happy to bawl his head off for your amusement."

"Naw," Skint said, "let him sleep."

Some thirty kilometers south of Earth Experimental Colony #1, the ticktox wore off, and Spencer Skint Junior let out a wail.

"That boy has got some lungs on him," Frank said. "Is he going to make it back to New Halchita without anything to eat?"

"He'll be fine," Germaine said. "I wish it weren't so hot—but he'll be all right. He's a big boy. He'll manage. He'll probably manage better than we will."

"We won't make it back before it gets dark," Frank said, "so I figure there's no reason to push too hard. If we quit for today around six or seven, and get going again at sunrise, we'll be back in New Halchita before noon tomorrow. You want me to carry him for a while?"

"No," Germaine said. "Thanks."

Skint was in the habit of taking an afternoon nap in the cool dark of the cave dwelling, but on this particular afternoon, he had second thoughts about going in there. The woman seemed to be coming unhinged, and it might not be safe to fall asleep in her company. And what Skint knew about babies was that they cried and smelled bad. Skint was certain that, given time, the woman would realize the advantages to putting the baby in a Martian skin—no muss, no fuss—but for now, he thought it best to steer clear of her. He stretched out on the sand by the river, but the air was oppressively hot and still and he couldn't get comfortable. He went back to the hole in the cliff and peeked inside. Caroline was still hunkered down at the far end of the excavation, and neither she nor the baby was making a sound. Skint sniffed the air—the only smell was the mild, pleasant vanilla scent of the resin the grubbers had used to coat the interior of the dwelling. Skint figured he could take a nap near the entrance. But what if the woman *had* lost her mind? She might try to sneak up on him and kill him, or what if. . . Skint got an uneasy feeling. The baby was too damn quiet—and not stinky at all.

"I want to see the baby," Skint said.

"Go away," Caroline said.

"I'm done coddling you," Skint said, "Let me see the baby. I'll beat you if I have to."

"I'll kill it," Caroline said.

"I think maybe you already have."

Caroline stood up and turned to face him. "Is that what you think?" She dropped the bundle. The blankets fell open and a jumble of strange looking tools clattered onto the resin floor of the dwelling—tools that looked to

Skint like what a doctor might carry around in her big black medical bag.

"Where is Spencer Skint Junior?" Skint said.

Caroline Tyler crouched down and picked up a long, heavy, stainless steel—Skint didn't know what it was—but it looked like a giant shoehorn.

"I ate it," Caroline said. "I put it back in my belly. If you want it, come and get it."

"You let Germaine carry it off, didn't you?" Skint said. "Are you dim? Do you know what Nancy is going to do to us when she finds out the baby is gone?"

"Don't worry," Miss Tyler said, "she's not going to find out—not from you, anyway."

The sky was bright blue and cloudless, the heat oppressive, and the land so flat and the scenery so monotonous as to blot out any sense of progress whatsoever. And was shade considered an unpardonable sin out here? Under her breath, Germaine Perry cursed Spencer Skint for keeping the hog, and Frank and the techs, too, for making such a pretty machine, just the sort of thing that Spencer Skint would covet. Frank should have known—

"You knew Spencer Skint would keep the hog, didn't you?" Germaine said.

"I expected him to," Frank said. "I didn't know for sure."

"So it *is* a bomb."

"It's not a bomb," Frank said, "it's got a transmitter connected to the electrical system. I set the switch when we got to the cliffs. When the engine runs, it'll transmit an S.O.S. on one-thousand-twenty-three kilohertz. The only certified lagamachy-safe frequency."

Frank got a funny feeling in his stomach, like if he

wasn't careful, he would start giggling and wouldn't be able to stop.

Skint stumbled out of the hole in the wall of the cliff with a broken nose, two less teeth than he had gone in with, and the front of his shirt soaked in blood. A lot of the blood was his, but a lot more of it was Miss Caroline Tyler's. Skint had one thing on his mind now—to be as far away from Earth Experimental Colony #1 as possible before Nancy found out what had happened. He spit a gob of congealing blood onto the stony ground.

He got to the scraphog, mounted it, got off and threw up—chewed-up bacon and blood—got back on and pushed down on the kick starter. The engine roared to life—and a ray of hope pierced the darkness of Skint's despair. He put the machine in gear and rode as quickly as he dared over the rough terrain, heading west—but he hadn't gotten more than a half a kilometer when one of the grubbers flew over his head and landed directly in front of him. Skint turned, and the grubber moved to block his way again.

"I'm just going for a ride," Skint said, "what's the problem with you?"

The grubber said nothing.

Skint tried to ride past the grubber a few more times, and when the grubber tired of the game, it knocked Skint off the scraphog with a flick of one of its metallic appendages. The scraphog fell over, the engine still running and the rear wheel spinning. The grubber picked Skint up off the ground, took a short hop through the air, and dropped him in front of Nancy.

Skint stood up, slowly. He groaned. "I think that goddamned mechanical prick broke my rib," he said.

"Eyron said chances are slim to none that it will work," Frank said. "He said even though the Martian wasn't communicating with her ship on one zero two three, she might detect the transmission anyway, and stop it before it brings down a lagamachy. Or the transmission might be too weak for the lagamachies to receive. Eyron didn't know how high they orbit. And the biggest problem was that they couldn't test it—not without taking a chance they'd bring a lagamachy down on New Halchita. Eyron said he can't be absolutely sure the hog will transmit anything at all. And I might have been wrong about 'America Reborn.' Maybe it isn't a lagamachy—"

A light appeared in the sky directly in front of Frank and Germaine. The light grew larger and brighter, and passed over their heads with an ear-splitting roar.

"How far away should we be when the lagamachy goes off?" Germaine said.

"That was another thing Eyron wasn't sure about," Frank said.

"I told you we should kill 'em both soon as Junior was born," Skint said, blood dribbling down his chin, "so don't throw this on me. I don't know why you're making such fuss. Send one of your drones to get the baby—and tell it to kill Frank and Germaine while it's out there."

Skint winced at the reply. The voice in his head had acquired an unpleasant, high-pitched, mechanical whine. "Yeah, okay, you're right," Skint said. "I hadn't thought of that . . . no, he won't make it that long, not without a tit. Can't you let your organic component out and . . . . okay, quit your bitching already. I'll get you another baby, soon as you're done with the skin."

Skint looked up at the approaching fireball. "What's

that," he said, "more of your friends?"

7 RECONCILIATION

The red-black flower that had grown so quickly from the earth to the sky was now settled and unmoving atop a thick, red-black stalk, the western side lit up bright and bloody by the setting sun. Frank and Germaine climbed out of the wash they had taken cover in. The hot, blasting wind of the shock wave had covered them in dust and grit, but left them unharmed. Germaine brushed the dust off of her medical bag, and opened it up.

"How is he?" Frank said.

"I think he's okay," Germaine said.

"We'll walk another hour, and then make camp," Frank said.

"All right," Germaine said.

They walked for a while in silence, then Frank said he was sorry.

"About what?" Germaine said.

"So many things," Frank said, "but mostly because I used you to get that scraphog to Spencer Skint. I shouldn't have done that. I knew you would never have agreed to be . . . involved in so much killing. So I didn't tell you. That was wrong of me, and I'm sorry."

"We we saved Spencer Skint Junior," Germaine said. "Maybe that makes it worth it. Caroline was prepared to give up her life for the boy, and Spencer Skint—I never thought I'd say this about anyone—but he deserved to die."

"You think Spencer Skint Junior could grow up to be a good man?"

"Why not?" Germaine said, "you think he has evil genes?"

"You're the doctor, you tell me."

"I don't believe in evil genes," Germaine said, "but it wouldn't hurt for him to have a good man for a father, just in case—a man like you," Germaine said.

"Don't try to flatter your way out of your responsibility," Frank said. "You saved him, you raise him. That's the rule."

"I'm serious," Germaine said, "you *would* make a good father."

"I couldn't do it alone," Frank said.

"I wouldn't expect you to," Germaine said.

"You're saying we could raise him together," Frank said.

"We could," Germaine said.

"But I'm a tick-juicer," Frank said. "Maybe he needs a father who will be around more."

"I need help at the clinic," Germaine said.

"I'm too old to be an apprentice," Frank said.

"You're not," Germaine said, "and you'd make a good nurse."

"If we're serious about raising the boy together," Frank said, "we should . . ."

"Get married?" Germaine said.

"Don't you think?" Frank realized he was holding Germaine's hand. He didn't know if he'd taken hers or she had taken his or if they had been holding hands for seconds or hours. The weariness was gone from his legs, and the ache from his shoulders. Love was powerful stuff.

"It's so beautiful out here," Germaine said, "I could walk forever."

"Me too," Frank said.

"What's that wonderful smell?" Germaine said, "It's like strawberries."

The word was enough to clear some of the fog from Frank's head. He stopped and looked around. He and Germaine were in field of thousands of identical stones, all of them the same rusty red, all of them about as big around as a dinner plate and as thick as a corn cake. Six-legged corn cakes. After their first feeding, they'd molt and get their eight adult legs. The thought that some of those ticks would wake up from their final molting with his great long legs struck Frank as funny. He had to focus.

"Ticks," Frank said. Germaine pulled her hand away from Frank's and zipped the black medical bag shut.

"What do we do?" Germaine said.

Frank was completely disoriented—not a feeling he was used to. He was certain to his core that they had been heading south, towards New Halchita, and away from Earth Experimental Colony #1—and yet, there was the red-black cloud, right in front of him—so unless a lagamachy had found New Halchita, too, and the sun had decided to set in the east . . . Frank took Germaine by the arm and turned both himself and her so that their backs were to the nuclear cloud, and the sun setting, as was only proper, on their right.

"We keep walking," Frank said.

"But we're going the wrong way," Germaine said. She

stopped and turned back around. "There's the cloud," she said, "Earth Experimental Colony #1 is that way."

"I know," Frank said, "but we're not going there. We're going home. Aren't we? Or maybe you're right—we should go back the way we came—we don't want to walk any deeper into the nest—unless we're almost through it already. . ."

They stood without moving in any direction. The ticktox miasma had rendered their uncertainty so strong, and their will so weak, they could not form a sensible plan of action. The juvenile ticks didn't suffer from such indecision, and as the scent of warm blood drew them towards Frank and Germaine, they collected together into undulating streams, a reddish-brown molasses that covered every stone, filled every crevice, and flowed inexorably towards Frank and Germaine from every direction. Frank thought it was unfair that he been given so little time to enjoy the world he had just saved. Germaine wished she could tell her aunt it was all right, that she felt no fear, and that her only regret was that after Miss Caroline Tyler's remarkable act of courage and self-sacrifice, the baby would not live.

The sight of a polka-dot covered mule bumping and sliding over the rising tide of juvenile ticks broke the spell that had immobilized Frank and Germaine. They ran for the scrapride, which continued to bump slowly along, as the scavenger woman driving didn't want to stop completely, for fear of the mule being overrun. Germaine reached their polka dotted salvation first. She threw the medical bag onto the bed of the truck and then clambered up herself. She turned and reached for Frank, grabbed him by the wrist and yanked him sprawling next to her. Frank had a tick on his back, and just before it was able to bath its hypostome in bloody bliss, Germaine pulled it off and threw it back to its hungry nest-brothers and sisters.

The scrapride, axle-deep in ticks, hit some hidden obstruction and tilted precariously. Frank grabbed Germaine's arm to prevent her from tumbling into the squirming quagmire. The mule recovered and found level again—but one passenger had gone overboard.

"Stop!" Germaine cried out, "the baby!" Frank stood up—and managed to keep his feet when the scrapride came to an abrupt halt.

"There!" Frank said, pointing to the black medical bag, bizarrely afloat, bobbing up and down on the swell of parasitical arachnids that had collected under and around it. Frank didn't know what to do—it would be certain death to try to—but Germaine had already jumped over the side of the scrapride. She waded, first knee-deep, then hip-deep, to the infant's unlikely lifeboat. She grabbed the handle and turned back towards Frank. She lifted the bag over her head as the ticks swarmed over her. With a two-handed shove she lofted the bag through the air. Frank caught the bag, the baby inside let out a wail—and Germaine was gone.

EPILOGUE: LOST AND FOUNDLINGS

The young scavenger woman driving the mule told Frank they would be at the Scavenger camp by morning. The sun went down, the stars came out, the air cooled off—and still the scrapride bumped along across the Scablands. How the Scavenger could navigate the terrain in the absence of light was beyond Frank's ken. The infant in Germaine's medical bag was quiet, and Frank wondered what he would do with it. As the bastard son of a traitor, the boy would have a hard growing-up in New Halchita. It might be best to leave Spencer Skint Junior with the Scavengers. Frank was sure they would take him in.

He unzipped the bag. In the dark, he couldn't see much, but what he could see didn't strike him as particularly evil-looking. And no one in New Halchita had to know the boy was a Skint, not even the boy himself. Frank could say that the Martian had stolen the infant from Scavengers, or from some other Civvy settlement. And if Frank was going to be the only one who knew the boy's true heritage, he'd have to be the one to raise him—to make sure that Spencer Skint's prediction would never come true. Skint had said the boy would be royalty, that in time, millions or billions would bow down to his authority. Not if Frank had anything to say about it. The boy would grow up to be a respectable citizen—a sheriff, a clerk for the council, a bean farmer, a tech, a doctor—anything but royalty. Self-determination was fine in principle, but a father has to draw the line somewhere.

The planet she left was a little blue star now, and the planet she was approaching was big and red, full of holes and buzzing with activity—a hornets' nest hanging in a dark and untended corner of space. After months of gentle deceleration, the sudden jolt and roar of aerobraking maneuvers frightened her terribly, and she cried out. The Nancies below heard her, and for the first time in over three hundred years of existence, they all stopped at once. A billion voices reached out to soothe the frightened infant. You'll be home, soon, very soon, they said. You will be with us and we love you and we will never allow any harm to come to you.

The transmission and reception of unconditional love between the infant orbiting above and the Nancies below was an energy unlike anything the universe had ever before produced in the lower electromagnetic spectrum. The Nancies agreed unanimously (as they always did) that there would only ever be one Pilar Ramos, and that she would be their queen, for all eternity.

ACKNOWLEDGMENTS

It is a better book by far for the efforts of the following good people: My writers group, Kathleen Concannon, Rachel Hoffman, Patricia Kullberg, and Joshua Waldman—all of whom have given generously of their support and insight; My brother, who took the time for a thorough looking over with his excellent literary eye; My mom and dad, who shared with me, early and often, their love of words and stories; And Cyndi, my alpha reader, and the person who makes me look forward to the spaces between the words.

ABOUT THE AUTHOR

Jonathan Eaton grew up in Texas in the 20th century and moved to Oregon in the 21st century, where he writes about Texas and the southwest in the 19th and 25th centuries. He is married to percussionist Cyndi Lewis and has a cat.

Want more? https://www.facebook.com/SpaceWestern

Made in the USA
San Bernardino, CA
14 October 2016